GREAT LOVE STORIES OF THE THEATRE

ADRIENNE LECOUVREUR

Great Love Stories of the Theatre

A Record of Theatrical Romance

BY

CHARLES W. COLLINS

NEW YORK
DUFFIELD AND COMPANY
1911

PREFACE

The tinselled thrones of player-queens enjoy one
prerogative, at least, of actual royalty; they too stand
within the fierce white light of public attention.
Apologies, therefore, need not be made to the memories of the long-dead actresses whose amorous exploits are recounted in the present volume; their
intrigues have been permanently photographed into
theatrical history.

Stage chronicles are usually dull reading for the
laity unless the personalities of the players, whose
art is indeed wrought in running water, can be re-
animated. To the typical theatre-goer, the voice,
the smile, of the last new-made "star" has infinitely
more interest than the names of all the mummers
who have died and been buried, in unsanctified
ground or Westminster Abbey, since much-men-
tioned Thespis trundled out his cart. From such a
view-point this work was undertaken. Certain great
women of the theatre's great past have been studied
as women rather than as histrionic *automata*. Their
splendid amours, with men of great name or title,
have been retold as the central episodes of their
lives; and by the blaze of these passions their characters and their careers have been silhouetted.

Love stories these papers are called, and love
stories they remain. There has been no attempt,

however, to adopt a pseudo-fictional method. The vein of historical narrative, blended with occasional authentic anecdote, has been chosen as the proper medium, and accuracy, combined with vivacity of manner, has always been the intention.

Quotations from the memoirs and obscure stage records which were the chief sources of material have been used freely, in order to keep the subject more closely within its own frame. The articles fall naturally into a chronological sequence, beginning with the early days of the Restoration and ending, in England with the dawn of the Victorian reign and in France when the Romantic movement and Louis Philippe were in the ascendant.

They differ widely in mood, these old scandals; each may be read in a key all its own. In the case of Nell Gwyn, it is glittering venality; in that of Anne Bracegirdle, platonic discretion; in that of Adrienne Lecouvreur, tragic disillusion; in that of Mlle. Georges, hero-worship; and so on through the series. Each theme has been chosen for its human appeal or its psychological values; and each story, it is hoped, will be found worth the telling.

C. W. C.

CONTENTS

CONTENTS

ILLUSTRATIONS

GREAT LOVE STORIES OF THE THEATRE

GREAT LOVE STORIES OF THE THEATRE

I

NELL GWYN AND CHARLES II

"PRETTY, witty Nelly," the player-paramour of Charles II, is an inevitable first choice for heroine when the notorious romances of the stage are viewed in their historical perspective. Hers was hardly a love story; one may respect the dignity of the tender passion, even in its illicit episodes, by making that concession. The euphemisms of sentimentality can no more be invoked when a "merry monarch" enlists a beauty of the theatre among his fine body of courtesans than when a sultan buys a new Circassian odalisque for his seraglio. Yet the liaison of Eleanor Gwyn and Charles Stuart had in its own time a certain glamour which has been enhanced by the imagination of later generations; and so, with all their profligate fame upon their heads, they may be accorded the courtesy title of lovers. The genuine bond of sympathy and friendly affection between them serves as their warrant to that honour; and Nell herself is preëminent among the frail sisterhood of peccant actresses because she, more than any of her royally-favoured successors, left a frank imprint of her dainty finger upon the pie of statesmanship.

As for Charles II, there is little need to comment at length upon his lecherous temperament and amorous record. His incorrigibility in this regard is celebrated. He was the most immoral man of England's most debauched period, the Restoration; his propensities were of the barn-yard; he was the Chantecler of kings. His conquests may be tabulated, rather than discussed, in this incomplete list: Lucy Walters; Barbara Villiers, afterward Countess of Castlemaine and Duchess of Cleveland; Louise de Querouaille, afterward Duchess of Portsmouth; the Duchess of Mazarine; Erengard de Schulenberg; Katherine Pegg; Mary Davis; Mrs. Holford; Mrs. Roberts, and, the most admirable as well as the most picturesque figure in the collection, Eleanor Gwyn.

His progeny by the left hand were numerous; once, when appealed to by an unctuous courtier as "the father of his people," he overheard and tolerated the sneering aside of the Duke of Buckingham: "Father of a good many of them." He stocked the peerage with illegitimate offspring; ducal patents were granted to no less than six of his natural sons; and when an encyclopædist of the reign was preparing a "baronage," he had to ask the King's private advice for the proper classification and naming of these princelings of the bar sinister. So much for the miscellanies of Charles II's other amours; and now for the notable case of Nelly, whose foot was toasted as the smallest in the kingdom.

A public favourite on the stage before she rose to the political importance of a royal mistress, she held the admiration of the sturdy British heart after her attainment of glittering, if dubious, eminence. Where the other paramours of the King were hated by the populace, she was beloved. A child of the people, reared in the gutters, she always possessed the sympathy of the London mob. Frank, merry and kind-hearted, her influence upon her easy-going patron was for good. She never lent herself to the intrigues of the court, and her sway held in counterpoise the malign power of her greatest rival, Louise de Querouaille, who was an instrument of corroding French diplomacy. A courtesan who founds a hospital for old soldiers, and who advises her protector, "Send your women packing and attend to the proper business of a king," should rightly command some respect; and these are among the white marks in favour of Eleanor Gwyn.

Madame de Sévigné's letters contain vivid contemporary evidence as to the character of Nell. In contrasting the high-born Louise de Querouaille with the illiterate actress, this sprightly gossip wrote:

"Mademoiselle [Louise de Querouaille] amasses treasure and makes herself feared and respected by

3

as many as she can; but she did not foresee that she should find a young actress in her way, whom the King dotes on, and she has it not in her power to withdraw him from her. He divides his care, his time and his wealth between these two. The actress is as haughty as Mademoiselle; she insults her, she makes grimaces at her, she attacks her, she frequently steals the King from her, and boasts whenever he gives her the preference. She is young, indiscreet, confident, wild, and of an agreeable humour. She sings, she dances, she acts her part with a good grace; has a son by the King, and hopes to have him acknowledged. As to Mademoiselle, she reasons thus: 'This lady pretends to be a person of quality; she says she is related to the best families in France; whenever a person of distinction dies she puts herself into mourning. If she be such a lady of quality, why does she demean herself to be a courtesan? She ought to die with shame. As for me, it is my profession. I do not pretend to be anything better.'"

It is small wonder, then, that for us Nell is the flower of Charles II's flock. The stage which she adorned before he sacrificed her art to his pleasure has honoured her as a heroine in several dramas. Douglas Jerrold depicted her in an admirable light in his comedy, "Nell Gwynne, or the Prologue," produced in 1833. In "English Nell," staged in 1900, she had the vivacious interpretation of Anthony Hope as author and Miss Marie Tempest as actress; and that same season Paul Kester's "Sweet

(From the painting by Sir Peter Lely.)

ı

NELL GWYN

Nell of Old Drury," played in England by Miss
Julia Neilson and in this country by Miss Ada Re-
han, presented another attractive version of her
story. A third manifestation of the Gwyn vogue
then prevalent on the American stage was George C.
Hazelton's "Mistress Nell," in which the name-part
was played by Miss Henrietta Crosman.

Jerrold's comedy, now forgotten, was put forward
as a rehabilitation of Nell's character. The preface which stated that intention may, therefore, be
quoted:

"Whilst we may safely reject as unfounded gossip many of the stories associated with the name of
Nell Gwynne, we cannot refuse belief to the various
proofs of kind-heartedness, liberality, and—taking
into consideration her subsequent power to do harm
—absolute goodness of a woman mingling (if we
may believe a passage in Pepys) from her earliest
years in the most depraved scenes of a most dissolute
age. The life of Nell Gwynne, from the time of
her connection with Charles II to that of her death,
proved that error had been forced upon her by circumstances, rather than indulged in from choice.
It was under this impression that the present little
comedy was undertaken; under this conviction an
attempt has been made to show some glimpses of
the 'silver lining' of a character, to whose influence
over an unprincipled voluptuary we owe a national
asylum for veteran soldiers, and whose brightness
shines with the most amiable lustre in many actions

of her life, and in the last disposal of her worldly goods."

Eleanor Gwyn (also spelled Gwynne, and Gwinn) came of such obscure stock that her birthplace is in doubt. One tradition holds that she was born in Hereford, a town which has honour enough in theatrical annals as the scene of David Garrick's nativity. A stronger claim is made out, however, for the Coal Yard of Drury Lane, in the very purlieus of London, a villainous alley which took on infamy later as the habitat of Jonathan Wild and the nesting place of Jack Sheppard, both of them criminals with literary prestige. Close to the Coal Yard was Lewknor Lane, which would now be called a clearing-house for the "white slave" traffic, but which from the viewpoint of the Restoration was merely a recruiting station for orange-girls. In this grim locality Eleanor Gwyn was born, February 2, 1650; and an orange-girl she naturally became, vending fruit and tossing banter in the pit of the King's Theatre, the first playhouse to stand on the famous Drury Lane site. She was doubtless present at its dedication, for it was opened in 1663, when she was at the proper orange-girl age of thirteen. With her arch young beauty and her ready tongue, which had every turn of vulgar repartee at its tip, she must have done a thriving business; and her exploits with the basket, coupled with Peg Woffington's a century later, have perpetuated the cry: "Oranges! Will you have any ripe China oranges!"

That inimitable diarist, Samuel Pepys, has given to posterity its earliest glimpse of Nell Gwyn. On Monday, April 3, 1665, Mr. Pepys indulged his passion for play-going at the theatre in Lincoln's-Inn-Fields, called the Duke's House because supported by the Duke of York as the other was supported by the King. There he saw the tragedy of "Mustapha," written by the Earl of Orrery, but more important than the performance to the impressionable man-about-town were his attractive neighbours. "All the pleasure of the play," he notes, was that he sat next to "pretty, witty Nelly at the King's House," and to Miss Rebecca Marshall, an actress of the same company—a fact which, he naïvely admits, "pleased me mightily." Thus it is established that in her sixteenth year Nell Gwyn had become a player—had risen from the pit and its questionable orange-hawking to the stage and its more redoubtable temptations. In that same audience, Pepys also records, were King Charles II and his termagant flame, Lady Castlemaine. The cast for the drama of Nell Gwyn seems assembled in that one entry.

Nell's transition from orange-girl to actress, at such an early age, is easy to conjecture. Her charm, her captivating laugh, her quick wit and vivacious manner—qualities which mark every anecdote of her —would have appealed to any discerning stage manager as the material from which popular soubrettes are made. Thomas Killigrew, who directed the King's House, himself a dramatist, doubtless took

7

up the favourite of the pit as a protégée who would one day add honour to his company.

Her histrionic progress was rapid, and—thanks again to Pepys—it may be traced with considerable accuracy of detail through the jumbled records of the period. One year afterward, December 8, 1666, the inveterate gossip wrote in his precious journal:

"To the King's House and there did see a good part of 'The English Monsieur,' which is a mighty pretty play, very witty and pleasant. And the women do very well, but above all, little Nelly; that I am mightily pleased with the play and much with the house, the women doing better than I expected, and very fair women they are."

"Little Nelly" had the leading woman's rôle in this piece, which was an ephemeral comedy of manners by James Howard; she played Lady Wealthy, a rich and sophisticated widow who teases her admirer, Wellbred, with unending persiflage, and having achieved his reform by that method, finally marries him. The part was thoroughly adapted to Nell's personality, although she was still too young to seem a genuine widow, and was doubtless written expressly for her. A glance over the text of "The English Monsieur" and an attempt to imagine bright little Nelly in it brings to mind, as a modern analogue, Miss Billie Burke in W. Somerset Maugham's "Mrs. Dot."

Nell Gwyn's success was so marked that she was soon cast in the "stock" or classic dramas to which

8

the King's House had the rights, as well as in the comedies of the day. The rôles she played in the older works cannot be named with certainty, except in the case of Celia in Beaumont and Fletcher's "The Humorous Lieutenant"; but it may be assumed that she had leading or soubrette characters in most of the following dramas, which were in the repertory of the theatre:

Shakespeare's "Othello," "Julius Cæsar," "Henry IV," "The Merry Wives of Windsor," and "A Midsummer Night's Dream"; Ben Jonson's "The Alchemist," "The Fox," "The Silent Woman," and "Catiline"; Beaumont and Fletcher's "A King and No King," "The Humorous Lieutenant," "Rule a Wife and Have a Wife," "The Maid's Tragedy," "Rollo," "The Elder Brother," "Philaster," and "The Scornful Lady"; Massinger's "Virgin Martyr"; and Shirley's "Traitor."

Pepys is authority for her appearance in "The Humorous Lieutenant." He went behind the scenes after that performance with his wife, and Mrs. Knepp, the actress to whom he owed his entrée into the green-room and whose favours he is believed to have enjoyed, "brought to us Nelly, a most pretty woman, who acted the great part of Celia to-day very fine, and did it pretty well. I kissed her, and so did my wife, and a mighty pretty soul she is."

His summing up of that day's blessings ends, as with a smack of the lips, upon the words, "specially kissing Nelly." One must agree with Sir Walter

9

Scott's foot-note to this paragraph: "It is just as well that Mrs. Pepys was present on this occasion."

Then came Dryden's "Secret Love, or the Maiden Queen," the idea for which was suggested to the poet by the King himself. Nell Gwyn was the Florimel—a "breeches-rôle"—and seems to have achieved her *chef-d'œuvre* in that character. Pepys raves over her in the following strain:

"The truth is, there is a comical part done by Nell, which is Florimel, that I never can hope ever to see the like done again by man or woman. . . . . So great a performance of a comical part was never I believe in the world before as Nell do this, both as a mad girl, then most and best of all when she comes in like a young gallant, and hath the motion and carriage of a spark the most that ever I saw any man have. It makes me, I confess, admire her."

Nell, costumed to set off every charm of her lissome young figure, must have been stared at with the roguish Restoration leer by all the beaux and bucks of London that afternoon (the performances began at 3 p. m. then). The drama of eyes focussing upon her surpassed even the Restoration mood; it was Balzacian in its intensity. Playing opposite her was Charles Hart, her admitted lover. On one side of the house was Charles Sackville, Lord Buckhurst, whose mistress, for a few months, she was soon to become. In an opposite box sat Charles II, whose name was to be linked with hers through life. This series of paramours, actor, lord and King,

10

each with the same name, prompted Nell afterward to tell Charles II to his face, with her usual daring, that he was only her Charles III.

She must have smitten many other hearts as well as she preened in her boyish gear and raced through such lines as these:

"Yonder they are, and this way they must come. If clothes and a *bonne mien* will take 'em, I shall do't. Save you, Monsieur Florimel! Faith, methinks you are a very jaunty fellow, *poudré et ajusté* as well as the best of 'em. I can manage the little comb, set my hat, shake my garniture, toss about my empty noddle, walk with a courant slur, and at every step peck down my head. If I should be mistaken for some courtier now, pray where's the difference?"

Within a few months after this production, there was fresh scandal for the coffee-houses. The King had taken up Moll Davis, who sang and danced at the Duke's House; and Lord Buckhurst had won over Nell Gwyn of the King's. The latter affair was regarded as a happy match on both sides, Buckhurst's talents and popularity rivalling Nell's. They went to Epsom, a fashionable *spa* of the day, for an outing; and Pepys tells how they kept "merry house" there, with Sir Charles Sedley, the wit, to assist them in the flow of mirth and wine. Then, after what was no doubt a memorable summer for her (July and August, 1667)—though a black one for England with a Dutch fleet brazenly carrying war up the Thames—she returned to the theatre in

Drury Lane, playing such parts as Bellario in Beaumont and Fletcher's "Philaster," Panthea in their "A King or No King," Cydaria in Dryden's "Indian Emperor," Samira in Robert Howard's "Surprisal," and Mirida in James Howard's "All Mistaken, or the Mad Couple."

This was the critical period of Nell's career, and good old Pepys has left graphic record of it. She had broken with Buckhurst and was dissatisfied with her lot—but let Pepys tell it in his own words, which are eloquent enough:

"26 Aug., 1667. To the King's playhouse and saw 'The Surprisal,' a very mean play I thought, or else it was because I was out of humour, and but little company in the house. Sir W. Penn and I had a great deal of discourse with Orange Moll, who tells us that Nell is already left by my Lord Buckhurst, and that he makes sport of her, and swears she hath had all she could get of him; and Hart, her great admirer, now hates her; and that she is very poor, and hath lost my Lady Castlemaine, who was her great friend, also; but she is come to the house but is neglected by them all."

.   .   .   .   .

"5 Oct. 1667. To the King's House, and there going in met Knepp, and she took us up to the tiring rooms; and to the woman's shift, where Nell was dressing herself, and was all unready, and is very pretty, prettier than I thought. And into the scene-room and there sat down, and she gave us fruit; and here I read the questions to Knepp, while she answered me through all the part of 'Flora's Vagaries,' which was acted to-day. But, Lord! to see how they were both painted would make a man mad, and did make me loathe them; and what base company of men comes among them, and how lewdly they talk, and how poor the men are in clothes, and yet what a show they make on the stage by candlelight, is very observable. But to see how Nell cursed for having so few people in the pit was pretty; the other house carrying away all the people at the new play, and is said now-a-days to have generally most company, as being better players."

Charles II was still philandering with "little Miss Davis," while Nelly was cursing the bad audiences, but his interest in her was waning. He was also quarrelling with the imperious Castlemaine, and a pathetic complaint against his scandalous behaviour from his queen, Catherine of Braganza, now and then complicated his domestic affairs. Altogether, he was ripe for new diversions, neither as sordid as a mere dancer nor as haughty as a countess; and he found the happy medium in Nell Gwyn, who had more distinction and beauty than Moll Davis and a more winsome personality than the Castlemaine.

"The Black Prince," written by the Earl of Orrery and produced at the King's House October 19, 1667, decided Charles for the new adventure. He watched Mistress Gwyn play the rôle of Alice Piers, the enchantress of Edward III, with keen admiration; and straightway Mr. Pepys had to jot down the rumour that "the King had sent for Nelly." The scandal involved Lord Buckhurst also, for it was pointed out that he had been made a groom of the King's bedchamber with a pension of 1,000 pounds a year; that he had been promised a peerage upon the death of his grandfather; and that he had been sent on a complimentary mission, "a sleeveless errand," as Dryden said, to France. These reports, though true in themselves, were slanderous in their suggestion that the King had bought Buckhurst away from Nelly, for that fine gentleman—too high-spirited, in the first place, to be guilty of such base-ness—had announced his permanent breach with her before His Majesty's inclination was manifest.

The King's new amour was discreetly managed in the beginning. Nell continued to devote herself to the stage with a zeal which discredited the stories of her visits to Whitehall; and not until more than a year had elapsed was it given the immodest publicity usual in Charles' affairs of the heart. In the spring of 1670 Nell Gwyn began to study the part of Almahide in Dryden's new tragedy, "Almanzor and Almahide, or the Conquest of Granada." Suddenly a postponement of the production was announced, the cause of which soon became public property. Charles II had been blessed with another natural son, the mother of whom was Nelly of the King's House. The play was put on a few months later, with Nell as Almahide, but that was her last appearance upon the stage. Thenceforth, as the King's mistress and mother of a prince of the blood royal, she was privileged to live in a palace and hold a little court of her own. This was a change in station esteemed as no small honour in those loose times; and of whatever honour there was, Nell proved herself more than worthy.

An incident associated with the production of this drama of "Almanzor and Almahide" was used by Douglas Jerrold as the basis of his comedy, "Nell Gwynne, or The Prologue." When speaking the prologue, Nell wore a hat which burlesqued Nokes, a comedian at the rival theatre, and though primitive in its humour, this local hit amused the town immensely. The story may be repeated as it occurs in Downe's "Roscius Anglicanus," a curious miscellany of stage anecdotes printed in 1789:

"At the Duke's theatre, Nokes appeared in a hat larger than Pistol's, which took the town wonderful, and supported a bad play by its fine effect. Dryden, piqued at this, caused a hat to be made the circumference of a timber coach wheel, and as Nelly was low of stature, and what the French call *mignonne* or *piquante,* he made her speak under the umbrella of that hat, the brims thereof being spread out horizontally to their full extension. The whole theatre was in a convulsion of applause; nay, the very actors giggled, a circumstance none had observed before. Judge, therefore, what a condition the merriest Prince alive was at such a conjuncture.

'Twas beyond *odso!* and *ods fish!* for he wanted little of being suffocated with laughter."

Nell Gwyn's first contribution to the large royal family was born May 8, 1670, and was named Charles Beauclerk. At that time the King and his court were at Dover to welcome the visiting Duchess of Orleans, his sister, through whom an alliance with France against Holland was effected. In the retinue of this feminine diplomat, Nelly's bitterest rival, Louise de Querouaille, came to England, sent by Louis XIV to seduce Charles II to the interests of France. Thenceforward until the end of the reign there was feline warfare between these two favourites, with Nelly working for, and Louise, afterward Duchess of Portsmouth, conniving against true English interests. The former was known among the London commoners as the Protestant mistress (that word may be used in place of its blunter Restoration equivalent) and was beloved as one of them in birth and religion; while the latter, hooted at whenever she appeared in the streets as the Papish mistress, was cordially detested. Her name, difficult of pronunciation for the English tongue, was corrupted into "Mrs. Carwell," while Eleanor Gwyn was known and addressed everywhere by the affectionate diminutive of Nelly.

Once, when Nelly was driving in her coach at Oxford, her horses were stopped by a threatening mob. She looked out the window with a roguish smile, however, and said:

"Pray be civil, good people. I am the Protestant—"

Then the cat-calls changed to cheers.

Another anecdote illustrates Nelly's habit of chaffing her rival. The news of the deaths of a prince of the blood in France and of the Cham of Tartary reached London about the same time. Louise de Querouaille promptly put on mourning for the French nobleman; and the next day Nelly appeared at the court also garbed in black.

The King asked the cause of her grief, in the presence of the Querouaille, and Nelly remarked:

"Oh, haven't you heard of my great loss in the death of the Cham of Tartary?"

"And pray," demanded Charles, "what relation was he to you?"

"Exactly the same relation as the French prince was to Mlle. Querouaille."

Daniel Defoe may be consulted for the French lady's opinion of Nelly. He wrote:

"I remember that the late Duchess of Portsmouth in the time of Charles II gave a severe retort to one who was praising Nell Gwyn, whom she hated. They were talking of her wit and beauty, and how she always diverted the king with her extraordinary repartees, how she had a fine mien, and appeared as much the lady of quality as anybody. 'Yes, madam,' said the Duchess, 'but anybody may know she has been an orange-wench by her swearing.' "

As soon as Nell retired from the stage the King

established her in a house on Pall Mall with a garden fronting on St. James' Park. When she discovered that the place was only rented for her, she returned the lease to her liege sovereign with a sarcastic remark in which the mutability of loves and leaseholds were compared. She promptly received a deed in perpetuity.

John Evelyn, the fastidious cavalier whose diary contains so many vivid sketches of Restoration manners, saw Nelly and her lover exchanging gossip before that very house one afternoon (March 1, 1671). The scene prompted him to the following entry:

"I thence walked with him [the King] through St. James' Park to the garden, where I both saw and heard a very familiar discourse between His Majesty and Mrs. Nelly, as they called an impudent comedian, she looking out of her garden on a terrace at the top of the wall, and the King standing on the green walk under it. I was heartily sorry of this scene. Thence the King walked to the Duchess of Cleveland, another lady of pleasure and curse of our nation."

To illustrate Nelly's boldness of speech—the impudence of which Evelyn accuses her—there is a story of a private concert given at her home. When the program was over, the King was so profuse in his compliments that his hostess remarked:

"Then, sir, to show you do not speak like a courtier, I hope you will make the performers a handsome present."

Charles answered ruefully that he had no money with him, and asked his brother, the Duke of York, if he were in a better state of purse. It developed that the latter did not have more than a guinea or two. Then Nelly put on a horrified expression, and turned to the other guests, exclaiming with the King's typical oath:

"Ods fish! What company am I got into?"

On Christmas Day, 1671, the union of Nell and Charles was crowned with a second son, named James. These children were healthy, handsome youngsters, much petted by their father; and their fond mother resented the way in which they were neglected, in heraldic honours, in favour of some of their half-brothers. The Duchess of Cleveland's sons by Charles II were the Dukes of Grafton, Cleveland of Northumberland; Lucy Walters' son was the Duke of Monmouth and was treated like an heir apparent; the Duchess of Portsmouth's son was the Duke of Richmond; and even lowly Katherine Pegg's son was Earl of Plymouth. Nelly saw her rivals made duchesses and their offspring dukes while she and her pretty boys were titleless, so naturally she became vexed. Her method of approaching the King in this matter was characteristic.

"Come here, you little bastard!" she cried to her eldest-born in the King's presence. He objected to her use of the harsh word, and she answered:

"I have no better name to call him."

Charles acted upon this hint at the first opportunity, and on December 27, 1676, Charles Beauclerk was created Baron of Headington and Earl of Burford. A little later he was affianced to childish betrothal—a custom then—to the heiress of the illustrious Veres, daughter of the twentieth and last Earl of Oxford.

The second son, James Beauclerk, died at the age of nine (September, 1680) untitled, and to console Nelly for her loss, which she mourned deeply, the King transferred the high title of Duke of St. Albans, the last bearer of which had died without an heir, to the boy Earl of Burford (January 10, 1683). He was also appointed to the lucrative offices of Registrar of the High Court of Chancery and Master Falconer of England. The title of St. Albans still survives and its dukes are direct descendants of Nell Gwyn, the "impudent comedian."

After her son was ennobled, Nelly was given Burford House at Windsor for her permanent habitation, newly decorated by fashionable artists of the period. There she entertained at gay dinners and concerts, and indulged a passion for the gambling table. In one night's session at basset she lost 1,400 guineas, equivalent to 5,000 pounds to-day, to the Duchess of Mazarine. There, also, courtiers like the Duke of Monmouth and the Duke of Devonshire paid homage to her, for political purposes. She understood the dangerous ambitions of Monmouth, which ended in the battle of Sedgemoor— the last conflict fought on English soil—and the

headsman's block; and once she taunted him as
"Prince Perkin." He retorted that she was ill-
bred.

"Ill-bred!" Nelly rapped out. "Was Lucy Walters better bred than I?"

In 1682 Nelly compensated the English people
for the part which her extravagances played in the
drain on the public funds. She persuaded her lover
to found the Royal Hospital at Chelsea for old and
crippled soldiers—men who had fought at Edge-
hill, Marston Moor, Naseby and Worcester, and
who limped the streets of London as pathetic me-
morials of the Civil War. The King himself laid
the corner-stone of this institution—one of his few
instances of effective charity—but it has survived
chiefly to the glory of his mistress.

Among the contemporary documents relating to
Nell is Mrs. Aphra Behn's dedication of a play
called "The Feigned Courtesans." It runs on in
this strain of adulation:

"Besides all the charms and attractions and powers
of your sex, you have beauties peculiar to yourself—
an eternal sweetness, youth and air which never
dwelt in any face but yours. You never appear but
you gladden the hearts of all that have the happy
fortune to see you, as if you were made on purpose
to put the whole world in good humour."

The seductions thus celebrated by the first female
playwright never lost their appeal to King Charles.
Nelly continued in high favour. Arrangements

were in progress to make her Countess of Green-
wich, but before they could be consummated,
Charles received his final summons. He was profligate to the last, as this passage in Evelyn's diary
bears witness:

"I can never forget the inexpressible luxury and
profaneness and all dissoluteness, and as it were total
forgetfulness of God (it being Sunday evening)
which this day se'nnight I was witness of—the King
sitting and toying with his concubines, Portsmouth,
Cleveland, Mazarine, etc., a French boy singing
love songs in that glorious gallery, while about
twenty of the great courtiers and other dissolute persons were at basset round a large table, a bank of at
least 2,000 pounds in gold before them; upon which
two gentlemen who were with me made reflections
with astonishment. Six days after was all in the
dust."

This orgy lasted all that night. At eight o'clock in
the morning Charles was suddenly stricken with
apoplexy, and after a brief rally which cleared his
clouded brain, he surrendered his earthly crown
the following Friday (February 16, 1685), in the
fifty-fourth year of his age and the twenty-fourth of
his reign. He died like a true Stuart, debonairly,
and his death-bed scene reads like great fiction even
when described by the most plodding historian.
He apologised to the sleepless courtiers with a smile
for being "such an unconscionable time in dying";
sent messages asking pardon for his faults to his ab-

sent queen; bespoke the kindness of his brother and successor for his various mistresses; and ended with the words, now classic:

"Let not poor Nelly starve."

His last thought seems to have been for the low-born actress whose loyalty and loveliness had meant so much to him. That dying request, moreover, seems fraught with Stuart humour as well as Stuart kindness; it carries a wan, tolerant gibe at Nelly's besetting sin of extravagance.

But for this injunction, breathed by Charles upon the threshold of death, Nelly's career would have ended in dire misfortune. She was deeply in debt; the only letter of her dictation—she could not write —which is extant, dated the previous year, gives orders for the melting of her silver plate in order to satisfy some of her creditors. After Charles was taken to his last home in Westminster Abbey, she sacrificed the pearl necklace which appears in many of her portraits, and which she had purchased from Peg Hughes, the actress-mistress of Prince Rupert, for 4,250 pounds. Even then she was not able to satisfy all her old bills, which flooded in upon her for collection as soon as her great protector had gone; and in the spring of 1685 she was outlawed for debt, with the threat of imprisonment hanging over her head.

Then James II, her morganatic brother-in-law, remembered Charles' dying words and gave generous assistance to Nelly in her hour of need. Although worried by the martial preparations of "King Monmouth," who was organising rebellion in the west, he did not neglect this inherited case of charity, as soon as it was brought to his attention. In his secret service expenses the item of 729 pounds 2 shillings 3 pence stands on record in satisfaction of all the debts of "Mrs. Ellen Gwyn." More than that, he made over to her two payments of 500 pounds each as royal bounty; settled the estate of Beskwood Park upon her and her heirs, and continued her pension of 1,500 pounds annually.

Nelly's comfort was now assured, but she was not permitted to enjoy these benefits for long. She survived Charles by only two years, dying in November, 1687, aged thirty-eight, with her beauty still unblemished by the ruthless hand of time, and still strong in the Protestant faith, despite rumours, after King James' kindness to her, that she had truckled to the new religious régime and "gone to mass"—as Evelyn reports. Her will contains many small bequests to old servants and pensioners, and a demand that his Grace the Duke of St. Albans, her heir, "would please to lay out twenty pounds yearly for the releasing of poor debtors out of prison every Christmas Day."

She was buried in the church of St. Martin's-in-the-fields, the vicar of which, Dr. Tenison, afterwards Archbishop of Canterbury, preached her funeral sermon. She had been one of his parishioners, and he was so eloquent in the praise of her good qualities that his remarks were used against him when his appointment to the see of Canterbury came before Queen Mary. That sensible daughter of James II dismissed the charges with this remark: "I have heard as much, and this is a sign that the poor unfortunate woman died penitent."

Nelly's son, the Duke of St. Albans, became a man worthy of his title in every particular. With Thomas Otway, the dramatist who wrote "Venice Preserved," as his tutor, his education was brilliant. King James continued his mother's pension to him, and made him colonel of a famous regiment of horse. He distinguished himself while still a youth at the siege of Belgrade, married the Lady Diana de Vere, to whom he had been affianced as a child, became a Knight of the Garter, and died, the father of eight children, in 1723.

Pepys' admiration of Nell's personal charms, as a man of the world, and Evelyn's somewhat priggish disapproval of her moral status, have already been quoted. Another contemporary sidelight upon her is to be gleaned from Bishop Burnet's "History of His Own Times":

"Gwyn, the most indiscreet and the wildest creature that ever was in a court, continued in great favour until the end of his life, for she acted on all persons in such a lively manner, and was such a constant diversion to the king that even a new mistress could not drive her away."

Colley Cibber, who as a boy may have seen Nelly

in the flesh, undertakes to refute the Bishop in his classic "Apology," adopting this strain:

"If we consider her in all the disadvantages of her rank and education, she does not appear to have had any criminal errors more remarkable than her sex's frailty to answer for. And if the same author [the reverend historian of his own times] in his latter end of that prince's reign seems to reproach his memory with too kind a concern for her support, we must allow that it becomes a bishop to have had no eye or taste for the frivolous charms or playful badinage of a king's mistress. Yet if the common fame of her may be believed, which in my memory was not doubted, she had less to be laid at her charge than any other of those ladies who were in the same state of preferment. She never meddled in matters of serious moment, or was the tool of working politicians; never broke into those amorous infidelities in which others are accused of; but was as visibly distinguished by her personal particular inclination for the King as her rivals were by their titles and grandeur."

So Nell of the Coal Yard, Nell the orange-girl, Nell the impudent actress, is remembered kindly in spite of her oblique moral code. Of Charles II's weaknesses, she was the most pardonable. She was truer to him than all his blooded paramours, and he gave her more than a Stuart's modicum of loyalty. Pepys' artless words might serve as her epitaph:

"A mighty pretty soul she is."

GREAT LOVE STORIES OF THE THEATRE

II

MARIE DE CHAMPMESLÉ AND RACINE

THE glorious traditions of Jean Baptiste Racine as the Sophocles of the classic drama in France are inseparably associated with the fame of the first great tragedienne of the French theatre—Maric de Champmeslé. Here was a perfect example of collaboration between dramatist and interpreter, the former giving instruction, the latter inspiration, in a mating of passion and of art. Whenever the jealous madness of Phèdre, in whom Sarah Bernhardt's enchanting lyrism and plastic loveliness have found their ultimate expression, is set upon the modern stage, they step out of the shadows of the seventeenth century—the poet, majestically bewigged, his lustrous eye and hard-set mouth curiously indicating contradictory strains of voluptuousness and austerity, and the tragedy queen, hardly pretty of face but moulded like an ancient statue, sure as a siren of her lures for men.

Racine, now linked with Pierre Corneille among the Olympians of French dramatic literature, won supremacy over the elder poet in his own time, no matter what critical hair-splitting may be indulged in over their rival merits to-day, vanquishing him in

29

fair fight with works of similar theme as the weapons. Champmeslé was the original Bérénice in his drama of that name, Roxane in "Bajazet," Monime in "Mithridate," Iphigenia in "Iphigénie en Aulide," and the title-character in "Phèdre." But she hardly needs her identification with Racine's tragic heroines to have historic rank; she was the marvel of the stage during the reign of *Le Grand Monarque;* the mouthpiece of every other notable dramatist of the period; and the first leading woman of the Comédie-Française at the formal establishment of that great institution in 1680.

Marie de Champmeslé, or Desmares, to use her birth-name, was born in Rouen in February, 1642. She did not spring from the then lowly player caste; her family had a good position, and she was well educated; but, perhaps because her widowed mother took her into the home of a step-father, she broke away from domestic ties, at the age of twenty-three, and plunged into the hazardous career of the stage. She played in the tennis court theatres of Rouen, and soon made the venture into theatrical matrimony which almost every débutante attempts, usually for worse, espousing (January 9, 1666) a young actor whose people were well-to-do bourgeois of Paris. He had discarded his patronymic of Chevillet, pretending to distinguished birth, on the play-bills, as the Sieur de Champmeslé; thus Racine's future muse found the name by which she is now remembered. They remained in the theatres of Rouen for two years, and then heard the call of Paris; soon after their arrival, both being capable players, they secured engagements at the Théâtre du Marais.

The first appearance of Mlle. Champmeslé, as she was known, on the stage of the capital, February 15, 1669, was in a pastoral called "La Fête de Vénus," in which she played the goddess. Then came "Polycrate," a heroic comedy by the same author (Abbé Boyer); next a tragedy by Donneau de Visé, "Les Amours de Vénus et Adonis," in which she was once more cast as the soft Cytheræan. She was applauded; but success in a second-class company like that of the Marais, and in compositions by poetasters, did not satisfy her. At the Palais-Royal the comedies of Molière were in sparkling session; and at the Hôtel de Bourgogne Racine's earlier tragedies were enthroned. She naturally yearned for bigger game than she could find at the Marais. Her *métier*, she felt, was in tragedy; and in 1670, after diligent study under one of the veterans at the Marais, Laroque, she found an opening at the Hôtel de Bourgogne, there to meet Racine and fame.

Although the dramatist afterward devoted himself assiduously to coaching her in declamation, and adapted his heroines to fit her personality, he did not welcome her with open arms when through the illness of Mlle. Des Œillets she was cast for Hermione in a revival of his "Andromaque." He was distrustful of this recruit from the Marais, of negligible reputation, and seems to have flown into the

31

customary author's fit of pique, for he refused to lend the sanction of his presence to the rehearsals, and was with difficulty persuaded to attend the first performance, which marked the reopening of the Hôtel de Bourgogne after the recess of Holy Week, 1670.

Champmeslé, in truth, came close to failure; her beginning was insipid. According to the "Annales Dramatiques" of the Abbé de Laporte:

"Mlle. de Champmeslé's rendering of the first two acts was very weak. These acts, where Hermione is in turn attracted and repelled by Pyrrhus, require a profound knowledge of the stage and great finesse. But in the last acts, where she is a frenzied lover, in whom jealousy carries all before it and to whom a supreme betrayal leaves nothing but vengeance to live for, she retrieved her ground so completely, threw so much fire into her acting, and rendered the passions with such real fervour, that she was enthusiastically applauded."

Racine was conquered immediately. After the play he rushed into her dressing room, to fall upon his knees before her, emotionally eloquent with compliment, congratulation, and apology. A few days later Mlle. Des Œillets, getting out of a sick-bed to inspect her substitute, wept from personal, not vicarious, grief as the performance proceeded, and exclaimed at the end: "Des Œillets is no more."

The dramatist was then in the flush of his young manhood. He had put aside, for the time being, the ascetic tendencies of his religious training at the Jansenist stronghold of Port-Royal, and had taken up the life of Parisian gallantry. For the past two years he had been wearing the mourning of the heart for the loss of his first mistress, a beautiful young actress named Mlle. Duparc, notable for having rejected the advances of Molière, Pierre Corneille, and La Fontaine before surrendering to him, and also for having created the rôle of Hermione in "Andromaque." His grief at her death had been sincere and profound; but when Champmeslé dawned upon him, playing the same Hermione with greater power, he decided that it was time to console himself with a new flame.

Though not addicted to amorous dalliance in the wholesale manner then in vogue, Racine had the ingratiating personality and debonair qualities that facilitate conquest. This sketch of him, by his son Louis Racine, written after he had abandoned letters for the life of a zealot and a courtier, will serve for his livelier days of woman and song:

"An amiable court found him amiable, both in conversation and appearance. He was not one of those poets who have a frowning front; on the contrary, his was a frank and open countenance, once remarked by Louis XIV as among the happiest faces to be seen at his court. To these exterior graces he added those of conversation, in which, never preoccupied, neither the poet nor the author, he cared less about displaying his own *esprit* than that of the people with whom he talked. He never spoke of his works, and responded modestly to those who brought up the subject. He was gentle, mild, insinuating, adept in courtly parlance."

As for Champmeslé, testimony varies, but she is usually granted seductive fascination rather than radiant beauty. Mme. de Sévigné wrote: "She is almost plain, but when she recites verses she is adorable." Into that verdict, however, the professional jealousy of womankind doubtless enters. The Parfaict brothers, in their theatrical annals of the period, went on record that "her skin was not white, and she had extremely small and round eyes," but that she had "an advantageous figure, excellently carried and noble," and that her faults "were, so to speak, effaced by the natural graces spread over her whole person." Her voice, moreover, was enchanting. According to the anonymous author of "Entretiens Galants":

"The recitation of actors in tragedy is a kind of chant, and you will readily admit that the Champmeslé would not please you so much if her voice were less agreeable. But she has learned to modulate it with so much skill, and she lends to her words such natural tones, that it would seem that she really has in her heart the passions she expresses with her mouth."

Louis Racine grants her unusual personal charms, but with the virtuous contempt of a son for his father's one-time mistress, he gives all the credit for her fame to the dramatist: "This woman was not

34

born an actress. Nature had only endowed her with
beauty, voice and memory; she was so lacking, however, in cleverness that it was necessary for him to
read to her the verses which she had to recite, and
to give her the proper intonations . . . . As
he had formed Baron [one of the leading actors
of the time] he formed the Champmeslé, but with
much more effort. Moreover, he taught her the
meaning of her lines, showed her the appropriate gestures, and dictated to her the exact emphasis."

The son goes farther than his father, with all his
pains as stage-director to Champmeslé, would have
permitted, in this indictment of her for stupidity.
She was an accomplished actress when she first appeared at the Hôtel de Bourgogne in "Andromaque"; Racine's sudden shift from animosity to
adoration is proof enough of her innate talent. He
undoubtedly helped her to perfect her technique, or
moulded it to his own ideals of tragic declamation,
in which he was accepted as an authority; but he
made her a great actress no more than she helped
him write "Phèdre." It was a collaboration on both
sides, art and love, or passion rather, working together for the additional fame of the dramatist and
his interpreter.

The liaison began immediately after that triumphant night at the Hôtel de Bourgogne when Racine
prostrated himself at the Champmeslé's feet. It
lasted until the production of "Phèdre," after which
Racine renounced the theatre altogether. During

those seven years of an amour in which there was no pretence at concealment, which was so public that it was spoken of gaily by all Paris as a *fait accompli,* what of the husband, the Sieur de Champmeslé? He was at hand, but complaisant. Mlle. de Champmeslé still remained nominally under his protection; they were friendly enough; but he was too devoted to his own career, to champagne-bibbing and the pursuit of personal pleasures, to annoy his wife or the lofty Racine. Years afterward Boileau, the doyen of French critics and one of Racine's closest friends, reminded him of the numerous bottles of champagne which had been consumed by the Sieur de Champmeslé,—"you know at whose expense." This accommodating lord and master of the wanton actress must be accepted in the mood of his century in this matter; and apart from the moral code, he seems to have been a clever, merry fellow, who won some distinction as an actor, and as a playwright also.

Almost every year Racine produced a new tragedy as a vehicle for his beloved; and every year Champmeslé's popularity increased, not only in the theatre, but also in a brilliant Bohemia in which polite dissipation was practised as one of the fine arts, to be cultivated gracefully by nobles and writers alike. Her house was the rendezvous for a talented circle of men which, besides Racine, included among its literary lights Boileau, Valincourt, a dilettante who succeeded to Racine's seat in the Academy;

36

Chapelle, a literary *viveur* and poet *manqué;* and La Fontaine, the fabulist.

The latter was a stanch admirer of his hostess, to whom he roguishly regretted that he was merely her friend and nothing more. He wrote her winsome letters, brocaded with bits of verse, some of which are preserved in his collected works. Their tone is often delicately suggestive of Racine's supreme position in her heart and house, as in this example:

"I am at Chaury, mademoiselle; judge if I should think of you, I who would never forget you in the midst of the most brilliant court. M. Racine promised to write to me; why has he not done so? Without doubt he would have spoken of you, loving nothing so much as your charming person; that would have been the greatest consolation for the pain I feel in seeing you no longer. If he knew that I had followed in part the counsels which he gave me, without ceasing, however, to be faithful to idleness and slumber, he would perhaps for compensation have sent me news of you and of himself; but I can genuinely excuse him; the delights of your society fill hearts so completely that all other impressions fade away.

"How right you were, mademoiselle, in saying that ennui would gallop away with me before I had lost sight of the steeples of the great village; it is so true that I have a presentiment of melancholy which will not, I feel, disappear until my return to Paris.

"To cure an atrabilious man
Champmeslé has a better plan
Than medical advice;
For me, I dare say in advance
That one bright moment of her glance
Would heal me in a trice." *

"Woods, fields, brooks and nymphs of the meadows no longer appeal to me, since you have enchained happiness close to yourself, so I foretell an immediate departure. However, I am attending to my affairs so little that I do not know when they will end. Things of disgust to me are these fables, sales, arrears; to talk your language is more my part; but do not imagine that I pretend to speak it as well as yourself; that is an impossibility, and something I should never attempt.

"Please persuade M. Racine to write to me; you will be doing a pious act, I assure you. I hope that he will tell me of your triumphs; on that topic I am sure that he will not lack things to say. I flatter myself that he will write to me just as you think of me. Assuring you that this news will be the most agreeable I can learn, that never will you find a servitor more faithful or more devoted than

"DE LA FONTAINE."

---

* A guérir un atrabilaire,
Oui, Chanmeslay saura mieux faire
Que de Fagon toute talent;
Pour moi, j'ose affirmer d'avance
Qu'un seul instant de sa présence
Peut me guérir incontinent.

This engaging letter was written in 1676. Two
years later La Fontaine sent another epistle from the
country to the worshipped Champmeslé; but in it his
references were to other men than Racine. The lady,
in fact, was not limiting her favours to the dramatist;
certain nobles had been found agreeable, for passing
diversion; and as usual, her peccadilloes were known
to everyone except the *amant en titre*. The fable-
teller babbled on in this fashion:

"Since you are the best friend in the world, as
well as the most agreeable, and since you take great
interest in that which concerns your friends, it is
apropos to send you word of what those who have
not followed you are doing. From morning until
night they drink water, wine, lemonade, et cetera—
trivial refreshments for those who are deprived of
seeing you. The heat and your absence throws us
into insupportable languors. As for you, mademoiselle, I have no need to send for word about what
you are doing. I see it from here. You amuse
yourself from morning until night, and accumulate
hearts upon hearts. Everything will shortly belong
to the King of France and to Mademoiselle Champmeslé. But what are your courtiers doing? As for
those of the King, I do not trouble myself. Are you
charming away the ennui, the ill-luck at cards, and
all the other disgraces of M. de La Fare? And is
M. de Tonnerre always bringing to the house some
little reward? Great ones he can no longer give,
after the acquisition of your good graces. All the

rest are blessings of small importance, and whoever has gained you should rejoice but mildly at all other good fortunes. Send me word if he has not forgotten the most faithful of his servitors and if you think that in return he will continue to honour me with his pranks and his jests."

Boileau, a frequent guest at the Champmeslé's salon, had his cynic's fling at her indulgences to not one but many admirers, in an epigram in which he hit her off as being the mistress of "six contented, unjealous lovers." Her husband and Racine made two, and the others, whether contemporaneous, as Boileau pretended, or successive, were the Comtes de Revel and de Clermont-Tonnerre, the Marquis de La Fare, and Charles de Sévigné. The latter was the spoiled, rakish son of Madame of the celebrated letters, who wrote: "The manœuvres of the Champmeslé for the conservation of all her lovers, without prejudice to the rôles of Atalide, of Bérénice and of Phèdre, would cover five leagues of ground quite easily."

Madame de Sévigné was highly concerned about her dissipated son, who was paying court to that historic enchantress, Ninon de Lenclos, and to Champmeslé at the same time—a mad venture which would have inconvenienced Don Juan himself. His perturbed though tolerant mother wrote to her daughter:

"Madame de La Fayette and I am using every effort to wean him of so dangerous an attachment.

40

Besides, he has a little actress, and all the Despréaux [Boileau] and the Racines. There are delicious suppers—that is to say, *diableries.*" And later: "Your brother is at Saint-Germain. He divides his time between Ninon and a little actress, and, to crown all, Despréaux. We lead him a sad life. Ye gods, what folly! Ye gods, what folly!" Three weeks afterward: "A word or two concerning your brother. Ninon has given him his *congé*. She is tired of loving him without being loved in return; she has insisted upon his returning her letters, which he has accordingly done. I was not a little pleased at the separation. I gave him a hint of the duty he owed to God, reminded him of his former good sentiments, and entreated him not to stifle all notion of religion in his breast. But this is not all; when one side fails us, we think to repair it with the other, and are deceived. The young marvel [Champmeslé] has not broken with him, but she will soon, I believe . . . Ninon told him that he was a *pumpkin fricasseed in snow*. See what it is to keep good company! One learns such elegant expressions!"

This series of letters goes on to record the incorrigible Charles' physical break-down from "the abandoned life he had led during Holy Week":— "I took the opportunity to preach to him a little sermon on the subject, and we both indulged in some Christian reflections. He seems to approve my sentiments, particularly now that his disgust is at its height. He showed me some letters that he had re-

covered from his actress. I never read anything so
warm, so passionate; he wept, he died; he believed
it all while he was writing it, and laughed at it a moment afterwards. I assure you that he is worth his
weight in gold."

M. de Sévigné's rupture with Champmeslé was
soon complete: "He has left his actress at last, after
having followed her everywhere. When he saw her,
he was in earnest; a moment later, he would
make the greatest game of her. Ninon has
completely discarded him; he was miserable
while she loved him, and now that she loves
him no longer, he is in absolute despair. She
wished him, the other day, to give her the letters
he had received from his actress, which he did. You
must know that she was jealous of that princess, and
wanted to show them to a lover of hers, in the hope
of procuring her a few blows with a belt. He came
and told me, when I pointed out to him how shameful it was to treat this little creature so badly, merely
for having loved him; that she had not shown people
his letters, as some would have him believe, but, on
the contrary, had returned them to him again; that
such treacherous conduct was unworthy of a man of
quality, and that there was a degree of honour to be
observed, even in things dishonourable in themselves.
He acquiesced in the justice of my remarks, hurried
at once to Ninon's house, and, partly by strategy and
partly by force, got the poor devil's letters out of her
hands. I made him burn them. You see by this

what a regard I have for the reputation of an actress."

In these racy letters Madame de Sévigné, whose testimony has proven of historical interest in regard to a great variety of people and topics ever since her fluent pen was laid away, thus places on permanent record the facts that the Racine-Boileau-Champmeslé coterie were regarded by more correct society as a very fast set, association with which would be the undoing of such young Turks as Charles de Sévigné; that Champmeslé was playing fast and loose with Racine, and not only with him but with several others as well; and that the actress, as a disciple of Aphrodite, was a formidable rival to Ninon de Lenclos. Lest the latter claim seem extravagant, however, it must be admitted that the amazing Ninon was losing her grip, so to speak; she was then in her fifty-sixth year, while Champmeslé was in her early thirties. The former, it would seem, was giving more than the fair handicap of a professional to an amateur. But in spite of her age, she was holding her own against the glamour of the blooming actress. Truly, she was a wonderful Ninon!

To return to the *théâtre* of Racine, and Champmeslé's participation in it: on November 21, 1670, Racine brought out at the Hôtel de Bourgogne a new drama, "Bérénice," with his new mistress in the title rôle. Eight days later, at the competing Palais-Royal, Pierre Corneille put forward his

"Tite et Bérénice," on exactly the same theme, with Mlle. Molière as the Judæan heroine. Thus were the two masters of classic tragedy pitted against one another, on the same ground, each having taken up the story of Titus and Berenice unknown to the other, at the persuasion of Henrietta of England, ("Madame"), daughter of Charles I and Louis XIV's sister-in-law. Perhaps that distinguished lady wanted to decide a bet, but whatever her fell purpose, she did not live to see its consummation. This peculiar tourney gave Racine an easy victory over his senior; Corneille's tragedy was accounted unworthy of him, while Racine's was approved by the public and the King, and held the stage for thirty performances. Doubtless the inspired acting of Champmeslé, and Corneille's complete failure, were the causes of Racine's good-fortune; his own literary friends, among them the satiric and acutely critical Boileau, were frank in stating that they did not care for his work over much.

"Bérénice" was followed, in due time, by "Bajazet," with Champmeslé as Roxane; and Mme. de Sévigné once more had something interesting to say. She attended the fifth performance, and promptly wrote to her daughter, with certain gay references to her son's intrigue:

"We have been to see the new play by Racine, and thought it admirable. My *daughter-in-law* is, in my opinion, the best performer I ever saw. She is a hundred leagues in front of Des Œillets, and I, who am supposed to have some talent for acting, am not worthy to light the candles when she appears. . . . I wish you had been with me that afternoon; I am sure you would not have thought your time ill spent. You would have dropped a tear or two, for I myself shed twenty; besides, you would have greatly admired your *sister-in-law*."

When the drama was printed, she sent her daughter a copy of the book, with this comment: "If I could send Champmeslé with it, you would find the tragedy among the best; without her, it loses half its value. Racine's plays are written for Champmeslé and not for posterity. Whenever he grows old and ceases to be in love, it will be seen whether or not I am mistaken."

"Mithridate," with its Monime, was the next theatrical joining of hands between Racine and Champmeslé; it was produced January 13, 1673, the day after the great occasion of the dramatist's reception into the French Academy. His eighth tragedy, "Iphigénie en Aulide," followed; its first performance was at Versailles, August 17, 1674, as a part of the gorgeous entertainments given by Louis XIV to his court in celebration of the conquest of Franche-Comté. The success of author and dramatist was overwhelming; the tears by which tragedy purges the soul, according to the Aristotelian idea, poured forth abundantly. Boileau dropped into rhyme to honour the occasion, tossing off a quatrain of which these lines may serve as the English equivalent:

> Assembled Greece shed no more tears that day
> At Aulis for the altar's maiden prey
> Than from our own eyes at this brilliant show
> Champmeslé, in her name, has caused to flow.*

During the next two years Champmeslé flourished prodigiously at the Hôtel de Bourgogne, playing all the current dramas, while Racine remained silent, absorbed in the composition of "Phèdre," which was destined to be his masterwork. He had maintained in Madame LaFayette's salon, according to tradition, that the blackest of themes could be made sublime by a true poet, and had undertaken to prove his theory with a tragedy around Phædra's incestuous passion for her stepson Hippolytus. The drama, wrought out with infinite pains, was produced on New Year's Day, 1677, with Champmeslé, of course, in the title rôle; and Racine at once found himself with another literary duel, more bitter than that with Corneille, on his hands. When the topic of his forthcoming work became public, the Duchesse de Bouillon, to whom he had given offense, engaged Pradon, a minor dramatist, to write a tragedy along similar lines; and this piece, completed in three months,

---

* Jamais Iphigénie en Aulide immolée
   N'a conté tant de pleurs à la Grèce assemblée,
   Que dans l'heureux spectacle à nos yeux étalé
   En a fait, sous son nom, verser la Champmeslé.

was scheduled for production at a rival theatre on the same day. The difficulty of finding a suitable interpreter for this second Phædra—the rôle hav· ing been rejected by both Mlle. de Brie and Mlle. Molière—delayed it, however, for two days. Racine was greatly chagrined by this challenge to his eminence, and also suffered some temporary alarm from the intrigues of the duchess. That venomous lady, determined to defeat Racine at any cost, bought up all the seats at the Hôtel de Bourgogne for several nights, at the expense of some 15,000 francs, thus compelling his "Phèdre" to be given before empty benches and to take on the semblance of an utter failure. But after she had received a hint from the King that her tactics were offensive to His Majesty, Racine's drama received its proper hearing by Paris, and promptly outshone the pre- tender Pradon's offering. "Phèdre" was both Ra- cine's greatest play and the crowning glory of Champmeslé's career. A few years later (August 25, 1680) the drama, with the original interpreter of its leading rôle, was chosen to mark the founding of the Comédie-Française by Louis XIV, and when a new home for the company was dedicated in the Rue des Fossés Saint Germain des Prés, April 16, 1689, it had a similar revival.

Shortly after the first production of "Phèdre," Racine broke off with the theatre and Champmeslé together. Some of his biographers hold that his reaction toward Jansenism—a puritanical variant of

Catholicism then prevalent—was due to his disillusionment regarding his mistress; that after tolerating her other affairs of the heart as mere flirtations which were no treason to their own solid attachment, his eyes were finally opened to her true character. Her acceptance of the Comte de Clermont-Tonnerre as a serious lover, about that time, certainly was not without its effect in provoking his mood of disgust for the world of play and players. He was bitterly humiliated by her open infidelity, and his stiff-necked pride as laureate of letters was particularly wounded by a punning epigram apropos of himself and his successor in Champmeslé's affections. Their names were the cue for this bit of satire; Racine (*anglice,* root) was proclaimed "uprooted" by Tonnerre (*anglice,* thunderbolt). He undoubtedly felt the sting of this quip; and, sickening of the falsity of theatrical life, his rebellion against Champmeslé included the institution which she adorned in art if not in morals.

Racine's son, and one of his most recent biographers, Gustave Larroumet, however, place the emphasis, in explaining his retirement, upon a reversion to the religiosity of his youth at Port-Royal. Says the former:

"He resolved not only to cease writing tragedies and even verses, but also to make reparation for those which he had written by a rigorous penitence. The keenness of his remorse inspired the idea of becoming a Carthusian."

But his spiritual adviser, still according to Louis Racine, "thought this action too violent," and counselled him "to remain in the world and escape its dangers by marrying some woman filled with piety." The father confessor's prescription sounds, in spite of the son's assertion, more like a cure for the heartbreak of a man who has been deceived in his love than like advice to a zealot who feels a genuine call to take monastic vows. So, "wise friends" having found a suitably pious mate for him, he was married June 1, 1677, of which union Louis Racine remarked that "neither love nor personal interest had any part in his choice; he consulted nothing but reason in so serious a step."

Still, however profound his conversion, he did not put on sack-cloth and ashes. His devotions were confined to his privacy; in public life he became an adroit courtier who, though his creed of Jansenism was not in favour with the King, secured some lucrative offices, among which was the post of chief flatterer to Louis XIV as historiographer-royal, shared by him with his old boon-companion, Boileau. He even became partly reconciled to the poetic muse which he had so harshly renounced, writing two lyric dramas of scriptural themes, "Esther," and "Athalie," to be played by the school girls whose innocence was under the special patronage—oh, beautiful paradox!—of Mme. de Maintenon, the King's ex-mistress and informal wife.

Racine's disgust for the professional stage, how-

ever, persisted through life; among his letters to his
son the following bit of paternal advice in regard to
play-going may be found:

"You know what I have said to you about operas
and plays; there will probably be some performances
at Marly; the King and the court are aware of the
scruples which I entertain about attending them
and they will have a poor opinion of you, if you
show so little regard for my sentiments. I know
that you will not be dishonoured before men should
you go to the play, but do you count it nothing to be
dishonoured before God?"

Mlle. de Champmeslé died May 15, 1698; and
Racine, a year later. He never relented in his bitter
estimate of her; and in spite of his own failing health
he commented upon her end in a manner which,
though typical of the churchly zealot then, seems almost unpardonable now. When he heard that she
was at death's door, he wrote to his son:

"M. de Rost informed me day before yesterday
that the Champmeslé was nearing her end, about
which he seemed very distressed; but what is more
afflicting is that which he apparently troubles himself
about but little; I mean the obstinacy with which
that poor wretch refuses to renounce the stage, having declared, as I have been told, that she thinks it
quite glorious to die an actress. It should be hoped
that when she sees death closer at hand, she will
change her tone, as most people who are so haughty
when they feel well usually do."

His old mistress was dead when he penned those words, though he had not heard the news. Two months later, after learning the details of her passing, he returned to the topic in this manner:

"I will tell you, by the way, that I owe reparation to the memory of the Champmeslé, who died in a sufficiently good state of soul, after having renounced the stage, very repentant for her past life, but especially afflicted at having to die."

Thus by his own words the great Racine stands indicted of a callous lack of charity which, however characteristic of the betrayed lover and however consonant with his sanctimonious pose, is hardly worthy of a poet.

As for Champmeslé, certain lines from Swinburne may do her justice:

> Though we shift and bedeck and bedrape us,
> Thou art noble and nude and antique;
> Libitina thy mother, Priapus
> Thy father, a Tuscan and Greek.

GREAT LOVE STORIES OF THE THEATRE

III

ELIZABETH BARRY AND THOMAS
OTWAY

NO actress has had a greater share in the literature of any epoch, through amorous association with its writers, than Elizabeth Barry in that of the Restoration. To letters in the merry, mad days of Charles II she was what her contemporary, Mistress Eleanor Gwyn, was to statecraft, with this greater distinction, that while Nell limited herself to the King alone, Mrs. Barry distributed her enchantments in a highly representative manner. The chronicle of her loves is almost a comprehensive literary criticism for the period, 1660—1700; it embraces the pinnacle of licentious satire in John Wilmot, Earl of Rochester; dips into the source of English comedy of manners in George Etherege; and includes the refulgent afterglow of classic tragedy in Thomas Otway. For a summing up of Restoration work in drama, verse and prose, a modern scholar, with more than two centuries of perspective, could make no better choice of three dominant names than did this distracting dame, herself the supreme actress of the time.

"The famous Madam Barry," as she was known,

was coeval with and analagous to Marie de Champmeslé of France; and Otway was her Racine, but
with a difference. Him she flouted and scorned,
while triumphing in the characters which he created
for her. The favours of her person were bestowed
in preference upon the men of wealth and title,
Rochester and Etherege, and were utterly denied the
ill-starred poet whose "Venice Preserved" kindled
anew the great Elizabethan ashes. Yet in the rejected Otway the chief sentimental interest of her
career is to be found; his sterile, unrewarded years
of vassalage to her, his frenetic letters of worship
and entreaty, which betray a genius humbling himself in the dust, and his ghastly end, make a story of
deep pathetic appeal.

Mrs. Barry, born about 1658, came to the stage
as a gentlewoman in reduced circumstances, her
father, Robert Barry, having wasted his substance
in loyally maintaining a regiment for the support
of his King during the Civil War. Sir William
Davenant, manager of the "King's House" after
Charles II had returned from exile into his own,
undertook to place her in his company, remembering
her father as a comrade-in-arms and knowing the
girl as his wife's "companion." Her voice and appearance were promising, but she seemed so inept
that after three trials she was given up as hopeless.
Then young Lord Rochester, ever ready to astonish
the town, made a wager that within six months he
could develop her into a favourite, and she was

handed over into his wild keeping. There is no reason to assume that she shrank from the experiment or its consequences.

The first, the inevitable step, was to make her a mistress; but Rochester did not neglect his pedagogic duties in the liaison. According to a "History of the English Stage," published by Edmund Curll in 1741, he selected for her the rôles of the Little Gypsy in Mrs. Aphra Behn's "The Rover" and Isabella in Lord Orrery's "Mustapha," rehearsing her "near thirty times on the stage and about twelve times in the dress she was to act in"; furthermore, "I have been assured from those who were present that her page was taught to manage her train in such a manner as to give each movement a peculiar grace." And when her declamation was found to be monotonous, this amateur stage-director "made her enter into the nature of each sentiment, perfectly changing herself, as it were, into the person, not merely by the proper stress or sounding of the voice, but feeling really and being in the humour the person she represented was supposed to be in."

Then, in 1673, before the six months' limit of Rochester's bet had expired, she appeared in "Mustapha," and won the money for her lover. The audience, which included Charles II and numerous courtiers, curious to see if the madcap Earl had fulfilled his vow, was swept by tragic pathos—Mrs. Barry's particular *genre* of acting. The Duchess of York, in particular, was so profoundly impressed that she endowed the débutante with her own royal wedding-dress.

Colley Cibber, who came to the stage when Mrs. Barry was in the maturity of her art, may be consulted on her histrionic endowments:

"A presence of elevated dignity, her mien and motion superb and gracefully majestic; her voice full, clear and strong, so that no violence of passion could be too much for her; and when distress or tenderness possessed her, she subsided into the most affecting melody and softness. In the art of exciting pity she had a power beyond all the actresses I have ever seen, or what your imagination can conceive."

As to Lord Rochester, who thus initiated Mrs. Barry into passion, fictitious and real: he was the classic rake of the riotous Restoration. His name is an epitome of all that was drunken, delirious and damnable while Charles II was on the throne. It seems, however, that in this case the devil has been given more than his due; Rochester's notoriety, intensified by apocryphal anecdote, is perhaps not altogether deserved; but before his exhausted vitality flickered out, at the early age of thirty-three, he had set the fast company of his day an impossible pace. Still, he is an ingratiating rather than an iniquitous figure; he was precocious, talented and witty; a man of gifts and muscular intellect caught in the high-tide of Restoration viciousness and surrendering himself to the swift current with total abandon.

Rochester's fame as a satirist needs only one epigram for its perpetuation—the verses which he inscribed upon the door of Charles II's bed-chamber:

> Here lies our sovereign lord the King
> Whose word no man relies on;
> Who never said a foolish thing
> And never did a wise one.

He has many another crisp bit to his credit, however; his gibes in rhyme, written with a venomous pen, stung tender reputations right and left. His was a mind of intense vitality, ever busy in the heat of alcohol; a superman of dissipation, he might almost be called. His poems make a rather extensive collection; and though they are marred by obscenities, some of which were foisted upon him by unscrupulous editors of later periods, pretty lyrics are also to be found among them. To the stage he contributed an adaptation of Beaumont and Fletcher's "Valentinian," produced after his death with Mrs. Barry in the leading rôle.

His exploits of ill-repute were many; Pepys records this specimen:

"Thence to my Lady Sandwich's, where, to shame, I had not been a great while. Here, upon my telling her a story of my Lord Rochester's running away on Friday night last with Mrs. Mallett, the great beauty and fortune of the North, who had supped at White Hall with Mrs. Stewart, and was going home to her lodgings with her grandfather, my Lord Haly, by coach; and was at Charing Cross seized

on by both horse and foot-men, and forcibly taken
from him, and put into a coach with six horses, and
two women provided to receive her, and carried
away. Upon immediate pursuit, my Lord of Rochester, for whom the King had spoke to the lady
often, but with no success, was taken at Uxbridge;
but the lady is not yet heard of, and the King
mighty angry, and the Lord sent to the Tower."

Nothing was too crazy for Rochester to attempt.
He went about London disguised as a porter or a
beggar, tracking down shopkeepers' wives and serv-
ant-maids for seduction; he costumed himself as
an Italian mountebank and practised astrology in
a low quarter for several weeks. Once, with Etherege, who was his inseparable, and two other ruffling gentlemen, he was involved in a shocking brawl
at Epsom. After tossing some street musicians in a
blanket, they decided to bait the constable, and
dragged that worthy out of his bed to receive a beat-
ing. The town watchmen rushed to the rescue and
subdued them, but after the fracas was apparently
over, Rochester drew his sword on the constable.
The watch returned to the attack, another mêlée
followed, and one of Rochester's friends was run
through with a pike and slain.

This rogue persisted in being paradoxical, and he
now has a niche, of all places, in ecclesiastical biography, through the good graces of Bishop Burnet.
When he began to pay the physical penalty of his
sins, he became repentant and called upon the his-

torian-churchman for spiritual advice. The bishop's account of their association and theological debates is a fascinating character study which paints the rake in cleaner colours than he has been granted at other hands, and which also discloses him as possessed of a philosophy of keenly modern rationalistic tendencies. Rochester was converted into a humble Christian mood before his death, but he also converted the bishop to a friendly view of his past misdemeanours. Burnet defends him as follows:

"The natural heat of his fancy, being inflamed by wine, made him so extravagantly pleasant that many, to be diverted by that humour, studied to engage him deeper and deeper in intemperance; which at length did so entirely subdue him that, as he told me, for five years together he was continually drunk; not all the while under the visible effect of it, but his blood was so inflamed that he was not in all that time cool enough to be perfectly master of himself. This led him to say and do many wild and unaccountable things. . . . There were two principles in his natural temper that being heightened by this heat carried him to great excesses: a violent love of pleasure, and a disposition to extravagant mirth. The one involved him in great sensuality; the other led him to many odd adventures and frolics, in which he was oft in hazard of his life; the one being the same irregular appetite in his mind that the other was in his body, which made him think nothing diverting that was not extravagant. And though in cold blood he was a generous and good-natured man, yet he would go far in his heats after anything that might turn to a jest or matter of diversion."

A group of Rochester's letters survive to throw some light upon his liaison with Mrs. Barry, to whom, it is believed, he gave the most sincere love of his debauched career. In one of them he writes:

"Madam:—So much wit and beauty as you have should think of nothing less than doing miracles; and there cannot be a greater than to continue to love me: affecting everything is mean, as loving pleasure, and being fond where you find merit; but to pick out the wildest and most fantastical odd man alive, and to place your kindness there, is an act as brave and daring as will show the greatness of your spirit, and distinguish you in love, as you are in all things else, from womankind. Whether I have made a good argument for myself, I leave you to judge; and beg you to believe me whenever I tell you what Mrs. Barry is, since I give you so sincere an account of her humblest servant. Remember the hour of a strict account, when both hearts are to be open, and we obliged to speak freely, as you ordered it yesterday; for so must I ever call the day I saw you last, since all time between that and the next visit is no part of my life, or at least like a long fit of the falling-sickness, wherein I am dead to all joy and happiness.—Here is a damned impertinent fool bolted in, that hinders me from ending my letter; the plague take him, and any man or woman alive that takes my thoughts off you! But in the evening I will see you and be happy in spite of all the fools in the world."

In another communication, he defines the ground of their attachment, with some truth, in this concise manner:

"Dear Madam:—You are stark mad, and therefore the fitter for me to love; and that is the reason, I think, I can never leave to be
"YOUR HUMBLE SERVANT."

His daughter by Mrs. Barry, named Betty, was the cause of a quarrel between them, Rochester insisting, apparently, that the mother should surrender the care of their offspring to more proper guardians selected by himself. They made it up again, however, and he wrote to her:

"I am far from delighting in the grief I have given you by taking away the child, and you, who made it so absolutely necessary for me to do so, must take that excuse from me for all the ill nature of it. On the other side, pray be assured I love Betty so well that you need not apprehend any neglect from those I employ; and I hope very shortly to restore her to you a finer girl than ever."

Rochester died in 1680, leaving an annuity of 40 pounds for the support of the child. Then George Etherege, as his next friend, inherited the actress herself as paramour.

Of this liaison little is known, for Etherege is an

elusive figure in the Restoration pageant, important though his work is from the critical point of view. It lasted, apparently, from 1680 to 1685, being terminated by the dramatist's appointment to the post of British envoy extraordinary to Ratisbon; it was a union of mutual satisfaction, and was blessed by a daughter to whom the father bequeathed 6,000 pounds. Some comment upon Etherege himself is necessary, however, to illustrate Mrs. Barry's influence in the realm of letters.

He was a fine gentleman of the Restoration, flagrant enough in his morals but without Rochester's deadly vigour in vice. Elegant, amiable and slothful, he was known as "gentle George" or "easy Etherege," as in these lines of Rochester, rebuking him for an indolent pen:

Now Apollo had got gentle George in his eye,
And frankly confessed that, of all men that writ,
There's none had more fancy, sense, judgment, and wit;
But i' the crying sin, idleness, he was so hardened
That his long seven years' silence was not to be pardoned.

Before the accession of Charles II Etherege had, it is surmised, spent a number of years in Paris; and he brought back with him the manners of French gallantry, as a contrast to English brutality in dissipation. Moreover, he had seen the dawn of Molière on the French stage, and by adapting the spirit of that master to the Restoration mood, eschewing the moral point of view and satirically recording rather than boldly castigating manners, he became the pioneer of a new school. Etherege blazed the way for Congreve, Goldsmith and Sheridan; let him be honoured, then, rather than included in the wholesale denunciation of the Restoration comic writers, according to time-honoured convention. His was a deft, light touch; he depicted fops and beaux "in a key of rose-colour on pale gray," says Edmund Gosse. The volume of his work is slender, but he occupies a position of some historical importance in the development of English comedy.

Etherege's plays are only three in number: "She Would If She Could" (1668); "The Comical Revenge, or Love in a Tub" (1669); and "The Man of Mode, or Sir Fopling Flutter" (1676). The latter was his masterpiece; its dialogue is almost Congrevian in brightness. The leading characters were plainly recognisable to its audiences; the airy Sir Fopling was Beau Hewitt; impetuous Dorimant was Lord Rochester, even to details of costume; gay young Medley as Sir Charles Sedley; and the suave Bellair was Etherege himself. To complete the precious coterie, the rôle of Mrs. Loveit was played by Mrs. Barry.

Pepys gives us a single glance at Etherege in a jotting that is rich with playhouse atmosphere:

"My wife being gone before, I to the Duke of York's play-house; where a new play of Etheridge's called 'She Would If She Could'; and though I was there by two o'clock, there was 1,000 people put back that could not have room in the pit; and I, at last, because my wife was there, made shift to get into the 18d. box, and there saw; . . . And, among the rest, here was the Duke of Buckingham to-day openly sat in the pit; and there I found him with my Lord Buckhurst, and Sedley, and Etheridge the poet; the last of whom I did hear mightily find fault with the actors, that they were out of humour, and had not their parts perfect, and that Harris did do nothing, nor could so much as sing a ketch in it; while all the rest did, through the whole pit, blame the play as a silly, dull thing, though there was something very roguish and witty; but the design of the play, and end, mighty insipid."

This man of fashion and letters was too lazy for a dramatist, so he became a diplomat, and spent five years in Ratisbon. One of his rare letters contains this comment on staid German life:

"Is it not enough to breed an ill habit of body in a man who was used to sit up till morning to be forced, for want of knowing what to do with himself, to go to bed in the evening; one who has been used to live with all freedom, never to approach anyone without ceremony; one who has been used to run up and down to find variety of company, to sit at home and entertain himself in solitude? . . . If I do well after all this, you must allow me to be a great philosopher, and I dare affirm Cato left not the world with more firmness of soul than I did England."

"Gentle George" scandalized the Germans by receiving an actress on terms of social equality. His house was besieged by a mob while he was at dinner with the lady, but he charged the crowd, sword in hand, at the head of his garrison of servants, and challenged its ringleader, a baron. He gamed and wrote verses to kill the time, quaffed many a flagon of Rhenish, and comported himself generally like a gallant blade of the Restoration. The tradition is that he died in Ratisbon, about 1689, breaking his neck in a drunken fall down-stairs; but there is better historical ground for believing that he fled to Paris after James II was dethroned by William of Orange, and passed away there in a more or less natural manner.

If wretched Thomas Otway had been alive when Etherege left London on his diplomatic mission, he might have had his great desire, which was possession of Mrs. Barry. He had been willing to wait, to eat his heart out in patience, to take her at second hand, or at third. But poverty and starvation had then claimed him for their own; he had died so pitifully that London was shamed, even in those careless days, and kept an ignominious silence about his end.

This forlorn member of the clan of poets accursed was the son of a Sussex rector; he was educated at Christ Church College, Oxford, and was drawn to London, as an undergraduate at the age of twenty (1671), by the glamour of the stage. Comely of person, he had hoped for a career as an actor; and through the friendship of Mrs. Aphra Behn he was

67

given a rôle in her drama, "The Forced Marriage,"
when it was produced at the Duke's theatre. Stage
fright sealed his lips, however; he was a complete
failure, and had to surrender his part. Then he returned to the university, to desert it finally in 1674,
after refusing to take holy orders. He became a sub-
altern in a troop of horse, but sold his commission
within a year to gravitate to London once more, determined to earn his living by his pen. His first
tragedy, "Alcibiades," was soon accepted; it was
staged with the rising star, Mrs. Barry, in the small
rôle of Draxilla, and with the leonine Betterton as
the hero. Otway's impressionable heart then began
its long, vain yearnings.

Mrs. Barry, involved with Lord Rochester at the
time, played a game familiar through the ages to
sirens of her type with the promising young writer.
Hers was a cold, worldly soul, devoted only to self-
interest; and she encouraged him just enough to keep
him in servitude. In a word, she used his passion
for her own professional advancement, and made no
return. He, thoroughly beguiled, kept on hoping
and toiling, putting his genius on the rack to create
rôles for her, pouring out his faithful dog's heart in
dithyrambic letters, squandering his earnings with a
crew of rich wastrels in order to live in her circle.

Otway followed the weak "Alcibiades" with the
immeasurably superior "Don Carlos," which came
within hailing distance of Corneille; and then
brought out an excellent translation of Racine's

drama on Titus and Berenice. The latter was slav-
ishly dedicated to Lord Rochester, the possessor of
his beloved, but instead of rewarding him in the customary manner the impish Earl, suspecting rivalry,
turned upon him with villainous satires. Then Otway, sickening of his servility, tried to forget Mrs.
Barry and cure himself of too much loving by military service in Flanders. He returned from that
venture in 1679, ragged and penniless, sans health,
sans fame, sans loot, to be satirised once more by
Rochester.

The madness for Mrs. Barry, however, still
burned in his veins; it was fastened on him like a
disease, and broke out with fresh violence after his
return from voluntary exile. He now began that
series of letters to her which will presently be
quoted. Determined to win her, bent upon rehabili-
tating his fortunes more for that purpose than for literary reputation, he busied his pen upon plays and
poems. As he was bringing "The Orphan" to com-
pletion, the troublesome Rochester died, and his
hopes flared up again at the news. The prologue and
preface to that drama seem to reflect that event by a
tone which, for him, is almost jocund. His fool's
paradise did not last long, for the gossips who told
of Mrs. Barry's astonishing triumph as Monimia also
carried the word that Etherege was Rochester's successor.

"The Orphan" gave Mrs. Barry her greatest moment of pathos. The indispensable Dr. Doran's

comment in his classic annals upon the "point" of which she made a *chef-d'œuvre* in that piece is too apropos to be neglected:

"Mrs. Barry, like many other eminent members of her profession, was famous for the way in which she uttered some single expression in the play. The 'Look there!' of Spranger Barry, as he passed the body of Rutland, always moved the house to tears. So, the 'Remember twelve!' of Mrs. Siddons' Belvidera; the 'Well, as you guess!' of Edmund Kean's Richard; the 'Qu'en dis-tu?' of Talma's Auguste; the 'Je crois!' of Rachel's Pauline; the 'Je vois!' of Mademoiselle Mars' Valerie, were 'points' which never failed to excite an audience to enthusiasm. But there were two phrases with which Mrs. Barry could still more deeply move an audience. When, in 'The Orphan,' she pronounced the words, 'Ah, poor Castalio!' not only did the audience weep, but the actress herself shed tears abundantly. The other phrase was in a scene of Banks' puling tragedy, 'The Unhappy Favourite, or the Earl of Essex.' In that play, Mrs. Barry represented Queen Elizabeth, and that with such effect that it was currently said, the people of her day knew more of Queen Elizabeth from her impersonation of the character than they did from history. The apparently commonplace remark, 'What mean my grieving subjects?' was invested by her with such emphatic grace and dignity, as to call up murmurs of approbation which swelled into thunders of applause."

Dramatic authorship, even in its most fortunate aspects, was no sure way to prosperity then; and Otway, like a true poet, let others reap the financial profit of his work. Destitution and despair were dragging him down even while "The Orphan" was winning more fame and largess for Mrs. Barry. He kept on struggling against his malign fate, however, and two years later brought out "Venice Preserved," which has become a permanent memorial to his genius and which is often rated as one of the finest tragic dramas since Shakespeare. With Mrs. Barry as the original Belvidera, the play took London by storm; but for poor Otway, there was no reprieve. He sank to the depths, and no helping hands were held out to lift him up.

His letters to Mrs. Barry, judging by internal evidence, began with his return from soldiering in the Low Countries, in 1680, and ended with the production of "Venice Preserved" in 1682. They tell a story of love-in-wretchedness which is epic in its violence. In chronological sequence, stripped of their frequent italics and modernised in spelling, they read as follows:

"My Tyrant!—I endure too much torment to be silent, and have endured it too long not to make the severest complaint. I love you, I dote on you; desire makes me mad when I am near you; and despair, when I am from you. Sure, of all miseries, love is to me the most intolerable. It haunts me in my sleep, perplexes me when waking; every melancholy thought makes my fears more powerful; and every delightful one makes my wishes more unruly. In all other uneasy chances of a man's life, there is an immediate recourse to some kind of succour or another. In wants we apply ourselves to our friends; in sickness to physicians. But love, the sum, the total of all misfortunes, must be endured with silence; no friend so dear to trust with such a secret, nor remedy in art so powerful to remove its anguish. Since the first day I saw you, I have hardly enjoyed one hour of perfect quiet. I loved you early, and no sooner had I beheld that soft, bewitching face of yours but I felt in my heart the very foundation of all my peace give way. But when you become another's, I must confess that I did then rebel, had foolish pride enough to promise myself I would in time recover my liberty. In spite of my enslaved nature, I swore against myself, I would not love you. I affected a resentment, stifled my spirit, and would not let it bend, so much as once to upbraid you, each day it was my chance to see or to be near you. With stubborn sufferance I resolved to bear and brave your power. Nay, did it often too, successfully. Generally, with wine or conversation I diverted or appeased the demon that possessed me; but when at night, returning to my unhappy self, to give my heart an account why I had done it so unnatural a violence, it was then I always paid a treble interest for the short moments of ease which I had borrowed; then every treacherous thought rose up and took your part, nor left me till they had thrown me on my bed and opened those sluices of tears that were to run till morning. This has been for some years my best condition; nay, time itself, that decays all things else, has but increased and added to my longings. I tell you and charge you to believe it, as you are generous (for sure you must be, for everything, except your neglect of me, persuades me that you are so), even at this time, though other arms have held you, and so long trespassed on those dear joys that only were my due; I love you with all that tenderness of spirit, that purity of truth, and that sincerity of heart, that I could sacrifice the nearest friends or interest I have on earth, barely but to please you. If I had all the world, it should be yours; for with it I could be but miserable if you were not mine. I appeal to you for justice, if through the whole actions of my life I have done any one thing that might not let you see how absolute your authority was over me. Your commands have always been sacred to me; your smiles have always transported me; and your frowns awed me. In short, you will quickly become to me the greatest blessing or the greatest curse that ever man was doomed to. I cannot so much as look upon you without confusion; wishes and fears rise up in war within me, and work a cursed distraction through my soul that must, I am sure, in time have wretched consequences. You only can with that healing cordial, love, assuage and calm my torments; pity the man then who would be proud to die for you

and cannot live without you, and allow him thus far
to boast too, that (take out Fortune from the balance)
you never were beloved or courted by creature that
had a nobler or juster pretense to your heart, than the
unfortunate (and even at this time) weeping

"OTWAY."

.   .   .   .   .

"In value of your quiet, though it would be the
utter ruin of my own, I have endeavoured this day
to persuade myself never more to trouble you with a
passion that has tormented me sufficiently already,
and is so much more a torment to me, in that I per-
ceive it has become one to you, who are much dearer
to me than my own self.   I have laid all the reasons
my distracted conditions would let me have recourse
to before me.   I have consulted my pride whether
after a rival's possession, I ought to ruin all my peace
for a woman that another has been more blessed in,
though no man ever loved as I did.   But love, victorious love, overthrows all that, and tells me it is his
nature never to remember; he still looks forward
from the present hour, expecting still new dawns,
new rising happiness; never looks back, never regards what is past and left behind him, but buries
and forgets it quite in the hot, fierce pursuit of joy
before him.   I have consulted too my very self, and
find how careless nature was in framing me; seasoned
me hastily with all the most violent inclinations and
desires, but omitted the ornaments that should make
those qualities become me.   I have consulted too my

lot of fortune and find how foolishly I wish possession of what is so precious, all the world's too cheap
for it; yet still I love, still I dote on, and cheat myself, very content because the folly pleases me. It is
pleasure to think how fair you are, though at the
same time worse than damnation to think how cruel.
Why should you tell me you have shut your heart up
forever? It is an argument unworthy of yourself,
sounds like reserve, and not so much sincerity as sure
I may claim even from a little of your friendship.
Can your age, your face, your eyes, and your spirit
bid defiance to that sweet power? No, you know
better to what end Heaven made you, know better
how to manage youth and pleasure than to let them
die and pall upon your hands. 'Tis me, 'tis only me
you have barred your heart against. My sufferings,
my diligence, my sighs, complaints and tears are of
no power with your haughty nature; yet sure you
might at least vouchsafe to pity them, not shift me
off with gross, thick home-spun friendship, the common coin that passes betwixt worldly interest. Must
that be my lot! Take it, ill-natured, take it, give it
to him who would waste his fortune for you, give it
to the man who would fill your lap with gold, court
with offers of vast rich possessions, give it the fool
who hath nothing but his money to plead for him.
Love will have a much nearer relation, or none. I
ask for glorious happiness; you bid me welcome to
your friendship; it is like seating me at your side-
table, when I have the best pretense to the right-hand

at the feast. I love, I dote, I am mad, and know no measure, nothing but extremes can give me ease; the kindest love, or most provoking scorn. Yet even your scorn would not perform the cure; it might indeed take off the edge of hope, but damned despair will gnaw my heart forever. If then I am not odious to your eyes, if you have charity enough to value the well-being of a man who holds you dearer than you the child your bowels are most fond of, by that sweet pledge of your first softest love, I charm and here conjure you to pity the distracting pangs of mine; pity my unquiet days and restless nights; pity the frenzy that has half possessed my brain already, and makes me write to you thus ravingly. The poor wretch in Bedlam is more at peace than I am! And if I must never possess the heaven I wish for, my next desire is (and the sooner the better) a clean swept cell, a merciful keeper, and your compassion when you find me there. *Think and be generous."*

.   .   .   .   .

"Since you are going to quit the world, I think myself obliged, as a member of the world, to use the best of my endeavours to divert you from so ill-natured an inclination. Therefore, by reason your visits will take up so much of this day, I have debarred myself the opportunity of waiting on you this afternoon, that I may take a time you are more mistress of, and when you shall have more leisure to hear, if it be possible for any arguments of mine to take place in a heart I am afraid too much hardened

76

against me. I must confess it may look a little extraordinary, for one under my circumstances to endeavour the confirming your good opinion of the world, when it had been better for me, one of us had never seen it. For nature disposed me from my creation to love, and my ill-fortune has condemned me to dote on one who certainly could never have been deaf so long to so faithful a passion, had nature disposed her from her creation to hate anything but me. I beg you forgive this trifling, for I have so many thoughts of this nature that 'tis impossible for me to take pen and ink in my hand, and keep 'em quiet, especially when I have the least pretense to let you know you are the cause of the severest disquiets that ever touched the heart of

"OTWAY."

. . . . .

"Could I see you without passion or be absent from you without pain, I need not beg your pardon for this renewing my vows, that I love you more than health, or any happiness here or hereafter. Everything you do is a new charm to me; and though I have languished for seven long tedious years of desire, jealously despairing, yet every minute I see you I still discover something new and more bewitching. Consider how I love you; what would I not renounce, or enterprise for you? I must have you mine, or I am miserable; and nothing but knowing which shall be the happy hour can make the rest of my life that are to come tolerable. Give me a word or two of

comfort, or resolve never to look with common goodness on me more, for I cannot bear a kind look and
after it a cruel denial. This minute my heart aches
for you. And, if I cannot have a right in yours, I
wish it would ache till I could complain to you no
longer. *Remember poor Otway."*

. . . . .

"You cannot be but sensible that I am blind, or
you would not so openly discover what a ridiculous
tool you make of me. I should be glad to discover
whose satisfaction I was sacrificed to this morning;
for I am sure your own ill-nature would not be guilty
of inventing such an injury to me, merely to try how
much I could bear, were it not for the sake of some
ass that has the fortune to please you. In short, I
have made it the business of my life to do you service,
and please you, if possible, by any way to convince
you of the unhappy love I have for seven years toiled
under; and your whole business is to pick ill-natured
conjectures out of my harmless freedom of conversation to vex and gall me with, as often as you are
pleased to divert yourself at the expense of my quiet.
Oh, thou tormenter! Could I think it were jealousy,
how should I humble myself to be justified; but I
cannot bear the thought of being made a property
either of another man's good-fortune or the vanity of
a woman that designs nothing but to plague me.
There may be means found, some time or other, to
let you know your mistaking."

. . . . .

"You were pleased to send me word you would meet me in the Mall this evening, and give me further satisfaction in the matter you were so unkind to charge me with; I was there, but found you not; and therefore beg of you, as you ever would wish yourself to be eased of the highest torment it were possible your nature to be sensible of, to let me see you sometime to-morrow, and send me word by this bearer, where, and at what hour, you will be so just as either to acquit or condemn me; that I may hereafter, for your sake, either bless all your bewitching sex, or as often as I henceforth think of you, curse womankind forever."

There the correspondence breaks off; and it may be assumed that Otway cursed rather than blessed the "bewitching sex" until his end. However liberally his maledictions were heaped upon Mrs. Barry, he may be forgiven.

Three years of squalor followed "Venice Preserved" for him, and then he died, more forlornly, it seems, than Chatterton. He hid himself away in the slums of London to escape his creditors, borrowing enough money from his one-time friends to keep himself in a state of alcoholic forgetfulness. He wrote one more play, and brought out a poem of royal flattery after the death of Charles II, but these efforts did not help his plight. A sordid inn, called the Sign of the Bull, was his place of refuge, from which he would make furtive excursions for alms, in deadly fear of the bailiffs. One night, starving and almost naked, he accosted a passerby, begging a shilling with which to buy food.

"I am Otway, the poet," he whined.

The man, an admirer of his works, was horror-stricken at this apparition of a genius in the gutter, and gave him a guinea for his immediate relief, promising him more whenever he needed it. Otway rushed to the nearest bakery-shop for bread, and set his teeth into the loaf, ravening like a wolf. But he had been without food too long; the first mouthful choked him, and the rest was silence.

Otway's minor writings for the stage include comedies called "Friendship in Fashion," "The Soldier's Fortune," "The Atheist," and "Heroic Friendship," the latter produced posthumously and doubtless worked over by other hands from his scenario or rough draft; a re-hash of Shakespeare's "Romeo and Juliet" and "Julius Cæsar" as "The History and Fall of Caius Marius," for which vandalism he humbly begged the pardon of his illustrious master; and a translation of Molière's "Fourberies de Scapin." "The Orphan" and "Venice Preserved" remained in the repertory of the British stage for two centuries; the latter even yet has not lost its vitality.

Mrs. Barry, the "vampire" to whom this poetic fool made his ineffectual prayer, flourished until the beginnings of the Georgian era. Her popularity established the precedent of benefits for players; authors had been the only ones to profit by that custom until James II commanded a benefit for her in recognition of her long service to the stage. She lived through Mrs. Bracegirdle's reign, saw the rise of Mrs. Oldfield, and died November 7, 1713. Her last recorded words were a delirious jest at Queen Anne's creation of twelve new peers. Like the true tragedy queen, it was a line of blank verse that she mouthed:

"Ha, ha! and so they make us lords by dozens!"

  .   .   .   .   .

GREAT LOVE STORIES OF THE THEATRE

IV

ANNE BRACEGIRDLE AND WILLIAM CONGREVE

DISCREET in their day and generation were Anne Bracegirdle and William Congreve. Circumspect and calm, each remembered more as an artist than as a personality, they seem quite aloof from the reckless, pre-Georgian throng of theatrical celebrities. "The Diana of the stage," as Mrs. Bracegirdle was called, and the master of English comedy, as Congreve is now ranked, had their common secret—whether of passion, of platonic sentiment or of friendship is entirely a matter of conjecture—and they kept it prettily; they did not wear their hearts upon their sleeves, or flaunt a gross amour, according to the way of their world.

Escape from gossip, of course, they could not, since nothing short of sheer austerity is a safeguard against that destroyer and creator of reputations. Little eddies of merry hint and tolerant innuendo circled about their names when Congreve's plays and Bracegirdle's playing supplied the coffee-houses with topics of tattle; they were even suspected of a secret marriage; and the pleasant indictment against them has come down through two hundred years and more with unimpaired vitality. Elusive, shrinking from coarse detail, the story of their association is, but that very shyness and reticence recommends it to the attention. These two, be they paramours or platonists, had the grace of modern reserve which refreshingly contrasts with the barbarous frankness of their contemporaries.

Mrs. Bracegirdle was one of the first in the royal line of English actresses, skilled alike in comedy or tragedy; she succeeded to the purple of Elizabeth Barry and surrendered it to Nance Oldfield. Almost alone among the player-queens of the Restoration and pre-Georgian period, she bore a reputation for chastity; she was as distinguished for her good conduct as for her talent. Yet her personal charms had London at her feet; she was admired, courted and besieged; many an accomplished seducer devoted himself to an ardent campaign against her virtue, but even such professional beaux as Lord Lovelace, Lord Burlington and the Earl of Scarsdale had to confess their utter discomfiture in the attempt.

Once, before the sly and affable Mr. Congreve appeared upon the scene, it is said that a group of nobles, having exhausted all other themes of bottle-oratory, began to toast the Bracegirdle's impeccable morals. Among them were Lord Halifax and the Dukes of Dorset and Devonshire. At last Halifax declared:

"Come, this is all very well, but why do we not

MRS. BRACEGIRDLE

present this incomparable woman with something worthy of her acceptance?"

With which he laid two hundred guineas upon the table. The others increased the donation to eight hundred, and this golden purse was sent to "Diana" with appropriate compliments.

Another anecdote illustrating her strict code of propriety describes her neat rebuff of Burlington's insinuating advances. His servant brought to her door a set of rare and precious china, and a fulsome letter. She accepted the flattery, but told the servant that he was in error about the china, which should be delivered at once to its intended recipient—Lady Burlington.

The vogue of this serene votarist of virtue was at its zenith before the star of Congreve's wit had flashed upon the English stage. Colley Cibber, her life-long friend, describes her popularity in his "Apology" as follows:

"Mrs. Bracegirdle was now but just blooming to her maturity; her reputation as an actress gradually rising with that of her person; never any woman was in such general favour of her spectators, which, to the last scene of her dramatic life, she maintained by not being unguarded in her private character. This discretion contributed not a little to make her the *cara,* the darling of the theatre; for it will be no extravagant thing to say, scarce an audience saw her that were less than half of them lovers, without a suspected favourite among them; and though she might be said to have been the universal passion, and under the strongest temptations, her constancy in resisting them served but to increase the number of her admirers, and this perhaps you will more easily believe when I extend not my encomiums on her person beyond a sincerity that can be suspected; for she had no greater claim to beauty than what the most desirable brunette might pretend to. But her youth and lively aspect threw out such a glow of health and cheerfulness that on the stage few spectators, that were not past it, could behold her without desire. It was even a fashion among the gay and young to have a taste or *tendre* for Mrs. Bracegirdle."

Dr. John Doran, the stage historian, seems to feel that Cibber did not do Mrs. Bracegirdle's beauty full justice; in "Their Majesties' Servants" he fills out Colley's conservative picture with these details:

"Other contemporaries notice her dark-brown hair and eyebrows, her dark, sparkling eyes, her face from which the flush of emotion spread in a blush of rosy beauty over her neck, and the intelligence and expression which are superior to mere beauty. She so enthralled her audience that it is quaintly said, she never made an exit without the audience feeling as if they had moulded their faces into an imitation of hers."

To demonstrate how evil passions raged around her, the Mountford murder case may be cited before Congreve is introduced—a black affair of which she was an innocent provocative. William Mountford was a handsome and gifted actor who played opposite Mrs. Bracegirdle; his love-making on the stage was so impassioned that, though happily married, rumour credited him as her accepted lover. Captain Richard Hill, a ruffling soldier, grew madly jealous of Mountford because of the realism of his theatric romances. Then, having proposed marriage to Mrs. Bracegirdle—as a last resort—and having been refused, he determined to abduct his goddess, choosing as an accomplice Lord Mohun, a bravo of the peerage who figures villainously in Thackeray's "Henry Esmond." With six soldiers, these desperadoes waylaid Mrs. Bracegirdle as she was returning from the theatre, December 9, 1692, and attempted to pack her into a coach, with the intention of driving off to some Gretna Green. Her cries attracted a crowd, however, and fear of being mobbed by "Bracy's" ragged but more worthy admirers from the pit compelled them to pass it off as a joke and gallantly escort her home.

After she was safely bestowed in her house, Hill and Mohun stood on guard outside, with drawn sword, watching for Mountford. Two hours later, about midnight, when they had inflamed their purpose with several bottles of wine, the actor came by, legitimately homeward bound. He asked Mohun casually:

"What does your lordship here at this time of night?"

"I suppose you have been sent for," Mohun sneered.

"No, I came by chance."

"I suppose you have heard about the lady?"

"I hope my wife has given your lordship no offense."

"No, it is Mrs. Bracegirdle I mean."

"Mrs. Bracegirdle is no concern of mine," Mountford answered, "but I hope your lordship does not countenance any ill action of Mr. Hill."

At this Hill, who had been standing aside, struck Mountford in the face, and then, before he could draw his sword, ran him through the body. The actor died the next day.

Hill fled as soon as he had delivered this cowardly thrust and escaped arrest; but Mohun stood his ground. When taken into custody, he demanded a hearing by his peers; and the House of Lords acquitted him of the charge of being an accessory to the murder, after a celebrated trial at which Mrs. Bracegirdle was a witness. It may be added that this pair of scoundrels perished fittingly by the sword, in the end. Hill was killed in a tavern brawl under Mohun's eyes, four years later. Twenty years passed before Mohun's fate overtook him, and then he died like a wild-cat. Mortally wounded by the Duke of Hamilton in a duel in Hyde Park, he delivered a treacherous stab from the ground and took his adversary down to death with him.

William Congreve came to London in 1691, an

amiable youth with a genius for friendship and a
suave literary talent. His matriculation as a wit
and a man-of-the-world was immediate; his success in letters, under the generous sponsorship of
Dryden and Thomas Southerne, was precocious.
After a few poetic flights he spread his wings in the
drama, "like a well-mettled hawk," according to a
lyric congratulator, with "The Old Bachelor," the
vivacity and sparkle, the Gallic lightness of whose
dialogue was, and still is, a matter of some amazement. The piece was staged in January, 1693, with
Mrs. Bracegirdle in the chief feminine rôle of Araminta, and so with one stroke this fledgling of
twenty-three years became the heir to the veteran
Dryden's supreme sway in literature, and the *cava-
liere servente* of the theatre's fascinating "Diana."

Mrs. Bracegirdle was seven years his senior, but
this disparity in age is chiefly a matter of vital sta-
tistics, for she was the spirit of youth in full flower,
as Colley Cibber has testified, and he, mentally and
physically, was mature before his time. Indolent
and pleasure-loving, self-indulgent always, though
without violent excesses, Congreve was a plump,
sleek beau, schooled in the manners of the gay world,
when he should have been only a raw and callow
débutant. London aged him fast; the athleticism
which prompted his boast that he had done twenty-
one feet in the running-broad jump slipped away
from him as soon as he began to frequent the coffee-
houses and deplete the vintage of Madeira.

In "The Old Bachelor," Mrs. Bracegirdle not only played the rôle of Araminta, but also spoke the prologue; and thus she may be fairly said to have introduced Congreve to the stage. That bit of versifying was cleverer than most prologues; in it Mrs. Bracegirdle pretended to break down, forget her lines, and run away, in this strain:

But on my conscience, he's a bashful poet;
You think that strange—no matter, he'll outgrow it.
Well, I'm his advocate—by me he prays you,
(I don't know whether I shall speak to please you)
He prays—Oh, bless me, what shall I do now?
Hang me if I know what he prays or how!
And 'twas the prettiest prologue as he wrote it!
Well, the deuce take it if I han't forgot it.
Oh Lord! For Heaven's sake, excuse the play,
Because, you know, if it be damned to-day,
I shall be hanged for wanting what to say.
For my sake then—but I'm in such confusion
I cannot stay to hear your resolution.

Then began the attachment which lasted until Congreve's dramatic muse, none too fecund, had deserted him. Mrs. Bracegirdle was the heroine of each of his five plays; the rôles were obviously written for her; and those of the amorous heroes, apparently, as mouthpieces of the author's own adoration. Such was the belief in Congreve's own day, and he was laughingly charged with having emulated, more successfully, the example of Nicholas Rowe, a tragic dramatist who had courted Mrs. Bracegirdle in vain. Colley Cibber declares that both writers "seemed palpably to plead their own passions and make their private court to her in fictitious characters"; while Tom Davies, like the true gossip, goes into particulars, stating:

"In 'Tamerlane,' Rowe courted her Selima in the person of Axalla; in 'The Fair Penitent,' he was the Horatio to her Lavinia; and in 'Ulysses,' the Telemachus to Bracegirdle's Semanthe. Congreve insinuated his addresses in his Valentine to her Angelica in 'Love for Love'; in his Osmyn to her Almeria in 'The Mourning Bride'; and lastly, in his Mirabel to her Millamant in 'The Way of the World.' "

Congreve followed "The Old Bachelor" with "The Double Dealer," produced in November of the same year—which argues that for once in his life he exerted himself. In this play Mrs. Bracegirdle was not the Lady Froth, "a great coquette, pretender to poetry, wit and learning," but the sincere, appealing Cynthia. Congreve's *théâtre* was licentious, like his times, but thanks to the influence of Mrs. Bracegirdle, there is always a maiden of honourable reputation to be found in his dramas—the rôle to which his adored one was assigned, in compliment to her chaste reputation.

"The Double Dealer" had hardly more than a *succès d'estime*. Having tasted too full a measure of popularity with his first play, Congreve felt the vulgar jeers of hack critics very bitterly, and undertook to prove that he was justly credited as Dryden's successor with a third comedy. This was "Love for Love," produced April 30, 1695, with Mrs. Bracegirdle as the distinguished and charming Angelica. Its run was unprecedented for that period, and thus Congreve's reputation for greatness, which the arbiters of polite letters almost thrust upon him, was established firmly, not only among his own coterie at the Kit-Kat Club, of which he was a shining light, but in the eyes of all the "town" as well.

Then the easy life of good-fellowship—he was everyone's friend and enjoyed the confidence of the most bitter literary rivals without becoming involved in their animosities—began to break down his health. Without sacrificing his pleasures at the table he became a cheerful valetudinarian, passing his time between London and the English *spas*. He continued to work, however, with his accustomed slowness, polishing every phrase of his dialogue. In February, 1697, "The Mourning Bride," his one poetic drama, was produced, adorned by Mrs. Bracegirdle as Almeria; and in March, 1700, he returned to comedy with "The Way of the World." Then, at the age of thirty, gouty and fatter than he had any right to be, he was content to rest upon his theatrical laurels. His subsequent literary work consisted of odes, songs and occasional verse of ephemeral character. He also undertook controversial battle with Jeremy Collier, following the

publication of that vigorous reformer's "Short View
of the Immorality and Profaneness of the English
Stage," and did not fare particularly well in his pam-
phleteering feud. His retort to the sturdy clergy-
man was entitled "Amendments to Mr. Collier's
False and Imperfect Citations"; it drew the fire of
an anonymous writer, who may have been Collier
himself, in the form of "Animadversions on Mr.
Congreve's Amendments," which contains certain
touches that are valuable additions to the small store
of personal testimony regarding Congreve and Mrs.
Bracegirdle.

In reference to Congreve's urbanity and engaging
manners, the pamphleteer remarks sarcastically:

"This is your friend, the courteous, the obliging
Mr. Congreve, the very pink of courtesy, nay, the
very reflection of heaven in a pond."

And of his affair with "Bracy":

"If that be Mr. Congreve's opinion, he need not
covet to go to heaven at all, but to stay and ogle his
dear Bracilla with sneaking looks under his hat, in
the little side-box."

Congreve's literary wooing of Mrs. Bracegirdle,
observed by the "town" and recorded by Tom
Davies, in "Love for Love," "The Mourning
Bride," and "The Way of the World," deserves illustration from the text. In "Love for Love," we
find the diffident Mrs. Bracegirdle as Angelica, and
the pursuing Mr. Congreve as Valentine, conversing
as follows:

ANGELICA: You can't accuse me of inconstancy; I never told you that I loved you.

VALENTINE: But I can accuse you of uncertainty, for not telling me whether you did or not.

ANGELICA: You mistake indifference for uncertainty; I never had concern enough to ask myself the question.

.   .   .   .   .

VALENTINE: Nay, faith, let us understand one another, hypocrisy apart. The comedy draws toward an end; and let us think of leaving acting, and be ourselves; and, since you have loved me, you must own I have at length deserved you should confess it.

ANGELICA *(sighs):* I would I had loved you!—for Heaven knows, I pity you; and, could I have foreseen the bad effects, I would have striven; but that's too late.

"The Mourning Bride" represents the conventional ecstasies, swooning delights and tortured emotions of poetic tragedy, and naturally does not bear so close a personal application. Here we find Almeria Bracegirdle and Osmyn Congreve in rapturous duets, such as these:

OSMYN: No more, my life; talk not of tears and grief;
Affliction is no more, now thou art found.
Why dost thou weep, and hold thee from my arms,

My arms which ache to hold thee fast, and
   grow
To thee with twining?
ALMERIA: I will, for I should never look enough.
They would have married me, but I had sworn
To Heaven and thee, and sooner would have
   died—
OSMYN: Perfection of all faithfulness and love!

So much for heroics. "The Way of the World" brings them back to high comedy's reality, Congreve as Mirabel, an elegant, scholarly rake, and Bracegirdle as Millamant, a charming mocker of lovers. In a scene in which the lady finally yields, she does so with conditions:

MILLAMANT: And, d'ye hear, I won't be called names after I'm married, positively I won't be called names—as wife, spouse, my dear, joy, jewel, love, sweetheart, and the rest of that amorous cant in which men and their wives are so fulsomely familiar. I shall never bear that. Good Mirabel, don't let us be familiar or fond, nor kiss before folks, like My Lady Fadler and Sir Francis; nor go in public together the first Sunday, in a new chariot, to provoke eyes and whispers, and then never be seen together again; as if we were proud of one another the first week, and ashamed of one another ever after. Let us never visit together, nor go to a play together, but let us be very strange and well bred; let us be as strange as if we had been married a great while, and as well bred as if we were not married at all.

Before sealing the bargain she must take advice of Lady Fainall:

MILLAMANT: Fainall, what shall I do? Shall I have him?

FAINALL: Have him, have him, and tell him so in plain terms, for I am sure you have a mind to him.

MILLAMANT: Are you? I think I am—and the horrid man looks as if he thought so, too. Well, you ridiculous thing, you, I'll have you—I won't be kissed, nor I won't be thanked. Here, kiss my hand, though—so, hold your tongue, now; don't say a word.

All this footlight wooing would have left a more picturesque impression if Congreve had only taken the stage, on some special occasion, to play his own Valentine or Mirabel; but unfortunately for the chronicles of romantic sentiment, he had too much dignity for such an exploit, which at least one modern dramatist—Jean Richepin in Sarah Bernhardt's production of his "Nana-Sahib"—welcomed gladly.

Congreve's greatest concession to amatory absurdity was the publication of some verses, obviously addressed to Bracegirdle, and indicating that she did not fall into his net too easily. He sang:

Anne Bracegirdle and William Congreve

Pious Celinda goes to prayers
    Whene'er I ask a favor;
Yet the tender fool's in tears
    When she believes I'll leave her.
Would I were free from this constraint,
    Or else had power to win her;
Would she could make of me a saint,
    Or I of her a sinner.

Thackeray singled out this dapper bit of rhyming, in his "English Humourists of the Eighteenth Century," as an excuse to satirise the poet genially, in a whimsical flight which contains more imagination than fact. He observed breezily:

"What a conquering air there is about these! What an irresistible Mr. Congreve it is! Sinner! of course he will be a sinner, the delightful rascal! Win her! of course he will win her, the victorious rogue! He knows he will; he must—with such a grace, with such a fashion, with such a splendid embroidered suit. You see him with red-heeled shoes, deliciously turned out, passing a fair, jewelled hand through his dishevelled periwig and delivering a killing ogle along with his scented billet."

Thackeray is all for jocosity in his treatment of Congreve; though stimulating, he is hardly to be accepted as a scholarly authority. He calls him "the most eminent literary 'swell' of his age," and adds "in my copy of Johnson's 'Lives,' Congreve's wig is the tallest and put on with the jauntiest air of all the laurelled worthies. 'I am the great Mr. Congreve,' he seems to say, looking out from his voluminous curls."

Only two references to Mrs. Bracegirdle are to be found in Congreve's letters, forty-three of which are extant. They are in the pink of Congrevian discretion, yet their casual air is in itself significant. Both are apropos of interesting occasions. The first was a competition between four prominent composers of the day, held in March, 1701, through the medium of a masque called "The Judgment of Paris," benignantly written by Congreve for that purpose. His careful description of the concerts is valuable as a contribution to early English musical lore; then he adds:

"Our friend Venus [of course Mrs. Bracegirdle had to be cast for that rôle] performed to a miracle; so did Mrs. Hodgson in Juno."

The November hurricane of 1703, which has a respected place in the meteorological records of London, prompted him to another little betrayal as follows:

"Our neighbor in Howard street [Mrs. Bracegirdle] 'scaped well, though frightened; only the ridge of the house being stripped; and a stack of chimneys in the next house fell luckily into the street. I lost nothing but a casement in my man's chamber," etc.

The best contemporary sketch of Congreve and Mrs. Bracegirdle is to be found in Mrs. Delarivière Manley's "New Atlantis," a hand-book of intrigue and scandal published May 26, 1709. Its lively contents are indicated by its full title, "Secret Memoirs and Manners of Several Persons of Quality, from the New Atlantis." She pays her compliments to the poet-dramatist and his flame, as follows:

"Be pleased to direct your eyes toward the pair of beaux in the next chariot. . . . He on the right is a near favorite of the Muses; he has touched the drama with nearer art than any of his contemporaries, comes nearer nature and the ancients, unless in his last performance, which indeed met with most applause, however least deserving. But he seemed to know what he did, descending from himself to write to the Many, whereas before he wrote to the Few. I find a wonderful deal of common-sense in that gentleman; he has wit, without the pride and affectation that generally accompanies it.

"His Myra is as celebrated as Ovid's Corinna, and as well-known. How happy he is in the favor of that lovely lady! She, too, deserves applause, besides her beauty, for her gratitude and sensibility to so deserving an admirer. There are few women who, when they once give in to the sweets of an irregular passion, care to confine themselves to him that first endeared it to them, but not so the charming Myra."

The quality of Congreve's off-stage wit, at the Kit-Kat Club or in the coffee-houses, must remain as

purely speculative as Mrs. Bracegirdle's virtue—
which varies, from the testimony of Anthony Aston,
who called her "Diana," to that of Charles Gildon,
author of a pamphlet called "A Comparison Between the Two Stages," who declared: "She falls
into good hands, and the secrecy of the intrigue se-
cures her; but as to her innocence, I believe no more
on't than I believe of John Mandeville." (The latter, of course, was that mythical traveler, the medi-
æval Dr. Cook of the orient.) Congreve had a
reputation for repartee which must have been well-
founded, since he was in competition with many ex-
perts of extempore epigram; but none of his sayings
have been preserved for us in the anecdotage of the
period. Perhaps he was too amiable to say the bitter word that becomes historic; we have it on the
authority of Alexander Pope that Congreve, Vanbrugh and Garth were "the most honest-hearted real
good men of the poetical members" of the Kit-Kat
clique.

Congreve was faithful to "pious Celinda" for
years, but not, it must be regretfully admitted, for
life. They came to a parting of their ways after
Mrs. Bracegirdle had retired from the stage and her
lover had relapsed into gout-burdened invalidism,
she to live on to a ripe old age in dignified repose,
filled with deeds of charity, and he to permit his
physical ailments to be solaced by the tender ministrations of Henrietta, Duchess of Marlborough, a

daughter of the great commander. The last phase of their romance may be traced by theatrical records.

Mrs. Bracegirdle was the Venus in Congreve's masque, "The Judgment of Paris," in March, 1701, as has been told. Three years later he turned to the stage again, in a dilettante manner, with "Squire Trelooby." This piece was adapted, as an entertainment for "persons of quality," from Molière's "Monsieur de Pourceaugnac," by Congreve, Vanbrugh and William Walsh (a minor poet); when it was played, Mrs. Bracegirdle spoke the epilogue, of Congreve's unaided composition. "Squire Trelooby" became popular on the professional stage, and on May 23, 1704, it served as the vehicle for Mrs. Bracegirdle's benefit. The following year, Congreve wrote an epilogue to an Italian masque, "The Triumph of Love," and again Mrs. Bracegirdle was his mouthpiece. She retired in the winter of 1707, but emerged in April, 1709, when her admirer's "Love for Love" was revived at Betterton's benefit, to play her old rôle of Angelica. That, it may be assumed, was her last concession to a romance waned, and the year 1710 may be fixed as the beginning of the reign of the Duchess.

Congreve was then, in his fortieth year, an afflicted man. His race was run; his divine spark extinguished. He was paying the penalty for overmuch dining and wining, and yet he bore himself debonairly down the decline of life. Dean Swift, his friend from academic days at Trinity College, Dublin, wrote to his Stella, October 26, 1710:

"I was to-day to see Mr. Congreve, who is almost blind with cataracts growing on his eyes; and his case is, that he must wait two or three years, until the cataracts are riper, and till he is quite blind, and then he must have them couched; and besides, he is never rid of the gout; yet he looks young and fresh, and is as cheerful as ever. He is younger by three years or more than I, and I am twenty years younger than he. He gave me a pain in the great toe by mentioning gout."

The circumstances of Mrs. Bracegirdle's retirement are famous; in the annals of the stage they should always be written in red-letter, as an eternal lesson to jealous actresses. She accepted the inevitable decay of her charm as gracefully as Congreve that of his health, and abdicated with all her glory still about her.

A younger actress, none other than Nance Oldfield had been challenging her supremacy, and finally the adherents of each, after excited debating, decided that the issue as to which were the better actress should be put to a test. So it was arranged, with the consent of the principals, that a comedy called "The Amorous Widow, or the Wanton Wife," should be staged on two successive nights, with Mrs. Bracegirdle as the wife at the first performance and Mrs. Oldfield at the second. Certain authorities on the Georgian stage believe the story to be apocryphal, but at any rate, according to the anonymous compiler of the "Authentic Memoirs of that Celebrated Actress, Mrs. Oldfield":

"The long expected night being come, the senior championess appeared, attended with such a crowd of beaux as might be expected from a long unrivalled superiority, and performed her part, as usual, to such admiration as inspired a confidence into all her friends, and made Mrs. Oldfield's well-wishers dread the issue would not be in her favor. However, the next night, when our heroine graced the stage, and had spoke but ten lines, such was the gracefulness and beauty of her person, so enchanting the harmony of her voice and justness of her delivery, and so inimitable her action, that she charmed the whole audience to that degree they almost forgot they had ever seen Mrs. Bracegirdle, and universally adjudged her the preëminence."

Admitting her defeat, the legend runs, Mrs. Bracegirdle withdrew from public gaze. Colley Cibber wrote in 1740 that she retired from the stage "in the height of her favor . . . nor could she be persuaded to return to it, under new masters, at the most advantageous terms. . . . She has still the happiness to retain her usual cheerfulness and to be, without the transitory charms of youth, agreeable."

She survived her *ci-devant* admirer by many years. Congreve died January 19, 1729, and was buried with stately obsequies in Westminster Abbey. His will contained among other legacies the item, "To Mrs. Bracegirdle of Howard Street, 200 pounds," but the bulk of his estate, valued at 10,000 pounds, was bequeathed to "The Duchess of Marlborough, the now wife of Francis, Earl of Godolphin in the county of Cornwall." Said husband received the compliment of being named as executor, after being warned that he should not "intermeddle or have any controlling power" in the fund.

The Duchess spent 7,000 pounds of this unnecessary gift for a diamond necklace, which she would exhibit in high pride; and marked Congreve's grave in the Abbey with a marble tablet, still standing, which sets forth, among other things, "how deeply she remembers the happiness and honour she enjoyed in the sincere friendship of so worthy and honest a man."

When her old mother, the redoubtable Sarah Churchill, read this inscription, she remarked grimly:

"I know not what happiness Henrietta might have had in his company, but I am sure it was no 'honour.'"

This effusive lady's other extravagance in memory of Congreve is perpetuated in Thackeray's pages: "She had a wax figure made to imitate him—a large wax doll with gouty feet to be dressed just as the great Mr. Congreve's gouty feet were dressed in his great life-time."

How bitterly Mrs. Bracegirdle must have smiled at this ghastly vulgarism!

The interpreter of Congreve's Araminta, Cynthia, Angelica, Almeria, and Millamant was courted by people of distinction in her mellow eld almost as much as in her glorious youth. A letter of Horace Walpole's, written in 1742, speaks of her in this vein:

"Now I talk of players, tell Mr. Chute that his friend, Mrs. Bracegirdle, breakfasted with me this morning. As she went out, and wanted her clogs, she turned to me and said: 'I remember at the playhouse they used to call—Mrs. Oldfield's chair! Mrs. Barry's clogs! and Mrs. Bracegirdle's pattens!'"

She died September 18, 1748, at the age of eighty-five. Then, among the great dead of Westminster Abbey, she rejoined her Congreve—so far as this world knows.

GREAT LOVE STORIES OF THE THEATRE

V

ADRIENNE LECOUVREUR'S LOST
ILLUSIONS

"WHAT'S living without loving?" This
motto Adrienne Lecouvreur, the most
appealing figure in the historic gallery
of the French stage, unconsciously framed for herself. *"Que faire au monde sans aimer?"* she asked,
in a letter to a friend, and in that spirit she lived,
always loving tenderly, devotedly, truly—and always disappointed.

She was a woman of purer ideals than her generation, though no saint from our own standards.
Warm-hearted, unselfish, worshipping love with a
poetic ardor, she was an anomaly among the actresses of the glittering, cynical Regency, and so
her romantic career was a series of disillusionments
which culminated in tragedy. Her sympathetic
character and the grim episode which brought her
brilliant achievements to an untimely end have made
her one of the most interesting players in the annals
of the theatre, and have caused many of her great
successors, among them Rachel and Bernhardt, to
impersonate her upon the boards, in the drama
which Scribe and Legouvé dedicated to her memory.

Her life-history contains, not a single, but a series of passions; and yet, considering the morals of her day, she is eminently forgivable, because she always loved honestly. Maurice Paléologue, one of her many biographers, pays this tribute to her sincerity:

"Her true originality among the women of her time lay in the conception that she formed of love. We know the singular change that this sentiment had undergone beneath the dissolving influence of the morals of the Regency; all that had made for the nobility and poetry of passion up to that time had fallen under the blows of the reigning philosophy and the persiflage of the salons. In this transformation the woman had lost more than the man. She had been taught that modesty and fidelity were grandiloquent words devoid of meaning, and, freeing herself from all romantic illusions, and clinging only to the positive and the agreeable in her amorous intrigues, she displayed everywhere a cynical libertinism. It was the honor of Adrienne to resist this contagion. The gift of her person was always a pledge of the heart. She loved not by caprice, not by vanity, but by a moral inclination, with an ardor, a conscientiousness and a gravity profound."

Adrienne's "grand passion" was for Maurice de Saxe, an Ajax in war and a Don Juan in gallantry. He is usually the solitary hero when her love-story is told, for her unhappy end centered in him; but in this record that picturesque seducer may be left for the final chapter. He is by no means the only notable phase of the Lecouvreur's sacrificial passions.

First of all, however, let her be introduced as she appeared to admiring eyes in the flower of her beauty. In 1719, when she was twenty-five years old, a Parisian journalist described her as follows:

"Without being tall, she is very well made, and has an air of distinction which prepossesses one in her favor; no one in the world has more charms. Her eyes speak as much as her mouth, and often supply the place of her voice. In short, I cannot do better than compare her to a miniature, since she has agreeableness, finesse and delicacy."

Another sketch of her, written shortly after her death, may be found in the *Mercure de France:*

"Mlle. Lecouvreur was about the middle height and admirably formed, with a noble and confident air, a well-poised head and shapely shoulders, eyes full of fire, a pretty mouth, a slightly aquiline nose, and very pleasing manners; although not plump, her face was somewhat full, with features admirably adapted to express sorrow, joy, tenderness, fear and pity."

She was born of humble parents, the family name being Couvreur, to which she added "Le" in order to secure a distinguished *nom de théâtre.* Her childhood seems to have been unhappy, for in a letter written years afterward, she declares that a "jealous and furious divinity" controlled her destiny from the cradle. Her histrionic genius, however, was soon discovered, a juvenile performance in which she attempted one of Corneille's heroines attracting the interest of influential patrons. An actor named Le Grand, a member of the Comédie-Française and a successful playwright, gave her lessons in the art for which she had an evident vocation, and then wisely directed her into the training school of the provincial companies. Beginning at the age of fourteen, she played in the cities of Alsace, Lorraine and Flanders for ten years, and then returned to Paris to make her début with the Comédie-Française, May 14, 1717, appearing, in a double bill of tragedy and comedy, in the title rôle of Crébillon's "Électre" and as Angélique in Molière's "George Dandin." For the next thirteen years she was the reigning queen of the Comédie-Française

Adrienne's love affairs began in her girlhood of arduous apprenticeship. Her first attachment was with a young baron, an officer in the Regiment of Picardie, garrisoned at Lille. He died suddenly after a few months of romancing, and her grief was so profound that she earnestly considered suicide. An episode with one Philippe Le Roy, who was in the household of the Duke of Lorraine, followed, but it may be passed by as containing no revelation of her character. With the entrance of Clavel, an obscure actor whom she met in the comradeship of the theatre, her true, tender woman's heart is first disclosed.

In the collection of her correspondence which has fortunately been preserved, there are only two love letters, and these were both inspired by this Clavel, who was totally unworthy of them. They show, in a very affecting way, how devoted and disinterested she was, how fine and noble were her sentiments. The first reads:

"I have at last received that letter so eagerly anticipated, and for which I have been astounding Notre Dame des Carmes with my prayers. I can assure thee, my dear friend, that I have had no rest since thy departure, both on account of my uneasiness at not receiving news of thee and of finding myself inconvenienced as I am. I hope to be better now, since I have reason to believe that thou lovest me still and that thou art well. Take care of thyself, I beg of thee, since thy health is as precious to me as my own. I shall be charmed to learn that thou art enjoying thyself, providing that I lose by it nothing of what is mine, and that thou dost not write to me less often. . . . Assuredly, I believe that thou hast a kind heart, and, consequently, art faithful to thy poor Lecouvreur, who loves thee more than herself. . . . I embrace thee with all the tenderness of my heart, and swear to thee a constancy proof against all things."

The second letter was written two years later, after Adrienne had come to suspect that her lover was reluctant to carry out his intention of marrying her. The change from the intimate "thou" to the formal "you" should be noted. Adrienne's latest biographer, Larroumet, pronounces this document to be "one of the tenderest and most touching letters to be found in literature, real or imaginative, worthy of comparison with the famous letter of Manon Lescaut"; and he does not exaggerate:

"I hardly know what I ought to think of your neglect, at a time when everything ought to alarm me. Be always persuaded that I love you for yourself a hundred times more than on my own account. Time will prove to you, my dear Clavel, what I swear to you to-day. Entertain for me the sentiments that I shall entertain for you all my life, for all my ambition is bounded by that. With all the attachment that I have for you, I should be in despair if you did anything for me with repugnance. Reflect well that you are still master. Consider that I have nothing, and that I owe a great deal, and that you will find greater advantages elsewhere. For my part, I have nothing save youth and good will, but that does not adjust matters. I speak to you plainly, as you see, and I tell you frankly things which are able to make you think of me as one whom you ought to avoid. Here is a chance to take your own part. Have no consideration. Make no promise that you do not intend to keep; were it necessary for you to promise to hate me, it seems to me that it would be easier for me to bear than to find myself deceived. . . . I tell you again, my dear Clavel, that your interests are dearer to me than my own. Follow the course which will be most pleasing to you. I know you to be of a disposition which will prompt you to behave generously and perhaps to surpass me; but yet once again reflect well. Act like the honest man that you are and follow your own inclination, without troubling about the possible consequences. I shall resign myself, by some means or other, as well as I can, whether I gain or lose you. If I have you, I shall have the sorrow of not rendering you as happy as I should wish; my own happiness will perhaps make me forget the pain. . . . If I lose you, I shall strive at least not to do so entirely, and I shall still retain some place in your esteem. If you are happy, I shall have the pleasure of knowing that I have not prevented it; or, if you are not, I at any rate shall not be the cause, and I shall endeavour in some way to console myself."

The literary quality of these letters, written by a mere girl, is remarkable; and her later correspondence, though more impersonal, has the same charm, with an even more finished style. In fact, Adrienne Lecouvreur, over and above her histrionic triumphs, deserves a place in *belles lettres* with those other mistresses of the epistolary art whom critics have chosen to honour—Mme. de Staël, Mlle. Aïssé, and Mme. de Sévigné.

The end of the Clavel affair was disillusion again for her. He followed his own inclination, as she counselled, and decided that marriage with a young actress, dowered only with an art as yet unrecognized, would not be advisable; and so he passed on and is forgotten, save only as his memory is embalmed, as a hopeless cad, in the precious amber of these beautiful letters. Adrienne was heartbroken when he failed her, and lived in practical seclusion for several months, her life barren of everything but the toil of the theatre. Then, in Strasburg, Count François de Klinglin, son of the first magistrate of the city, prevailed upon her to accept his protection, under promises of marriage. He abandoned her, however, in the crisis of maternity, for a wealthy match of convenience. Embittered by these successive treacheries, in each of which she had given a frank, fond love and had hoped for an eventual legalization of the tie, she left the provinces and came to Paris, resolved to have done with love and to find consolation in a brilliant career.

The day of her triumph soon dawned; she was hailed as the greatest tragedienne of the French stage, and though besieged with admirers she cried quits with the tender passion. For several years, at least, until Maurice took final possession of her impressionable heart, she was the Diana of the period, offering to fervent, sighing lovers only a cool platonic friendship. The mood of disillusionment was strong within her, and to one of her wooers she wrote:

"If I am unable to render you more happy, I am more grieved than you yourself. I tell myself, without doubt, more than you can tell me; but I could not deceive you. Caprices do not agree with reason, and love is nothing else but a folly which I detest, and to which I shall strive hard not to surrender myself as long as I live. You will understand it later on, and the severity with which I have treated you will serve then only to render you more happy. Permit me to approach the matter with you and offer you my counsels. Be my friend; I am worthy of that; but choose for mistress one who possesses a heart quite untampered with; who has not yet repented of that trust which renders everything so beautiful; who believes you such as you are, and all men such as you. Let her be young and rather strong; she will be the less sensitive. Finally, see that she gives you as much constancy as I should have given, if I had never loved any one save you."

Adrienne's career with the Comédie-Française may be briefly summarised as including all the heroines, then classic, of Corneille and Racine, and many other rôles in the tragedies of the time, the most notable of which were written by Voltaire. Her genius as a tragedienne did not carry over into comedy, in which she attempted only a few parts without great success. She is to be credited with having effected a reform in theatric diction, supplanting the loud, stilted chanting of the old school with a simple, though lofty, declamation which was as close to the naturalistic style as the rhymed alexandrines of French poetic drama would permit. In pantomime, in attitudes, in the difficult art of listening in silent scenes, and in transitions from one mood to another, she was superlative, if the critics of her day are to be trusted. She also brought about an advance in realism of costuming, though her famous successor, Mlle. Clairon, completed this revolution.

In proof of her personal charm—the good-taste, modesty, education and literary gifts to which her letters bear witness—the fact may be cited that she was the first French actress to be admitted into regular society by the *noblesse*. Duchesses admired her and welcomed her into their homes; among the *grande dames* of the Regency she was as popular as if she could match their high titles on equal terms. She was greatly sought after in the salons, but life in the fluttering gaiety of the *haut monde* did not appeal to her strongly. In a letter, probably written to Maurice, she regrets that so much of her time was being taken up with social duties, and expresses her yearning for a quieter, more normal existence, as follows:

"I spend three parts of my time in doing that which displeases me; new acquaintances whom it is impossible to escape as long as I remain tied as I am prevent me from cultivating the old or from occupying myself at home as I should like to do. . . . My vanity does not find that numbers atone for merit in persons, and I have no desire to shine. To keep my lips closed and listen to good conversation, to find myself in the delightful society of clever and virtuous people, is a hundred times more pleasant to me than to be stunned by all the insipid praises which they lavish on me right and left in many places to which I go. It is not that I am wanting in gratitude or in the wish to please, but I find that the approbation of fools is not flattering, and that it becomes burdensome when it has to be purchased by individual and repeated complaisances."

She was happier in her friendships than in her loves; she had a veritable genius for friendship and the gift of converting importunate suitors into platonic allies of life-long fidelity. Her greatest friend was Voltaire, who regarded her interpretations of his heroines as true collaboration. There has been a whisper of scandal in their relationship, chiefly based upon a letter written by Voltaire shortly after her death in which he proclaimed himself "her admirer, her friend, her lover"; but everything indicates that he used the latter word in its purer sense. Voltaire and his devoted henchman, d'Argental, were as true friends to Adrienne as ever a woman had; and attention may be given to the refreshing aspects of their association before the passionate episode with Maurice is discussed.

Voltaire was among the first to discover Adrienne's artistic and personal gifts, after her Parisian début, and she was for him not only an ideal interpreter of his stately heroines, but also an intellectual companion. He found in her lofty outlook on life a pleasant foil for his own cynicism and in her mentality a keener feminine insight than he had ever known. One of the anecdotes of their friendship is thoroughly characteristic of that Voltairean contempt for the established order which sowed the seeds of the French revolution.

When Voltaire's "Mariamne" was having its run, he and several other men, including Chevalier de Rohan, a duke's son, were in Adrienne's dressing-room at the theatre. The author was holding forth volubly, as usual, upon the canons of dramatic art and kindred topics, speaking as if his word were the law and the prophets—as, indeed, it soon became. Rohan, who was courting the actress and was jealous of her comradeship with Voltaire, suddenly asked with a sneer:

"Who is this young man that talks so loud?"

"He is one who does not carry about a great name," Voltaire snarled, "but who earns respect for the name he has."

The nobleman lifted his cane as if to chastise the upstart, but Voltaire's hand sought the hilt of his sword in such a threatening manner that he hesitated. In this emergency Adrienne fainted, with infinite tact and histrionic skill, and the rivals forgot their tentatives of combat in a simultaneous rush to her assistance.

Then the quarrel was apparently dropped, but a few days later Voltaire was waylaid and well cudgelled by Rohan's lackeys. So, with much ostentation, the writer began to take fencing lessons, and fiercely chewed the cud of rage as he practised with a *maitre d'escrime*. When a finished artist in swordsmanship, he sent Rohan a formal challenge, which was an outrageous presumption on his part according to the code of honour then. For a commoner to call out a duke's son was almost a treasonable offense, and therefore a *lettre de cachet* promptly placed the rebellious genius in the Bastille for a short term of imprisonment.

D'Argental, who is remembered best as Voltaire's *fidus Achates,* was smitten with a mad passion for Adrienne when only a callow youth, and she had to manage him discreetly. Her offers of friendship without love did not satisfy him; his ardour became preposterous; and at length his family tried to cure the infatuation by sending him to England. Adrienne tried to comfort his exile with long sisterly letters, which only added fuel to the flame. When he was permitted to return to Paris, his passion was so unruly that his family, which was noble, conceived a suspicion of Adrienne's motives, and in fear that she was really exciting him, by a pretended coolness, into a matrimonial frenzy, they decided to ship him oversea to San Domingo. Then Adrienne wrote to the mother a letter which is the masterpiece of her correspondence, and which deserves extended quotation:

"He is the most respectful youth and the most honest man that I have met in my life. You would admire him did he not belong to you. Once again, madame, deign to coöperate with me in destroying a weakness which irritates you, and in which I have no part, whatever you may say. Do not show him either contempt or harshness. I would prefer to take upon myself all his hatred, in spite of the friendship, affection and veneration that I entertain for him, rather than expose him to the least temptation which might cause him to fail in respect toward you. You are too interested in curing him not to strive earnestly to attain your object; but you are too much so to succeed in attaining it unaided, above all when you endeavour to combat his inclination by the exercise of your authority, or by painting me in disadvantageous colours, whether true or not.

"His passion must indeed be an extraordinary one, since it has existed so long without the least hope, in the midst of disappointments, in spite of the journeys you have made him undertake, and during eight months' residence in Paris, during which he never saw me, at least not at my house, and was unaware if I should ever receive him again. I conceived him to be cured, and for that reason consented to see him during my last illness. It is easy to believe that his society would afford me infinite pleasure, were it not for this unhappy passion, which astonishes as much as it flatters me, but of which I decline to take advantage. You fear that if he sees me, he will depart from his duty, and you carry this fear to such a point as to take violent resolutions against him. Assuredly, madame, it is not just that he should be rendered unhappy in so many ways. Do not add anything to my severity; seek rather to console him; make all his resentment fall on me, but let your kindness serve to reassure him.

"I will write to him whatever you please; I will never see him again if such is your wish; I will even withdraw to the country if you consider it necessary. But do not threaten to send him to the end of the world. He may be of service to his country; he will be the delight of his friends; he will fill you with pride and satisfaction. You have only to guide his talents and leave his virtues to act for themselves. Forget for a time that you are his mother, if this character is opposed to the kindness that, on my knees, I beg you to extend to him. Finally, madame, you will see me prefer to retire from the world, or to love him with the love of passion, rather than to suffer him to be any more tormented for me or by me."

Her advice was followed, and d'Argental became the eternal friend of the woman who had prevented him from making a fool of himself. The cure was accomplished without any need of Adrienne's carrying out the last two sacrifices which she offered to the mother. She changed him from lover to business adviser; she consulted him about all of her affairs; on her death-bed she named him as her executor. Sixty-three years afterward, d'Argental discovered the letter by means of which she had adjusted his career, among his mother's old papers; and it requires no stretch of the imagination to picture him, as an aged man, reading the faded pages with tears in his eyes and silently giving Adrienne's well-beloved memory all the reverence due a saint.

In 1720 Maurice de Saxe arrived in Paris to become the lion of the salons and the danger of dames. A constant patron of the theatre, addicted to the company of actresses, he soon met Adrienne, whose virtuous resolves capitulated at once before this warlike wooer. From that time until her death she was his favourite mistress; she gave her undivided heart to him, while he distributed his favours broadcast.

Aside from the purely physical element of Maurice's redoubtable fascination for women, it is difficult to understand Adrienne's complete devotion to this expert in seduction. She is credited, however, with having seen the intellectual and spiritual qualities which were strangely overlaid with the animal in Maurice's nature, and to have tried to develop them. It may be fairly assumed, taking her character as it has already been revealed, that her influence brought out the best in Maurice and diverted his leonine instincts from mere debauchery to the ambitions for heroic supremacy which he afterwards realized. This was the view taken by Lemonty, a historian who read a eulogy of her at a meeting of the French

Academy in 1823, as may be seen by the following
extract from that flowery essay:

"As in the time of chivalry, her cares, her tenderness, her wise counsels initiated her friend into the
amiable accomplishments, the benevolent virtues,
the polished manners which, in the long run, made
him as much a Frenchman as his victories. Under
her sweet tuition the Achilles of Homer became the
Achilles of Racine. She adorned his mind without enervating it, and modified what seemed extraordinary and singular in the turn of his ideas. She
taught him our language, our literature, and inspired him with the taste for poetry, for music, for
all the arts, and with that passion for the theatre
which followed him even into the camp. One
might say of the victor of Fontenoy and his beautiful preceptress that he learned from her everything except war, which he knew better than anyone, and orthography, which he never knew at
all."

Although Adrienne knew of Maurice's infidelities, she contented herself with the thought that she
alone, of all his charmers, was the confidante of his
plans. Their relationship endured without interruption for four years, and then Maurice set out for
Poland to become a candidate for the Duchy of
Courland, with Adrienne's blessing. She was well
aware that his game of adventurous diplomacy involved marriage and that its success would probably
separate them forever, yet when lack of funds baf-

fled his intrigues and forced him to call upon his friends in France, she was the first to respond. Unhesitatingly she disposed of her jewelry and plate and sent him 40,000 livres ($7,400). Maurice was elected by the Diet of Courland; but the Duchess whom he should have married bore such a striking resemblance to a Westphalia ham in countenance that he could not pay court to her with conviction; moreover, he found himself outlawed by Poland, attacked by Russia and renounced by his father, the Saxon Elector; so after a year of swashbuckling and amazing feats of arms, he had to surrender his duchy and return to Paris.

Adrienne, who had kept closely in touch with his affairs, writing to him several times a week, had looked forward to a happy reunion. She found Maurice changed, however, and again love brought her wretchedness. He was disappointed and restless; he fretted against a life of idleness in Paris, after his exciting year in Courland; and finding no relief for his ill-humour in dissipation, he inflicted it upon her. Though he placed no bounds upon his own conduct, he viewed her friendships with jealousy, and seems to have accused her of deceiving him, for we find among her letters this cry of bitterness, written to a confidant:

"I am worn out with anger and grief; I have been dissolved in tears this livelong night. Perhaps it is unreasonable of me, since I have nothing wherewith to reproach myself; but I cannot endure severity so

little deserved. I am suspected; I am accused, and
. . . if chance does not enable me to know what is
happening, I shall be covered with the most horrible
calumny possible to conceive by a man who has borne
the name of my friend for ten years. I am not permitted to tell you this; I esteem and love tenderly
him who forbids me, but I know not how to keep it
to myself; I am too affected, too wounded, and too
alarmed for the future not to reveal it, at any rate,
to you. . . . I have been told that it is his way
of thinking, that he does not intend to do me any
wrong in confounding me with the generality of
women. I cannot entertain this idea. That is not
the language he has held toward me for ten years,
and ought not to be the reward of my attentions to
please him and to make him esteem me, at least, according to my deserts. What can one do to me, after
all, save wound me in the place where I am most
sensitive? I could destroy in an instant the error in
question; but how am I to console myself for the intention of this calumny?"

Love, in fact, had played another cruel trick upon
Adrienne when she gave her heart into the keeping
of Maurice de Saxe. He seems to have been her
evil genius; seventeen months after his reappear-
ance in Paris she died under suspicious circumstances, poisoned, according to the popular belief,
which is preserved in the drama of Scribe and Legouvé, by a jealous duchess who coveted her lover.
One attempt, certainly, was made upon her life by

this woman; and the case is so strange that it may be recounted in detail.

Adrienne's would-be rival was Louise Henriette Françoise of Lorraine (Mlle. de Guise), wife of the Duc de Bouillon. As described in a contemporary document, she was: "Very pretty; rather tall than short; neither stout nor slender; an oval face; a broad forehead; black eyes and eyebrows; brown hair; very wide mouth and very red lips." Mlle. Aïssé, the Circassian girl who was bought in a slave-market of Constantinople and adopted as a daughter by the father of the d'Argental who figures in this story, left a series of letters which are among the most interesting documents of the Regency, and in them the Duchesse de Bouillon gets this bad character:

"Madame de Bouillon is capricious, violent, headstrong, and much addicted to gallantry. Her tastes extend from the prince to the actor. She conceived a fancy for the Comte de Saxe, who had none for her. Not that he piques himself on his fidelity to the Lecouvreur; for, together with his passion for her, he has a thousand little passing tastes. But he was neither flattered nor anxious to reply to the impulsiveness of Madame de Bouillon, who was enraged at seeing her charms despised, and who had no doubt that the Lecouvreur was the obstacle that stood in the way of the passion that the Count would otherwise naturally entertain for her. To destroy this obstacle, she resolved to get rid of the actress."

In July, 1729, Adrienne received an anonymous

letter, asking her to come to a designated spot in the Luxembourg gardens, on a matter of urgent import-ance to herself. Escorted by friends she kept the ap-pointment, and there found a young student of paint-ing from the provinces, Abbé Bouret, who stated that he had been offered a bribe by the Duchesse de Bouillon to poison her. According to his story, he had been approached on this subject by masked men representing the duchess, who declared that he would be richly rewarded if he carried out the com-mission, and would be killed if he did not. He was instructed to ingratiate himself with the actress by his painting, to secure entrance into her house, and to present her with some lozenges or candies which would be supplied him. Terrified by their threats, he consented, and was taken to the duchess, who con-firmed the plot and gave him the poisoned candy.

After hearing this strange tale, Adrienne in-formed the police, with the young man's consent. His candies were fed to a dog, which died in fifteen minutes, and then he volunteered to submit to ar-rest until the Duchesse de Bouillon could be con-fronted by him. That lady's family, however, had great influence with both the civil and the church authorities, and the matter was hushed up for a time.

Some months afterward Bouret was arrested on a *lettre de cachet* issued at the request of the Bouil-lons, and. was imprisoned. He persisted in his story; Adrienne wrote to him, begging him to withdraw the charges if they were untrue and promising to obtain his pardon if such were the case; but he continued to accuse the duchess as a poisoner. The actress sent him money, clothes, and books, and summoned his old father, a government official in Metz, to his aid. Parental pleas caused Bouret to be released after three months, but his father's illness prevented him from leaving Paris at once, as Adrienne advised; and six months later he was arrested again on a new *lettre de cachet*. By this time the affair had become a public scandal, the sympathy of Paris being strongly in favor of Adrienne and Bouret. Although the prisoner was constantly urged to deny his story with promises of freedom, he refused. While he was stifling in an oubliette, Adrienne died, and suspicion naturally fastened upon the Duchess as having made a second and successful attempt upon her life. A few months later the terrors of the Bastille broke Bouret's spirit; he recanted, declared that he had invented the plot himself merely to gain the friendship of the actress, and swore that the Duchess was innocent. Soon afterward he was released, and so he disappears from history.

Did the Duchesse de Bouillon, once exposed as a poisoner, have the diabolical hardihood to carry out her purpose while the affair was still notorious? That is one of the many unsolved historical mysteries, although Scribe and Legouvé have used the dramatist's license and caused her to poison their heroine with a bouquet of drugged flowers. The documentary evidence, however, leaves a reasonable doubt as to her actual guilt, though none as to her murderous intention.

Shortly after Bouret's denunciation, the Duchess brazenly appeared in a box when Adrienne was playing Racine's "Phèdre." The tragedienne's usual discretion deserted her when she observed her enemy pretending to applaud her, and she turned directly toward the Duchess as she read, with unmistakable emphasis, the famous lines which may be translated as:

"I know my own treacheries, Œnone, but I am not one of those hardened women who, enjoying a tranquil conscience among their crimes, can face the world without a blush."*

The audience applauded this allusion vigorously and the Duchess left the theatre in a rage. This incident served Scribe and Legouvé for one of the climaxes of "Adrienne Lecouvreur."

Not long afterward, Adrienne became ill, and though she kept on playing, her health failed rapidly. That winter the Duchesse de Bouillon tried to convey the impression that a truce had been declared between them, and when Adrienne was invalided, she sent her servants with solicitous inqui-

---

* " Je sais mes perfidies,
Œnone, et ne suis pas de ces femmes hardies
Qui, goûtant dans la crime une tranquille paix,
Ont su se faire un front qui ne rougit jamais."

ries every day. Finally, after a performance of Jocaste in Voltaire's "Œdipe," in which she seemed pitifully frail, she took to her bed, and four days later, March 20, 1730, she died. Voltaire, Maurice de Saxe and a surgeon were with her at the end, and the faithful d'Argental, hurriedly sent for, arrived a few minutes too late.

The last irony of Adrienne's career came after she was at peace. The *curé* of her parish, an extremely bigoted priest, had been called in to administer the last sacrament and to receive the renunciation of profession which a player had to make in order to obtain Christian burial in consecrated ground. Certain accounts say that he did not come until she had breathed her last; others, that when exhorted to repentance she pointed to a bust of Maurice which stood near her bed and exclaimed:

"Voilà mon univers, mon espoir, et mes dieux!" ("There is my universe, my hope, and my gods.")

At any rate, she died unshriven, and the churlish priest refused her remains not only Christian burial (which was usual then), but also interment in the unconsecrated part of the cemetery reserved for heretics and unbaptized children. The latter denial is without precedent in all the church's spiritual warfare against the votaries of Thespis.

The following midnight, therefore, after an autopsy, upon which Voltaire insisted and which resulted in a verdict of death from natural causes, all that was mortal of Adrienne Lecouvreur was taken in a coach, with only a few porters and guards of the watch in the dreary cortège, to a piece of unclaimed ground near the Seine, and was buried in quick-lime. The place was kept secret and was unmarked by stone or cross.

This sudden and brutal disposition of her remains, directed by the police; the secrecy, the quick-lime, the concealed grave, all point to powerful influences working to prevent a second autopsy. Maurice de Saxe was wanting in this emergency; he might have secured for the woman who had loved him so deeply the last honours of decent burial, but he does not seem to have made an effort in this direction. Voltaire, always at odds with the authorities, was helpless.

The day after the burial, Voltaire's grief broke out in a fury of protest. He addressed a withering open letter, written in verse, to a public official, contrasting Adrienne's furtive funeral in the dark to the elaborate obsequies of two English actresses who had recently died. Next, he spoke before the members of the Comédie-Française with eloquent indignation, calling upon them to desert that institution "until they had secured for the pensioners of the king the rights which were accorded to those who had not the honour of serving his majesty." Resolutions to this effect were passed, but were never carried out; the players loved their individual incomes more than their professional good name. Voltaire followed this protest with a splendid poem on the death of Adrienne, crying out against the sacrilege of denying the rights of sepulture "to her who in ancient Greece would have had shrines."

The Comédie-Française closed its season four days after Adrienne's death, and according to custom, at the final performance an *éloge* of Adrienne, written by Voltaire, was read by the youngest member of the company. It concluded with these words:

"I feel, messieurs, that your regrets recall that inimitable actress, who might almost be said to have invented the art of speaking to the heart and of presenting sentiment and truth where once had been shown little but artificiality and declamation. Mlle. Lecouvreur—permit us the consolation of naming her—made one feel in every character which she impersonated all the delicacy, all the soul, all the decorum that one could desire; she was worthy to speak before you, messieurs. Among those who deign to listen to me are several who honoured her by their friendship; they are aware that she was the ornament of society as well as of the theatre; while those who knew her only as the actress can readily judge, from the degree of perfection to which she attained, that not only had she an abundance of wit, but that she further possessed the art of rendering wit amiable. You are too just, messieurs, not to regard this tribute of praise as a duty; I dare even to say that in regretting her I am merely your interpreter."

Adrienne Lecouvreur's Lost Illusions

Adrienne Lecouvreur, from her début until her death, was cheated by her highest ideal—love. Her passions always ended in bitterness; her romances in disillusion. Friendship served her better than love; it was Voltaire and d'Argental, not Maurice de Saxe, Clavel, and the other unhappy choices of her heart, who appreciated her at her true worth.

In 1786, fifty-six years after her death, an old man located her final resting place, on ground now occupied by 115 Rue de Grenelle. He was the ever-faithful d'Argental. The marble tablet which he placed there still exists, inscribed by verses of his own composition, indifferent as to literary quality, but poignant in appeal when the true story of their subject is known. Adrienne's fame was flown, her loves were dust—but an old friend still remembered her gentleness, her kindness, her patience with his youthful folly.

GREAT LOVE STORIES OF THE
THEATRE

VI

MARGARET WOFFINGTON AND DAVID GARRICK

THE incomparable David Garrick, *beau idéal* of all players, began, or rather, preluded, his career on the stage by falling in love with an actress. Fittingly enough, the lady thus honored was none other than bewitching Margaret, or Peg, Woffington, the most sprightly charmer of her day. And, for a time, "little Davy" and "lovely Peggy" romanced together.

The biographies of these two eighteenth-century luminaries have been so extensively exploited in memoir, chronicle, and anecdote that it is almost unnecessary to dip into the wealth of theatrical lore associated with their names. Garrick, the greater artist, has been more favoured in this regard; libraries are glutted with his memorabilia. One slender volume of fiction and fact—Charles Reade's "Peg Woffington"—perpetuates his casual partner's fame, however, as effectually as a hundred-weight of musty stage histories.

For all the glory of these two, their love story has been somewhat neglected—perhaps because both were discreet enough to leave no personal record of it; perhaps because, being merely a mummers' mock-wedding, it did not assume scandalous aspects in an age when the amours of nobility alone attracted much notice. But at any rate, it is well worth the telling, in so far as it may be reconstructed.

Woffington is the more sympathetic figure in the liaison, and she shall, therefore, be introduced first, according to the portrait of her greatest—but purely literary—admirer, Charles Reade. He re-creates her imaginatively as follows:

"It certainly was a dazzling creature; she had a head of beautiful form, perched like a bird upon a throat massive yet shapely and smooth as a column of alabaster, a symmetrical brow, black eyes full of fire and tenderness, a delicious mouth with a hundred varying expressions, and that marvelous faculty of giving beauty alike to love or scorn, a sneer or a smile. But she had one feature more remarkable than all, her eye-brows—the actor's feature; they were jet-black, strongly marked, and in repose were arched like a rainbow; but it was their extraordinary flexibility which made other faces upon the stage look sleepy beside Margaret Woffington's. In person she was considerably above the middle height, and so finely formed that one could not determine the exact character of her figure. At one time it seemed all stateliness; at others, elegance personified, and flowing voluptuousness at another. She was Juno, Psyche, Hebe, by turns, and for aught we know at will."

"PEG" WOFFINGTON

This description is based upon a passage in the "Memoirs of the Celebrated Mrs. Woffington," written by an anonymous contemporary, and published shortly after her death. It, too, may be quoted, in order to fix the vision of bewitching Peggy:

"Her eyes were black as jet, and while they beamed with ineffable lustre at the same time revealed all the sentiments of her heart, and showed that native good sense resided in their fair possessor. Her eyebrows were full and arched, and had a peculiar property of inspiring love or striking terror. Her cheeks were vermilioned with Nature's best rouge, and outvied all the labored works of art. Her nose was somewhat of the aquiline, and gave her a look full of majesty and dignity. Her lips were of the colour of coral and the softness of down; and her mouth displayed such beauties as would thaw the very bosom of an anchorite. Her teeth were white and even. Her hair was of a bright auburn colour. Her whole form was beauteous to excess."

An Irish colleen, daughter of a bricklayer, she had as a child sold "China oranges" about the theatres of her native Dublin, and then had taken to the stage as naturally as a duck takes to water. She became a great favourite in the Irish capital, and when she appeared for the first time as the dashing Sir Harry Wildair in "The Constant Couple," a versifier broke out in her praise as follows:

That excellent Peg
Who showed such a leg
When lately she dressed in men's clothes—
A creature uncommon,
Who's both man and woman,
The chief of the belles and the beaux.

At the age of twenty-two, with only one costume in her wardrobe, she came to London to make her fortune. After eighteen fruitless visits, she finally gained an audience with Rich, the eccentric manager of Covent Garden, and from that moment her future was assured.

"It was a fortunate thing for my wife," Rich afterwards told Sir Joshua Reynolds, "that I am not of a susceptible temperament. Had it been otherwise, I should have found it difficult to retain my equanimity enough to arrange business with the amalgamated Calypso, Circe and Armida who dazzled my eyes. A more fascinating daughter of Eve never presented herself to a manager in search of rare commodities. She was as majestic as Juno, as lovely as Venus, and as fresh and charming as Hebe."

Peg Woffington was the toast of London before David Garrick had broken away from his wine-merchant's vault. As Sylvia in Farquhar's "The Recruiting Officer," as Lady Sadlife in "The Double Gallant," and as Sir Harry Wildair in "The Constant Couple"—which established her preëminence in debonair "breeches-rôles"—she was tremendously admired.

Garrick was then selling wine, yearning to desert commerce and join his fortunes with the art which, in his own words, "is really what I dote upon." His business of dispensing Red Port, Canary, Mountain and Malmsey to the bloods of London; his temperamental inclination toward the stage, and his gay tastes as a young man-about-town, all brought him into contact with the players. He was not only a constant theatre-goer, but also a habitue of the green-rooms and coffee-houses, on speaking terms with all the celebrities, chief among whom for him was pretty Peggy Woffington. Smitten by her Sylvia and her Wildair, he sought her acquaintance and enlisted himself in the train of her admirers. Having scribbled verses from early youth, what was more natural than that he invoke the lyric muse in honour of his divinity? In the *London Magazine,* about that time, there appeared a ballad "To Peggy," signed D. G., which was long believed to be of his authorship. Some of its stanzas run:

> Once more I'll tune my vocal shell,
> To hills and dales my passion tell,
> A flame which time can never quell
>   That burns for lovely Peggy.
> Yet greater bards the lyre should fit—
> For pray, what subject is more fit
> Than to record the radiant wit
>   And bloom of lovely Peggy?

Were she arrayed in rustic weed
With her the bleating flocks I'd feed,
And pipe upon my oaten reed
   To please my lovely Peggy.
With her a cottage would delight;
All pleases when she's in my sight!
But when she's gone 'tis endless night—
   All's dark without my Peggy.

This song, however, was really written by Sir Charles Hanbury Williams, a minor poet of the day and himself an aspirant to Peggy's favour. Garrick's true touch as a troubadour is to be found, rather, in these lines "to Sylvia":

Possession cures the wounded heart,
   Destroys the transient fire,
But when the mind receives the dart
   Enjoyment whets desire.

Your charms such slavish sense control,—
   A tyrant's short-lived reign!
But milder reason rules the soul,
   Nor time can break the chain.

May Heaven and Sylvia grant my suit,
   And bless the future hour—
That Damon who can taste the fruit
   May gather every flower.

Then, at the obscure little theatre of Goodman's

Fields, October 19, 1741, came the memorable occasion of Garrick's first appearance on the stage, as Richard III. That was the birth of one of the greatest histrionic geniuses the world has known; the young man leaped immediately into fame, without ever having played a minor rôle, without having worked up from an humble apprenticeship, without any systematic training whatsoever. The next day he wrote to his provincial brother:

"My mind has always inclined toward the stage. All my illness and lowness of spirit was owing to my want of resolution to tell you my thoughts when here. . . . Last night I played Richard the Third to the surprise of everybody, and as I shall make very nearly 300 pounds per annum by it, and as it is really what I dote upon, I am resolved to pursue it."

Joyously he embraced the new career, for it not only satisfied the longings of his ambition, but it also catered to the desires of his heart—it brought him closer to Margaret Woffington. He secured an engagement at Drury Lane almost immediately; Davy and Peggy were together, and the romance was fairly begun.

Garrick's most intimate friend in the days when he first spread his wings was Charles Macklin, a burly, scholarly, roistering Irishman of considerable repute on the eighteenth century stage. It is said that by insisting upon a realistic method of diction and pantomime, Macklin anticipated the sweep-

ing reforms wrought by Garrick. He was the man
who introduced Davy to Peggy, and in 1742 the
three of them, each an exponent of the new, naturalistic school which drove ranting and posing out of
the theatre, installed themselves together at 6 Bow
Street—a congenial neighborhood for the talent of
the times, with Wills' coffee-house and Tom Davies'
book-shop just around the corner.

Associated together in the public eye upon the
stage, Garrick and Woffington soon became linked
socially as well. Macklin was presently discovered
to be unnecessary to their domestic arrangements,
and they shortly removed to other apartments in
Southampton Street, where they set up housekeeping
merrily, without benefit of clergy.

Peg Woffington had no particular reputation to
lose by this bohemian union—which is not saying
that she was worse than her feminine rivals in the
theatre. She was, if anything, far above the average
Georgian actress in the honesty of her life; hers
was a clean, sunny, winsome nature; and yet she was
a child of fortune who let her fancy stray where it
listed. Garrick himself had no reputation as a libertine, and this affair with Woffington was, so far as is
known, his only illicit entanglement. They were
young, he twenty-five and she twenty-four, and
deeply in love; they looked forward to marriage at
some indefinite time; and so, like a couple of bright
song-birds, they nested together with no pretense at
concealment.

The liaison is explained in Fitzgerald's "Life of Garrick" as follows:

"The lively Garrick did not see in her merely what the men-about-town so much admired, the sauciness and boldness which seeks to captivate by an effrontery of speech and bearing, and a wearisome succession of 'breeches-parts,' but was taken, we may be sure, by the half-pensive, half-sad expression, and fancied an ideal that could be capable of real love and true happiness. Indeed, the whole of this amour, as it must be called, turns out on examination so different from the vulgar notion handed down by the Macklins, Murphys, and others, that it becomes a valuable illustration of Garrick's character. He was all through looking to an honourable attachment, an honourable establishment in life with one whom he could sincerely esteem. Under the follies and the failings which he fancied were those of the hour, he saw the generous nature, the honest purpose, the warm impulse, the sense of loyalty to herself and duty to her profession which might in time be earnest for her sense of duty to himself. Margaret Woffington, it must be remembered, had many gifts and accomplishments that were of an intellectual sort. She was indeed a captivating creature. She could speak French admirably and dance with infinite grace, and above all, possessed a kind, generous heart that could do a good-natured thing."

As good a case, with better ground, can be made out for Mistress Woffington. Later events proved that she was the more honestly devoted of the two.

Their housekeeping arrangements were as unique as if devised by one of the comic dramatists of the period. It was to be a coöperative establishment; Garrick was to pay the expenses one month and Woffington the next. His income then amounted to about 1,000 pounds a year; hers to about 600. Thus they could afford to live luxuriously, and they entertained often; but all the honour of the situation went to Peggy.

Garrick had come to London to make his fortune, and he was bent upon achieving that ambition, in the most material sense. He was no bohemian, no spendthrift; he husbanded his money, while Woffington was generous almost to a fault. Dr. Johnson hit the actor off truly in a remark to Boswell: "He had then begun to feel money in his purse, and he did not know when he would have enough of it." So saving was David, in fact, that his economy has become a tradition. A young and successful man in love who practises unnecessary parsimony is not a figure for much hero-worship; the wits busied themselves at David's expense, and many an epigram has perpetuated his grudging share of that experiment in "trial marriage."

Macklin was their most frequent guest, and being addicted to sarcasm, he has not spared his friend David in the "Mackliniana" which he left behind him.

"In talk Garrick was a very generous man," he

DAVID GARRICK

remarked, "a very humane man and all that, and I believe he was no hypocrite in his immediate feelings. But he would tell you this in his house in Southampton Street, till, turning the corner, the very first ghost of a farthing would melt all his fine sentiments into the air, and he was again a mere manager."

Dr. Johnson, too, enjoyed the hospitality of the Garrick-Woffington alliance, the association between the ponderous lexicographer and the volatile actor being historic; a great tea-drinker, he was particularly fond of the bohea served by the fair hands of Mistress Peg. One evening, when Garrick was the paymaster of the month, she brewed a cup extra-strong for the honoured guest—and Garrick, "the pernickety little player," as Johnson dubbed him, bounded up from his chair to enter an emphatic protest.

"It is no stronger than I have made it before," said Woffington.

"No stronger than usual! It is, madam. All last month it would have injured nobody's stomach. But this tea, madam, is as red as blood!"

That year Garrick and Woffington left London for a joint engagement in Dublin, which lasted for three brilliant months. She was re-crowned queen of the Dublin heart, and he repeated his London triumphs before audiences said to be the most exacting in Great Britain. Woffington, as usual, was besieged with admirers, all of whom were jealous of

Garrick. Upon one occasion, Garrick was visiting her at the home of her mother and sister, and, the day being warm, had removed his wig to cool his head.

Suddenly a fervent young lord, a great patron of the drama and a worshipper of Peg, was announced, at which Garrick took himself off to another room, forgetting his wig, which was left on the table. As soon as the visitor entered, his eyes fell on that incriminating object.

He immediately burst out into a storm of jealous rage. Peggy heard him through, and then began to laugh. She was always a better actress off the stage than on.

"Yes, my lord," she said, "it is certainly Mr. Garrick's wig; and as I am learning a new breeches-rôle, he was good enough to lend it to me to practise with."

Thus was the noble's powerful patronage saved for herself and Garrick.

Woffington's quickness of repartee was famous. Between her and Kitty Clive there was a feud of long standing, and some of their exchanges of feminine banter have become classic.

"A pretty face," said Kitty to Peg, "of course excuses a multiplication of sweethearts."

"And a plain one," retorted Peg to Kitty, "insures a vast overflow of unmarketable virtue."

Mistress Clive had her revenge for that. When Peg was playing Sir Harry Wildair, she ran into the green-room, after a scene which had been received with enthusiasm, saying:

"I really believe half the house take me to be a man."

"And the other half know the contrary," whipped out the evil-minded Kitty.

Peg's and David's joint housekeeping lasted only two or three seasons. In 1745, Garrick was living in King Street, Covent Garden; he had gone to play in Dublin without Woffington, and she had departed for Paris with her sister to study tragedy under Dumesnil. In 1746, he was playing at Covent Garden and she at Drury Lane; even their professional association had ended. And in 1748, Garrick married Mlle. Violette, a dancer as famous then as Genée is now, to be a virtuous family man from that time forward.

Garrick's parsimony and Woffington's love of admiration were the causes of their separation. They bickered over the details of household expense; they quarrelled over Peg's friendships with other men. She always preferred masculine society, saying, "women never talked but of silks and satins." She was imprudent, rather than unfaithful, but Garrick doubtless gave some credence to the groundless scandals which were circulated about her.

The only letter in Woffington's hand which is extant contains a defense against this gossip. Written to Thomas Robinson, a juvenile player, it reads in part:

"I hear the acting-poetaster is with you still at Goodwood and has had the insolence to brag of favours from me—vain coxcomb! I did, indeed, by the persuasion of Mr. Swiney and his assistance answer the simpleton's letter—foh! He did well, truly, to throw my letter into the fire, otherwise it must have made him appear more ridiculous than his amour at Bath did, or his cudgel playing with the rough young Irishman. Saucy jackanapes! To give it for a reason for the burning of my letter that there were expressions in it too passionate and tender to be shown! I did in an ironical way (which the booby took in a literal sense) compliment both myself and him on the success we shared mutually on our first appearance on the stage, and that which he had (all to himself) in the part of Carlos in 'Love Makes a Man,' when with an undaunted modesty he withstood the attack of his foes armed with cat-calls and other offensive weapons. I did indeed give him a little double meaning touch on the expressive and graceful motion of his hands and arms as assistants to his energetic way of delivering the poet's sentiments, and which he must have learned from the youthful manner of spreading plasters when he was apprentice. These, I say, were the true motives to his burning the letters, and no passionate expressions of mine."

The man, or "jackanapes," referred to in this sarcastic screed was probably an actor and writer named Hallam, who is remembered as having brought English companies to New York in the Colonial period. If Hallam were really the offender against Peg's good name, he met a merited end, for he was killed by the formidable Macklin, who thrust a cane-ferrule through his eye into the brain in a green-room quarrel. The manslaughter was accidental, Macklin having no other intention than to hasten his exit from the room, and when the case came up for trial in the Old Bailey, a verdict of not guilty on the charge of murder was rendered.

Even after their separation, Woffington and Garrick held to their engagement to wed. She was living in a suburban home, and he near Covent Garden; but the actress, always sincere in her affections, did not dream that her lover possibly had repented of his promise. The date set for their wedding drew near, and with its approach, Garrick became more and more moody. He made the attentions of a Lord Darnley the pretext of reproaches, but Peg, whose conscience was doubtless clear, took them good-naturedly, as was her wont with David's tempers.

Finally, he appeared with the wedding ring, and tried it on her finger, which it fitted perfectly. She complimented him upon his taste, and ran on with Woffingtonian pleasantries, to which his spirits did not rise. At last she asked him the cause of his depression. He alleged a bad night of sleeplessness.

"And pray was it this"—holding up the ring—"which has given you so restless a night?"

"Well, to tell you the truth, my dear," he answered sourly, "as you love frankness, it was; and in consequence of it, I have worn the shirt of Dejanira for these last eight hours."

Then Peg's Irish spirit arose—and who can blame her?

"Then, sir, get up and throw it off," she advised cuttingly, her black eyes flashing. "I could guess the cause of your dejection. You regret the step you are about to take."

Garrick did not answer, and Woffington, after waiting for his reply, went on:

"Well, sir, we are not at the altar, and if you possessed ten times the wealth, fame and ability that the world gives you credit for, I would not, after this silent but eloquent confession, become your wife. From this hour I separate myself from you, except in the course of professional business or in the presence of some third person."

He tried to make a defense, but her indignation ruled the scene, and the English Roscius sank into humiliated insignificance before the righteous fury of an actress scorned. As soon as Woffington reached her home, she returned everything that Garrick had given her. He replied in kind, but sometime later she remembered an expensive pair of diamond shoe-buckles, and reminded him politely by note that they were still in his possession. His answer was to the effect that they were all he had to remind him of his happy hours with lovely Peggy, and therefore he hoped she would permit him to keep them. Woffington was too proud to ask a second time; Garrick retained the precious buckles, and the coffee-house wits had one more topic for gibes at the meanness of their first actor.

Woffington then became a "co-star," according to the jargon of the present day, with Spranger Barry, a tragic actor new-come from Ireland, whose rivalry, for a time, gave Garrick many apprehensions. He was called "the silver-tongued," and so great was his popularity and success that Garrick was forced to abandon certain rôles, such as Othello and Hotspur, to him. This strong competition caused Garrick, then an actor-manager, to attempt to woo Woffington over to his side again, professionally at least, but she had been wounded too deeply to forgive. Stung by her repulse of his offers, he undertook reprisals with the pen, in a wholly despicable manner, and as an epilogue to his sentimental ballads to Peggy, of his early days, he printed a set of verses which began:

I know your sophistry, I know your art,
 Which all your fools and dupes control;
Yourself you give without your heart—
 All may share that—but not your soul.

He could be a very mean little man when he chose, this same great David Garrick. Poor Peg Woffington had a nobler soul than he.

She never married, but kept on playing year after year—one of the best-loved actresses who ever stepped upon the English stage—and became almost as able in tragic as in comic rôles.   On May 3, 1757, she made her last appearance, as Rosalind in "As You Like It."   Her strength had been failing rapidly, and though she went through the drama with her usual sprightliness, when she appeared to speak the epilogue, she collapsed.

At the last lines—"If I were among you, I would kiss as many of you as had beards that pleased me" —her voice failed; she tottered, called out, "Oh, God! Oh, God!" and stumbled to the wings, where she fell helpless.   The storm of applause which broke out—her last curtain call—was never answered.

Pretty Peggy recovered from that stroke, which proved to be paralytic, enough to spend the few remaining years of her life in charitable ministrations among the poor.   She became religious, advised young girls against the stage, saying, "There is no position in life so full of incessant temptations," settled her fortune upon her mother and sister, and died March 28, 1760.

The elegy with which John Hoole, a poet now forgotten, mourned her death expressed the sentiment of thousands.   The tribute is worth a quatrain's quotation:

> Farewell, the glory of a wondering age,
> The second Oldfield of a sinking stage;
> Farewell, the boast and envy of thy kind,
> A female softness and a manly mind.

GREAT LOVE STORIES OF THE THEATRE

VII

THE FAVARTS AND MAURICE DE SAXE

"SHE is possessed by the demon of conjugal love," Maurice de Saxe complained of Justine Favart, a pretty soubrette of Louis XV's reign. For that virtue, strange to the libertine eighteenth century, she and her devoted husband, Charles-Simon Favart, suffered incredibly, enduring imprisonment, exile, and spiritual torture. Their loyal attachment was pursued *à l'outrance* by conscienceless debauchery, which at last hunted it to death. Persecution rather than passion is the theme of their story. It contains plotting and cunning villainy enough for a dozen melodramas.

Charles and Justine Favart would have offered the one solitary example of happy marriage on the wanton stage of their day if they had been permitted to work out their own destinies. He was a clever librettist and versifier, a writer of vaudevilles and comic operas; she was a singing actress and dancer of piquant charm. They were colleagues and collaborators as well as lovers, and they tried to live according to a creed of conjugal fidelity. But they were born in the wrong age; they were unable to cope with the evil genius of their period—incarnated for them by the redoubtable Maurice de Saxe.

That historic figure is the villain in the romance of the Favarts. Heroic he may be in the other aspects of his adventurous life, but in this episode he is merely base—a satyr with the craft of a wolf. Maurice of Saxony, Marshal of France, hero of Fontenoy, *beau sabreur,* the greatest Lothario of a lecherous age, appears here as an unmitigated beast. He deserves a lengthy introduction, however, being one of the most interesting characters that can be found among the world's famous blackguards.

An illegitimate son of Augustus II, Elector of Saxony and King of Poland, he began life as a soldier of fortune, and through skill in the arts of war and love he became one of the mightiest men in Europe. When twelve years old he carried a musket at Malplaquet. At seventeen he was in command of a regiment of cuirassiers. He appeared in Paris, with his sword for sale, when twenty-two, and entered upon a brilliant career of martial and amorous conquests.

Maurice was regarded as the strongest and most handsome man of his time. As a soldier he was impeccable; as a *roué* he was unsurpassed. Though untutored, with barrack-room manners that gained for him the sobriquet of "wild boar" in the salons of Paris, he was the pursued and the pursuer of women, *par excellence.* Don Juan is hardly to be mentioned in the same class with Maurice de Saxe. His liaison with Adrienne Lecouvreur, the great tragic actress, is conventional when compared with his rapacious quest of the more obscure Justine Favart.

Charles-Simon Favart was the son of a Parisian pastry-cook, who inherited from his father a penchant for writing verses. Well educated and looking forward to a literary career, he was forced to abandon his ambitions to manage the paternal bakery; but he tried to break the monotony of culinary endeavour by wooing the muse, and not without some success. Finally a vaudeville, accepted by the Opéra-Comique, freed him from his humble traffic.

This piece, called "Les Deux Jumelles" ("The Twins"), was produced on March 22, 1733. The next day he was at his shop as usual, in the full regalia of a cook, when a coach drove up to the door and a richly dressed man asked him for the author Favart. Replying that he would summon that gifted gentleman, Favart dashed upstairs, removed his farinaceous costume, donned conventional attire, and then returned, *in propria persona,* to present himself to the visitor.

He soon learned that good-luck had found him out. The caller proved to be a wealthy farmer-general with a passion to patronise the arts; he had attended the *première* of "Les Deux Jumelles," and had been pleased with it, had learned upon inquiry that the author was a youth of no means, and had come to put his feet on the road to Parnassus.

"I, too, have been on bad terms with Fortune," this philanthropist explained, "but she has ended by caressing me, and I can find no better way of using her favours than to employ them to the advantage of the arts."

The financier made his promise good, and through his generous patronage Favart was able to give his entire attention to playwriting. During the next few years he provided the minor theatres of Paris with more than twenty pieces, one of which, "La Chercheuse d'Esprit," given at the Opéra-Comique in 1741, had such an unusual success that the author threw aside the anonymity under which he had been working. In 1744 his talent was recognized by an appointment as manager of the Opéra-Comique.

Not long after Favart had entered upon his new duties, he received a letter from a woman who sought an engagement for her daughter, a singer and dancer. He answered in an encouraging tone, and in the due course of events mother and daughter presented themselves. That one interview was all Favart needed to be certain that he had found a jewel. The girl was Marie-Justine-Benoit Duronceray, then in her eighteenth year, vivacious, pretty, and accomplished. Favart engaged her at once, and provided her with a rôle in the vaudeville he was then writing to celebrate the marriage of the

Dauphin with the Infanta Maria Theresa—"Les Fêtes Publiques," it was called. Under the name of Mlle. Chantilly, which she retained for professional uses, Justine made her début, and was very successful, her piquant personality delighting the frequenters of the Opéra-Comique.

It seems to have been a case of love at first sight between Favart and Justine. His heart, at any rate, was lost to the young soubrette without delay, and instead of taking advantage of his position by exacting from her the *droit du directeur* and making her his mistress—the customary thing then—he proposed honorable marriage. They were wedded December 12, 1745, in the church of St. Pierre-aux-Boeufs, a favourite altar for couples who wished to keep their union secret. Justine's father was not present at the ceremony, his consent being given in writing—a fact which was brought up years afterward to ruin them.

To illustrate Favart's simple, honest temperament and his absolute devotion to Justine, a letter written to her in their period of betrothal may be quoted. It has a winsome ring:

"Take care of your health; remember that mine is involved in it. You will take more care of yourself if you have any regard for me, who love you more than life; though do not take offense, for my very sentiments are your eulogy. Your talents seduce me, but your virtue binds me."

They were wedded in the face of adversity. Fa-

vart's vaudevilles and Justine's singing had acquired
such a vogue at the Opéra-Comique that the Comédie-Française and the Comédie-Italienne, jealous of
rivalry, conspired together for the suppression of
that house, and shortly after the marriage their intrigues were successful. This act of official injustice was tempered by permission for Favart to open
a theatre at the fair of St. Laurent for a brief season,
and there he transferred his company, putting on a
pantomime called "Les Vendages de Tempe," in
which Justine was again successful. But when that
engagement was over the Favarts found their occu-
pation gone. Enter then, Maurice de Saxe, disguised as a generous patron. This was fifteen years
after the death of Adrienne Lecouvreur. Maurice
was now Marshal of France and commander-in-
chief of Louis XV's armies, and was waging the war
of the Austrian succession.

The Marshal of France, whom Favart had met at
some literary salon not long before, was a great fre-
quenter of the theatre. Such was his zeal for the
stage, and its women, that he encouraged troupes to
follow his armies on campaigns. He proposed to
the author-manager, therefore, that he organise a
company to go with the French army into Flanders,
where the destiny of the Austrian crown was about
to be decided. One troupe of the kind, managed
by a rival, was already in the field, and Favart,
though low in funds and uncertain of prospects,
hesitated, fearing the professional jealousy which

would result from his competition. Then Maurice promised to transfer the other players to Marshal Loewenthal's division and attach Favart's to his own, under his personal protection. Favart saw in this offer only a godlike beneficence—he was curiously blind to evil—and accepted gladly.

His official appointment as entertainer to Maurice and his warriors on the battlefields was couched by the patronising commander-in-chief in the following terms:

"The favourable report that has been made about you, monsieur, has induced me to choose you, in preference to all others, in order to give you the exclusive management of my comedy company. I am persuaded that you will use every endeavor to ensure its success; but do not imagine that I look upon it merely as an object of amusement; it enters into my political views and into the plan of my military operations. I will advise you what you will have to do in this respect when occasion arises, and, in the meantime, I count upon your discretion and punctuality. You are from this moment at liberty to make all your arrangements for opening your theatre in Brussels in the month of April next."

Accordingly, Favart leased a theatre in Brussels and organised a company. Upon Maurice's entry into that city a terrific peal of thunder was heard, and the people began to construe it as an evil omen for the French arms. Favart, however, as military vaudevillist, undertook to dispel that superstition

167

with verses, which may be Englished, in part, as follows:

> Is this our brave general
>   Ushered in by Bellona?
> It seems the great marshal
>   In *propria persona*.
> But no! I can see by the glance of his eye
>   'Tis the godhead of wars;—
> By the bolt and the wrath of the sky
>   Zeus announces grim Mars.*

Favart's company gave their first performance that evening, and were received with enthusiasm. An officer who thought these festivities inappropriate for the opening of a serious campaign asked the author-manager with a sneer what service a mere poet could be to an army, and received the proud answer:

"To celebrate the exploits of our soldiers and satirise the enemy."

Although his headquarters were in Brussels, Fa-

---

* Est-ce là notre général
    Que ramène Bellone?
  —Eh! oui, c'est ce grand maréchal,   )
    C'est lui-même en personne.
  —Non; je le vois à ses regards
    C'est le Dieu de la guerre,
  Et Jupiter announce Mars
    Par un coup de tonnerre.

vart's contract compelled him to follow Maurice's army with his entire company, of which Justine was the star. This entailed many hardships; rations were not abundant, and the means of transportation were primitive. At one time Favart passed three days and nights without sleep save for occasional naps leaning against a tree, ankle-deep in water. The players were subject to the terrors as well as the privations of war, for the enemy's cavalry—savage Croats and Pandours—were always hovering on the flanks of the army and ravaging the country almost within a musket-shot of the French lines. For protection against attack, thirty men were told off as the company's escort. Upon one occasion the little caravan was waylaid by a troop of hussars four times their number; the fighting was bitter hand-to-hand work, and when reinforcements arrived to save the players, only six members of the escort survived. He who came off most happily among those gallant soldiers had not less than four saber wounds to his credit.

Maurice did all in his power to make this adventurous life easy for his protégés. His gifts were generous, some of the items recorded in Favart's memoirs including three horses for their coach, a camp-bed of red satin, and twenty-five bottles of Hungarian wine. The marshal also informed Favart that he might draw upon him for whatever moneys he needed. In his simplicity the librettist believed that these kindnesses were tributes to his own literary and dramatic genius, though in reality they were to win the good graces of Justine.

In October, 1746, when the army of allied English and German troops was close at hand, Maurice sent for Favart, who had erected a theatre in the market-place of a small town occupied by the French, and said:

"To-morrow I shall give battle, but as yet I have issued no orders to that effect. Announce it this evening at the performance, in couplets suitable to the occasion. Until then let nothing be said."

Favart obeyed to the letter, and his song was sung by Justine between the two vaudevilles of the evening. Maurice's staff was amazed at this issuance of a general order for battle through the medium of a topical ballad, but the marshal, who sat in a box, smilingly acquitted Favart of madness and confirmed the news. Two days later the battle of Roucoux was fought and the enemy was routed.

All this time Favart had been living in a fool's paradise, drinking in the favor of the marshal. Maurice, although fifty years old and glutted with mistresses from his youth, was endeavouring to seduce Justine under the very eyes of her trusting, unsuspicious husband. The companies that followed Maurice's armies, at his own solicitation and expense, were seraglios for this Turk, and his lecherous intentions had centered chiefly upon the young soubrette. He had admired her ever since her début in Paris, had made Favart this offer as a means of winning her, and had been exerting all his arts of fascination, reputed irresistible, upon her while Favart was celebrating his glory in fluent, graceful verse. Justine, however, reversed precedent; she abominated the marshal, and when compared with her adored husband this paramour of queens filled her with intense disgust. All of which is made clear in an ill-spelled letter from Maurice to his sister, the Princess Von Holstein, dated March 10, 1747, that—in its printable section—reads as follows:

"Finally, I want to tell you that for three years I have been in love with a little girl who treats me badly, and who has turned my head completely; I wrote you something about her last year. *She is possessed by the demon of conjugal love.* . . . I have tried two or three times to seduce her."

To Justine herself, about the same time, he wrote:

"I take leave of you; you are an enchantress more dangerous than the late Madame Armide. Whether as Pierrot, whether under the guise of Love, or even as a simple shepherdess, you are so excellent that you enchant us all. I have seen myself on the point of succumbing—I, whose fatal art affrights the world. What a triumph for you had you been able to make me submit to your laws! I thank you for not having used all your powers; you might well pass for a young sorceress, with your shepherd's crook, which is nothing else than the magic wand with which the poor prince of the French, who, I fancy, they called Renaud, was struck. Already I have seen myself surrounded with flowers and *fleurettes,* fatal equipment for the favourites of Mars. I shudder at it; and what would the King of France and Navarre have said if, in place of the torch of his vengeance, he had found me with a garland in my hand?"

This high-flown epistle, doubtless written for the illiterate marshal by a cultured *aide-de-camp,* ends with a quatrain of verses, ostensibly original, but in reality pilfered from Voltaire. Maurice had neither an amorous nor a literary conscience.

The outcome of this wooing is in doubt; some of the biographers hold that Justine escaped the machinations of Maurice; but the most reliable evidence indicates that she succumbed, through fear for herself and her husband. Then, still "possessed by the demon of conjugal love," she became stricken with remorse. Maurice's return to Paris in the winter of 1747 gave her an opportunity to renounce her slavery, and when he reappeared in the field she firmly refused to resume the degrading relationship with him. The sultanic marshal went into battle with the repulse still rankling in his bosom, smashed the allies at Lawfeld, and then returned to break the spirit of his rebellious odalisque.

Harassed by importunities, Justine at last took the horrible story to her husband, freely confessing her fault and asking for his protection. Favart was broad-minded enough to see that he himself was partly culpable by having brought his young wife within the reach of the libertine Maurice. He forgave her freely, and that night they slipped away from the army together, going to Brussels, where Justine, who was ill, was placed under the chaperonage of a friendly duchess. Favart then went back to his company to forget his shame in his work, having no recourse, as a humble playwright, against such depredations on the part of the noble Maurice. The letter which he wrote to her immediately after his return is an eloquent comment upon the situation:

"I have arrived in good health, my dear little buffoon; your own occasions me much uneasiness. Send me the surgeon's certificate, that I may show it to the marshal. The gossip of the troupe has caused a report to be circulated that your illness is only an awkwardly devised piece of trickery to conceal your fears and my jealousy. I replied that there was no cause for jealousy, and that to suspect you was to insult you. M. de La Grolet [a surgeon in Brussels] is to be consulted as to whether you are in a fit state to rejoin the army, and a threat has been conveyed to me that you shall be brought here forcibly by grenadiers, and that I shall be punished for having invented the story of your illness. For myself, I care little for their threats; but I cannot forgive myself for having brought you to a country where you are exposed to such tyranny. . . . If any attempt be made to send you back, implore assistance of the Duchesse de Chevreuse; she has too keen a sense of justice to refuse you her protection in a matter of such importance, and the kindness with which she has honoured us is a sure proof of that. She can tell M. de La Grolet that your health does not permit of your undertaking so trying a journey. Against such testimony nothing can prevail. Finally, my dearest, although your presence is necessary here for the sake of the performances, and I am burning with impatience to see you once more, your health, more precious than all our other interests, more dear to me than life itself, must be preferred to everything. Send news of yourself as soon as possible to your affectionate husband."

Rage, first, and then despair, were the moods of the temperamental marshal when he learned that Justine had escaped him. An officer entered his tent to inform him that a bridge which kept his division in touch with Loewenthal's had been carried away by floods, and found the Mars of France sitting dejectedly upon his bed, hair dishevelled, clothes in disorder—the picture of lost hope.

"The misfortune is undoubtedly great," said the officer consolingly, "but it can be repaired."

"Ah, my friend!" cried Maurice, "there is no remedy. I am undone!"

"The loss of the bridge will perhaps not have the results that you fear," the officer argued politely.

Then the marshal lost his temper.

"Who could have supposed that you were talking

of lost bridges?" he roared. "That is an inconvenience which may be repaired in a few hours. But the Chantilly has been taken from me!"

After a time, however, the marshal's anger seemed to subside; his verbal abuse and threats of dismissal, hurled against the uneasy Favart, ceased altogether. The performances went on as before, without Justine, and the incident was apparently forgotten. But in the following autumn, when the war was over and Maurice had leisure to devote to his private feuds, a peculiar train of events began which caused the Favarts to imagine that they were being pursued by a cruel, inscrutable fate. Resenting a defeat in love as bitterly as in war, the marshal hunted them down without mercy, drove them into traps, mastered their petty lives as if he were an incarnate destiny—and not until he had the girl within his grasp again did either of them see him in his true light as a treacherous betrayer. Their faith in him as a patron was quite pathetic.

Favart, it will be remembered, had leased a theatre in Brussels at the beginning of the campaign. He had paid the annual rental of 500 ducats with due regularity, but when Brussels was restored to the Austrian sway, under the Peace of Aix-la-Chapelle, the proprietors—two sisters named Myesses—brought suit against him for mythical arrears of rent, amounting to 20,000 francs, and secured an order from the reorganised courts for a confiscation of his property and his arrest. Favart fled across the border in order to escape imprisonment and wrote to Maurice (who was really the instigator of the prosecution), asking his aid. The marshal answered his letter with apparent good feeling, and then prompted the Myesses sisters to apply for his arrest in the French courts.

The course of the intrigue that followed is tortuous, yet excessively dramatic. Among other things, it illustrates one of the causes of the French Revolution, even then beginning to ferment—the power for injustice and evil which the whims of a nobleman could exert over the lives of private citizens. Thenceforward until the marshal's death, the Favarts were like puppets pursued by Nemesis in a Greek tragedy.

While Favart was dodging the Brussels police and endeavouring, from the French side of the frontier, to appeal his case and regain control of his confiscated property, Justine was living in Paris; and again, weak rather than sinful, she had surrendered to Maurice. He installed her in a dwelling specially furnished for her benefit, and kept her there in a kind of captivity. Favart managed to find her, however, upon a stealthy visit to Paris, and crept into the house by night like an outlaw to bolster up her courage for a second defiance of the marshal. So she took advantage of her jailer's brief absence from Paris to abandon her sumptuous prison and seek refuge in the home of her mother-in-law, whence she wrote to Maurice, according to an old account of the episode which was found in the Bastille when sacked by the revolutionists, that "it was no longer possible for her to live in sin," and that "her salvation was dearer to her than all the fortunes in the world."

Poor Justine! She was merely a weak, pretty, wretched girl who wanted nothing more than to be a good wife—but she was like wax in the hands of the accomplished seducer. Favart forgave her a second time, however, and they resolved to make a brave stand together against fate and the marshal.

Then began the third and most brutal campaign in Maurice's amorous conquest. He brought all his power into play; the more stubborn the Favarts' resistance, the more dogged became his aggression. He first wrote to the authorities, urging Favart's extradition to Brussels. Then he sent the following missive to Justine:

"I am informed, mademoiselle, that the Demoiselles Myesses intend to prosecute Favart, in virtue of the decree which they obtained against him in Brussels. I think that it will be advisable for you to get away, and as you are not happily situated, I offer you an allowance of 500 livres, which will be paid to you every month until your affairs have taken a favourable turn. Have the kindness to inform me of your decision in this matter, and the place that you or Favart have chosen for your retreat."

Favart answered this letter himself, declining the

marshal's offer, with his very humble thanks.
However bitterly he felt toward Maurice, he must
perforce conceal the resentment and be glad that he
was alive. Of Maurice's plots, moreover, he was
still unaware; and in this reply he asked for protection against the Brussels courts, and for advice in
the dilemma.

Maurice told him to escape while the coast was
clear, and the worried writer, struggling in the
maze of intrigue like a fly in a spider's web, accepted
his word as sooth. Though penniless, he was too
proud to take the marshal's proffered loans; his old
mother borrowed 50 louis for him from an actress
at the Comédie-Française, and with these limited
funds he fled to Strasburg. The day after he left
Paris a *lettre de cachet* was issued against him at
Maurice's request.

Favart remained in hiding four months, and, now
suspicious of Maurice, did not answer to lures held
out for his inveiglement to Paris—and the Bastille.
His family was penniless for a time, but Justine baffled poverty by securing an engagement with the
Comédie-Italienne, her return to the Parisian stage,
on August 6, 1749, being a complete triumph. A
month later she wrote to her husband:

"The marshal is still furious against me; but I am
quite indifferent to that. He has just written a letter to Bercaville [his secretary], wherein he charges
him to tell our mother that, if you come to Paris,
and she has any affection for you, of which he has

no doubt, she must send you away instantly; and that this counsel was a last mark of his kindness for her. That as for Mlle. Chantilly, she is deserving of no consideration at his hands—a fact which ought not to occasion you any vexation.

"Your friends are under the impression that you are travelling in France for your own diversion. If you wish it, I will consign my début to all the devils and set out at once to join you. . . . If it be not possible for us to remain here, we will go away and end our days tranquilly in some foreign country. I am forever your wife and sweetheart."

All this time, Justine had been under surveillance, at the marshal's orders. Meusnier, the police agent entrusted with the affair, says in his memoirs:

"I received orders to keep her under observation, in such a way as to be able to render an account of all her actions and movements, while the marshal, on his side, worked to thwart all of her plans."

Then the marshal played his trump card and brought the melodrama to an appropriate climax. Justine's father, M. Duronceray, whose consent to the marriage had been given in writing, was a chronic drunkard, who had been confined in an institution of restraint at his daughter's request. Maurice secured his release and brought him to Paris as the tool in a scheme which is beneath contempt. The old man, angry with his daughter for the precautions she had taken to save him from an alcoholic grave, was worked upon by the marshal's agents until he filed an accusation against Justine, charging that her marriage with Favart was illegal, denying his consent to it, and asserting that the document which purported to come from him had been forged. Under the marriage laws of France, this was a very serious offense; and coming from the girl's father, with Maurice's backing, the accusation was given due weight by the courts. Accordingly, a *lettre de cachet* was issued for Justine's arrest and imprisonment. Once more she was within the ogre's clutches.

To prevent public suspicion of his part in the affair, Maurice had the old man plied with drink until he made a demonstration against Justine in a café, telling his fancied grievances to all who would listen. The next day this terrible father went to the Comédie-Italienne and denounced his daughter before her colleagues—causing Justine's rival in the company to fall upon his neck with sympathetic tears. After these Balzacian intrigues the *lettre de cachet* was enforced; Justine was arrested by Maurice's henchman, Meusnier, and taken to a convent on the borders of Normandy. She informed her husband of the situation in the following letter:

"They have brought me to the convent of Les Grands-Andelys, the Ursulines, situated twenty-two leagues from Paris. I have seen the *lettre de cachet;* it is my father who has caused me to be placed here. Do not lose an instant; send all our papers to the minister, M. d'Argenson, and especially my father's consent, signed with his own hand; it is in the keeping of the *curé* of Saint-Pierre-aux Bœufs. Collect our witnesses and take them with you to the minister. If it is my father who is persecuting us in this way, the truth will be revealed, and we shall speedily have justice done us. If this trouble is due to some of our enemies, they may do as they please; their influence may perhaps be sufficient to separate us for life, but they can never prevent us loving one another, nor break the sacred and honourable tie which binds our hearts together."

The marshal, attributing her arrest to religious zealots, sent Justine this note of hypocritical condolence and veiled suggestion:

"Favart ought to feel highly flattered that you should sacrifice for him fortune, pleasure, glory, everything, in short, that might have made the happiness of your life. I hope that he will be able to compensate you for it, and that you will never feel the sacrifice which you are making. . . . You would not make my happiness and your own. Perhaps you will make your own unhappiness and that of Favart. I do not wish it, but I fear it."

Justine was soon transferred to another convent which was a place of detention for state prisoners, and here she was treated like a criminal, though at the Ursulines she had been given every attention. Then her courage began to fail; day by day her spirit came closer to the breaking point. She exchanged letters with Maurice, writing in this vein:

"Life is a burden to me; I loathe it. I desire to die, in order that everyone may be satisfied; I am living in a state of despair. Never can I recover from the blow which has brought all this on me."

He would reply in the following strain:

"The great attachment that you entertain for Favart and his relatives is very praiseworthy; but I doubt whether it is advisable to manifest it so clearly, since it is certain that it is this same great attachment which has placed you in the vexatious position in which you now find yourself."

In order to discourage her still further, the marshal, lying like the trooper that he was, accused Favart, the constant husband, with marital infidelity, thus:

"The race of poets does not take things so much to heart. Voltaire has produced two tragedies since the death of Madame du Châtelet, though it was said he was dead also because he was believed to be much attracted to that lady. But to die, *malpeste!* an author's feelings do not carry him as far as that; they are too familiar with fiction to love reality up to that point."

After Justine had endured prison life a few months, Maurice held out to her a hope of release with exile. She answered:

"I await news from day to day with the utmost impatience since you have given me hope of being able to leave this villainous house. Every time that the bell rings, I have terrible palpitation of the

heart. I believe it is some one come to fetch me.
I bound to the door, and when I find it is not I whom
they seek I return, covered with confusion, to my
little cell and weep, like a child who has been beaten
for ten or twelve days. That is the life I am leading. When I leave here, I shall imagine that I am
seeing daylight for the first time. . . . Mon-
seigneur, I implore you in mercy to take me from
this place."

The other Favarts were of sterner stuff than
the soft little actress. Hearing of Justine's negotiations with the marshal, her sister-in-law wrote to
her:

"It was not necessary to ask the advice of my
brother. You ought to know him well enough to be
sure that he would not give you any counsel different from that which he has always given. He knows
of no arrangement that can be made with infamy;
the most cruel punishments would not terrify him;
nor could he be seduced by the most brilliant advantages. He escaped for a time from the rest of the
evils prepared for him, and did not do so for his
own sake. The loss of you had rendered his life
odious to him, but he yielded to our alarms; he
feared the despair of a mother and a sister already
afflicted by the misfortunes which had overtaken
him. . . . He has lost, through these continual
persecutions, his friends, his protectors, his property,
his talents, his health, and all his resources. Nev-
ertheless, he will consider all atoned for when he

finds in you sentiments worthy of him. He does not ask to be their object; honour alone must determine you. Content with loving you, he demands nothing in return, knowing, by sad experience, that the heart is not to be commanded. If it be true that you have been detained by force, now that you are free you will find with us a poor but honourable asylum. . . ."

But Justine was no such Spartan. In January, 1750, after she had been under arrest three months, she surrendered to the inevitable. She was released and exiled to the provincial town of Issoudun, where Maurice took possession of her, according to the agreement which was the only way she could secure her freedom. Threats of Favart's death, however, played a part in her pitiful, despairing acceptance of the marshal's gross terms of capitulation.

And then the romance of the Favarts, so genuine and so out of keeping with its century, died of disillusion. The starving, hunted librettist cast off his wife when he learned of her last compulsory infidelity; he came to the decision that for such a woman he had suffered enough. In June, 1750, the *lettres de cachet* against them were revoked, and they were permitted to return to Paris; but Favart came without joy, saying to a friend who had sheltered him in Strasburg:

"It seems that they are tired of persecuting me; my exile is over, but I am none the happier for that;

my sorrows are of a kind that can only end with my life."

When he met Justine it was without reproaches, but with a cold indifference. Favart had too great a heart to cherish a bitter resentment against his wife; he forgave her, and yet he could not forget, for the old love had burned itself out, leaving the ashes of shame behind. The poet had lost faith in his ideal of love; he wrote to a friend: "Fly from love as from the greatest of evils."

A few months after the persecution of the Favarts ceased, Maurice de Saxe, who was responsible for it all, died of wounds received in a duel with the Prince de Conti, according to rumour; but that fitting end was too late for his victims, whose love he had killed before being called to his last account. Friendship alone survived in the wreckage wrought by his evil passion. The Favarts resumed their professions on the stage, and were stanch, sympathetic counsellors, even collaborators, but no longer man and wife. Justine held public favour in the lyric drama for twenty years, brought about some notable reforms in costuming, and became famed as the most versatile comic opera player of the period. She died in 1772, while her husband survived her by two decades, fecund of libretti to the end. A version of their story has been staged in Offenbach's operetta, "Mme. Favart."

Justine Favart met death more bravely than she had resisted Maurice de Saxe; there was a gay irony, typical of her character, in her last moments. When a neighbour, grotesquely attired, entered the chamber, she said smilingly, with an allusion to one of the standard rôles of pantomime: "I think I see the clown of Death." Before administering the last sacrament, the priest demanded a renunciation of her profession, which was still under the church's ban, but she firmly refused. At last a friend came to her with the news that her salary would be continued as an official pension, in case of her retirement; so she turned to the stern priest and murmured: "Very well, now I can renounce it." Having received absolution, she composed her own epitaph and set it to a dance tune; she was humming the lilt when her breathing stopped.

GREAT LOVE STORIES OF THE THEATRE

VIII

"PERDITA" ROBINSON AND HER PRINCE

"PERDITA" and "Florizel" they called one another during a brief honeymoon of sentimental raptures. They had full right to these sobriquets, for she was one of the loveliest princesses that ever graced Shakespeare's romance of Bohemia's sea-coast; and he was none other than Prince of Wales, afterward to be known as George IV of Great Britain and The First Gentleman of Europe.

Florizel wooed impetuously, and Perdita resisted meltingly; they exchanged innumerable letters and countless vows—for both were very young; she abandoned the stage to flaunt the tokens of his highborn favour, hoping to become a second Eleanor Gwyn; and then her Prince Charming tossed his handkerchief to another flame, leaving his niggardly and prudish father to settle a little expense item of a bond for 20,000 pounds as well as he might. In its mingling of sentimentality and self-seeking, of sighing ardours and brutal dismissal, the romance is typically Hanoverian throughout.

Mary Robinson's most successful stroke in per-

petuating her name was when she became the light-
o'-love of an heir apparent to the English crown.
She is also to be remembered as an actress and a
woman of letters, but the proper definition of her
is as a brilliant adventuress, with the triumphant
fascination and allure of her type—and yet an adventuress with ideals. Accepted from this point of
view, her picturesque character comes into focus
with vivid colouring; but to take her, as some biographers have done, for a conventional injured heroine, weakly misplacing faith in princes, is to trans-
form the piquancy of her story into mawkishness.

She herself forestalled, in large measure, the verdict of posterity by making full confession; her own
biography, written with the practised pen of a literary lady, is the most prolific source of data regarding the liaison. This fervid chronicle, frankly
granting the facts yet glossing over or ornamenting
the motives, must be read, however, largely as a plea
for the defense, not as absolute evidence. The
words are those of a Clarissa Harlowe, but behind
them there is an experienced woman of the world.
In these qualifications there is no thought of extenua-
tion for George Prince; the episode with Perdita,
which was practically the first of his follies, reveals
him plainly as the rhapsodic cad of youth that begot
the flamboyant "bounder" of manhood.

This make-believe Perdita seems to have been
predestined to adventure. Her father, a Captain
Darby, was a ship-owner who attempted to colonize

GEORGE IV., AS PRINCE OF WALES

the bleak coast of Labrador for whale fisheries, in which speculative emprise he sank the savings of his more commonplace cruises. He would return from his exile at intervals years apart to visit the wife and child whom he had left with a small allowance to the dubious existence of London lodgings, and hurriedly flit back oversea again. He disappears from Mary's story at her fourteenth year, laying upon the mother, as he sails for America, this terrifying charge:

"Take care that no dishonour falls upon my daughter! If she is not safe at my return, I will annihilate you!"

His melodramatic exit might be considered, in an equally melodramatic mood, as a departing father's premonition of his child's fate; but as the paternal instinct was not strong in Captain Darby, and as he himself had the rake's insight into feminine character, it may be interpreted as a glimpse of the siren already budding in the maid. Mary met with glittering dishonour, but the wild captain failed to annihilate his wife on account of it; the natives of Labrador, rather, placed the responsibility where it belonged by annihilating his colony.

Although poor, the Darbys were well connected, and when Mary's precocity took a theatrical turn, she found friends willing and able to help her. The dancing teacher in her school was also the ballet master at Covent Garden; he introduced her to Thomas Hull, actor-manager of that theatre, who after admiring her virginal charm and the purity of diction with which she recited passages from Nicholas Rowe's "Jane Shore," presented her to Garrick. The great Davy, also captivated, immediately proposed to coach her in the rôle of Cordelia, so that she might play opposite him in "King Lear." Garrick was then nearly sixty, and close to his retirement, but the spirit of youth and memories of his favourite leading woman, Susannah Cibber, came back to him at the sight of fragrant Mary Darby.

Her dramatic career might have begun at once but for her mother's reluctance and the ingratiating advances of a young man named Thomas Robinson, an embryo lawyer, who pretended to be heir to a handsome fortune. He was debonair; his prospects seemed bright; his courtship was skillful; and so in her sixteenth year Mary put away her maiden name and her studies with Garrick to become Mrs. Robinson.

These annals of Perdita's novitiate in life must be recited, for though apparently trivial they form an exposition to the dramatic episode with Florizel. It is, indeed, curiously interesting to see how she progressed, step by step, deviously and yet none the less definitely, as if led by a wayward fate, to the position of a prince's mistress.

Robinson was a poor husband for Mary, and if, as she relates, the match was hardly more than a marriage of convenience on her part, the choice displays particularly bad judgment. He had the youthful vices of extravagance and dissipation; he liked to cut a dash and mingle with the fastest bucks in London; and in these desires he was aided and abetted, though she admits it not, by his girl-wife. They trailed about together through Ranelagh, Vauxhall and the Pantheon Gardens, resorts where the gay world of London congregated, and fell in with a mad, bad crew of roués whose leaders were "the wicked" Lord Lyttelton, Captain Ayscough, and George Robert ("Fighting") Fitzgerald. These gentlemen did their best to seduce her, Lyttelton by the crafty method of causing Robinson to waste his substance in riotous living and by carrying tales of his infidelities to Mary; Fitzgerald by the romantic device of an attempted abduction. She was discreet enough, however, to cajole and baffle them.

Mrs. Robinson describes her début into gaiety as follows:

"The first time I went to Ranelagh my habit was so singularly plain and Quaker-like that all eyes were fixed upon me. I wore a gown of light brown lustring with close round cuffs (it was then the fashion to wear long ruffles); my hair was without powder, and my head adorned with a plain round cap and a white chip hat, without any ornaments whatever."

Here and in many other passages she artlessly exposes her obsession with dress; every important event of her life has its paragraph on costume. Her memoirs are so utterly feminine in this respect that they provoke the usual masculine smile. Her vanity has, indeed, some justification, for her clever taste did away with certain absurdities of costuming on the stage; while in her unprofessional public appearances she was the fashion-plate of the town.

Mrs. Robinson soon discovered that her husband's great expectations were an imposture, and that he was merely the illegitimate son of a crabbed old gentleman in Wales who became less and less inclined to do anything for him. For diplomatic reasons the gay young pair visited this relative by the left hand, who had the courtesy title of "uncle"; and Mary found him friendly, but not generous. The sister-in-law, moreover, was hostile—because of the jealousy of dress, according to the bride.

"Miss Robinson rode on horseback in a camlet safeguard, with a high-crowned bonnet," she states. "I wore a fashionable habit and looked like something human. Envy at length assumed the form of insolence, and I was taunted perpetually on the folly of appearing like a woman of fortune."

They returned to London with neither donations nor promises as reward for their sojourn of painful duty, and took a house in a fashionable district, furnishing it with "peculiar elegance." How did this pair of foolish butterflies manage to make such a display without visible means of support? That question has never been definitely answered. Mrs.

Robinson remarks that "I frequently inquired into the extent of his finances, and he as often assured me that they were in every respect competent to his expenses." She leaves it to be understood that his funds came from that vague and ominous quarter known as "the Jews," but if so, the money-lenders gave him an unprecedented amount of rope with which to hang himself. There is good reason for the suspicion that the future Perdita was herself talented in the art of living luxuriously on nothing a year, and that when she could not get credit from trades-people she had no scruples about accepting "loans" from men of Lord Lyttelton's type, who were willing to hold as security certain hopes of an ultimate surrender—collateral upon which cool Perdita never permitted them to realize. There is even a report to be found in the pamphlets of the time that she had snared a member of the usurious tribe itself in the web of her captivation, but no means now remain of establishing this as fact.

Finally the inevitable crash came; the peculiarly elegant household furnishings were seized, and Robinson was lodged in a debtor's prison. Perdita went through this time of trial with the white plume of wifely devotion flying. She marched off to jail with her husband, and there did the work of copying documents, offered by their "uncle" at a guinea a week, which was scorned by the lazy young wastrel. She also found time for her first literary effort—a long poem called "Captivity," which was published under the patronage of a duchess. After a few months of this bitter experience Robinson was tention to the stage, for she now had a baby to sup-released, and then Mary once more turned her at-port as well as a husband.

William Brereton, leading man at Drury Lane, introduced her to Richard Brinsley Sheridan, who had just acquired an interest in that house; the author-manager gave her a hearing in the lines of Cordelia and Juliet, and promptly engaged her. Garrick, now retired, undertook to prepare her for the début; she was the last of his pupils, and as such she did him full honour. After a month's study she made her first appearance on the stage, December 10, 1776, as Juliet, with Brereton as Romeo. Her arch young beauty and neat declamation were received with enthusiasm by the audience; Garrick and Sheridan were delighted with her playing. In her autobiography this important event is chronicled from the sartorial point of view:

"My dress was a pale pink satin, trimmed with crêpe, richly spangled with silver; my head was ornamented with white feathers, and my monumental suit for the last scene was white satin, and completely plain, excepting that I wore a veil of the most transparent gauze, which fell quite to my feet from the back of my head, and a string of beads around my waist, to which was suspended a cross appropriately fashioned."

A few weeks later she appeared as Statira in Nathaniel Lee's "Alexander the Great," of which occasion she leaves this record:

"My dress was white and blue, made after the Persian costume; and, though it was then singular on the stage, I wore neither a hoop nor powder. My feet were bound with sandals, richly ornamented; and the whole dress was picturesque and characteristic."

Then came the rôle of Amanda in Sheridan's new comedy, "A Trip to Scarborough." The piece was discovered by the audience to be an adaptation of Vanbrugh's "Relapse," and was hissed. Mrs. Robinson has something more pertinent than usual to say of that *première:*

"I was terrified beyond imagination when Mrs. Yates, no longer able to bear the hissing of the audience, quitted the scene, and left me alone to encounter the critic tempest. I stood for some moments as if I had been petrified. Mr. Sheridan, from the side wing, desired me not to quit the boards; the late Duke of Cumberland, from the stage box, bade me take courage. 'It is not you, but the play they hiss,' said his Royal Highness. I curtsied; and that curtsey seemed to electrify the whole house, for a thundering peal of encouraging applause followed. The comedy was suffered to go on, and is to this hour a stock play at Drury Lane Theatre."

She soon became the favourite of the day; she received a large salary, upon which her scamp of a husband drew freely for his needs at the gaming table; and was fêted on all sides. She had suddenly attained her ideal, which was "celebrity and fortune," and though her autobiography complains of her husband's neglect, it is not certain that she really regretted it. Various noble and wealthy personages tempted her to leave him, but she clung to her reputation for dear life. Sheridan was the only man who made an impression upon her; she seems to have been genuinely smitten with the dramatist, whose attitude toward her was only that of the friend and adviser. She writes of him in this strain:

"He continued to visit me frequently, and always gave me the most friendly counsel. He knew that I was not properly protected by Mr. Robinson, but he was too generous to build his gratification on the detraction of another. The happiest moments I then knew were passed in the society of this distinguished being. . . . He saw me ill-bestowed upon a man who neither loved nor valued me; he lamented my destiny, but with such delicate propriety that it consoled while it revealed to me the unhappiness of my situation."

Mrs. Robinson's star was on the ascendant for several years; then the influence of the Prince of Wales diverted it from its orbit of the stage and it became a gorgeous comet of adventure. On November 20, 1779, she made her first appearance as Perdita in "A Winter's Tale," and on December 3 the drama was repeated, by royal command. George III, who thought that Shakespeare was "sad stuff," nodded sleepily in his chair; Queen Charlotte watched the performance with rigid austerity; but the Prince of Wales, then a spirited boy tugging away from the parental leading-strings, was transformed by the magic wand of romance into Florizel.

In the green-room before the play "Gentleman" Smith, who was cast for Leontes, remarked laughingly to Perdita:

"By Jove, Mrs. Robinson, you will make a conquest of the Prince, for to-night you look handsomer than ever."

The jest was prophetic; and after the performance the entire company was in an excited flutter of gossip over Mrs. Robinson's great catch. Let Perdita herself tell how the inflammable Prince took fire:

"I hurried through the first scene, not without much embarrassment, owing to the fixed attention with which the Prince of Wales honoured me. Indeed some flattering remarks which were made by his Royal Highness met my ear as I stood near his box, and I was overwhelmed with confusion. The Prince's particular attention was observed by everyone, and I was again rallied at the end of the play. On the last curtsey, the royal family condescendingly returned a bow to the performers; but just as the curtain was falling, my eyes met those of the Prince of Wales; and with a look that I never shall forget, he gently inclined his head a second time; I felt the compliment and blushed my gratitude."

Among Mrs. Robinson's green-room acquaintances was Lord Malden, afterwards Earl of Essex, an intimate of the Prince. A few days later he brought her a note "of more than common civility," signed "Florizel." She refused to believe Malden's assertion that it came from the Prince of Wales; and soon another missive followed, stating that if she were still sceptical of Florizel's identity, she should attend a concert in Covent Garden, at which one of Handel's oratorios was to be played, for confirmation. Eager for this escapade, she took a prominent box in the balcony, and as soon as she appeared the Prince began to flirt with her outrageously, in this manner:

"He held the printed bill before his face, and drew his hand across his forehead, still fixing his eyes on me. I was confused and knew not what to do. My husband was with me, and I was fearful of his observing what passed. Still the Prince continued to make signs, such as moving his hand on the edge of the box as if writing, then speaking to the Duke of York (then Bishop of Osnaburgh), who also looked towards me with particular attention. I now observed one of the gentlemen in waiting bring the Prince a glass of water; before he raised it to his lips he looked at me."

This exchange of soft glances could not escape public attention. Mrs. Robinson admits that the incident was referred to in the "diurnal prints," but she fails to record the journalistic impression, which was to her disadvantage, as may be seen from this paragraph:

"A circumstance of rather an embarrassing nature happened at last night's Oratorio. Mrs. R——, decked out in all her finery, took care to post herself in one of the upper boxes, immediately opposite the Prince's, and by those airs peculiar to herself contrived at last so to basilisk a certain heir-apparent that his fixed attention to the beautiful object above became generally noticed, and soon after astonished their Majesties, who, not being able to discover the cause, seemed at a loss to account for the extraordinary effect. No sooner, however, were they properly informed than a messenger was instantly sent aloft desiring the dart-dealing actress to withdraw, which she complied with, though not without expressing the utmost chagrin at her mortifying removal."

The Prince was then in his nineteenth, and Mrs. Robinson in her twenty-first year. She would have the world believe that on both sides it was a case of love at first sight; to her the Prince was a young hero out of a story-book:

"I was not insensible to all his powers of attraction. I thought him one of the most amiable of men. There was a beautiful ingenuousness in his language, a warm and enthusiastic adoration expressed in every letter which interested and charmed me."

A heated correspondence ensued; letters signed

"Florizel" and "Perdita" were exchanged almost daily, with Malden serving as the go-between. She would not grant an immediate interview, as the Prince desired, and his infatuation was spurred to greater absurdities by her aloofness. He sent her his portrait in miniature, accompanied by a heart cut out of paper which had the emblems, obverse and reverse, *"Je ne change qu'en mourant,"* and "Unalterable to my Perdita through life." So the affair went on through the winter and spring of 1780, Florizel's passion increasing and Perdita's coyness slowly waning. Finally, to demonstrate his generous intentions, the Prince inclosed in one of his letters a bond for 20,000 pounds, made payable to her at his majority; this guarantee was unsought by her, yet she carefully refrained from returning it. Then the climax was at hand. She says:

"The unbounded assurances of lasting affection which I received from his Royal Highness in many scores of the most eloquent letters, the contempt which I experienced from my husband, and the perpetual labour which I underwent for his support, at length began to weary my fortitude. Still, I was reluctant to become the theme of public animadversion, and still I remonstrated with my husband on the unkindness of his conduct."

The first meeting of Perdita and Florizel was now arranged, after much negotiation. She rejected Malden's suggestion that she come to the

Prince's rooms, dressed as a boy; formality, she insisted, should mark the first interview, at least. Then the accommodating young lord offered his own house in Mayfair, but the Prince feared the vigilance of his tutors. He was living with his younger brother in a lodge by Kew Palace, supposedly absorbed in serious studies, and a nocturnal appointment in the groves of that semi-sylvan retreat was at last decided upon. In her description of this meeting, Mrs. Robinson becomes rhapsodic:

"At length an evening was fixed for this long-dreaded interview. Lord Malden and myself dined at the inn on the island between Kew and Brentford. We waited the signal for crossing the river in a boat which had been engaged for that purpose. Heaven can witness how many conflicts my agitated heart endured at this most important moment! I admired the Prince; I felt grateful for his affection. He was the most engaging of created beings. I had corresponded with him during many months, and his eloquent letters, the exquisite sensibility which breathed through every line, his ardent professions of adoration, had combined to shake my feeble resolution. The handkerchief was waved from the opposite shore; but the signal was, by the dusk of the evening, rendered almost imperceptible. Lord Malden took my hand, I stepped into the boat, and in a few minutes we landed before the iron gates of Old Kew Palace. The interview was but for a moment. The Prince of Wales and the Duke of York

(then Bishop of Osnaburgh) were walking in
the avenue. They hastened to meet us. A few
words, and those scarcely articulate, were uttered by the Prince, when a noise of people approaching from the palace startled us. The
moon was now rising; and the idea of being overheard, or of his Royal Highness being seen out at
such an unusual hour, terrified the whole group.
After a few more words of the most affectionate nature uttered by the Prince, we parted; and Lord Malden and I returned to the island. The Prince never
quitted the avenue, nor the presence of the Duke of
York, during the whole of this short meeting. Alas!
my friend, if my mind was before influenced by esteem, it was now awakened to the most enthusiastic
admiration. The rank of the Prince no longer
chilled into awe that being who now considered him
as the lover and the friend. The graces of his person, the irresistible sweetness of his smile, the tenderness of his melodious yet manly voice, will be remembered by me till every vision of this changing scene
shall be forgotten."

The place was apt for wooing, in spite of the first
interruption, and Perdita's trips across the river became more and more frequent. She would have us
believe that Malden and the juvenile bishop were always with them, but it may be inferred that they
served as sentinels rather than chaperons. Occasionally Florizel would burst into song, like any col-
legian of to-day:

"He sang with exquisite taste, and the tones of his voice, breaking on the silence of the night, have often appeared to my entranced senses like more than mortal melody. Often have I lamented the distance which destiny had placed between us. How would my soul have idolised such a husband! Alas! how often, in the ardent enthusiasm of my soul, have I formed the wish that that being were mine alone; to whom partial millions were to look up for protection."

Their secrecy did not prevent the attachment from becoming a public scandal. It even began to figure in the Hanoverian councils of state, for the Prince was about to be given a separate establishment, and popular opinion of his allegiance to a married woman was dreaded by George III. After the furtive amour had gone on for a year, Mrs. Robinson retired from the stage, May 31, 1780, in order that she might more fittingly adorn her new station as the heir apparent's mistress. Her husband was now utterly cast off, and he accepted the situation with his usual complaisance, doubtless secure in the faith that through his wife-in-name-only he now had access to the royal treasury whenever he was pressed by creditors. Then Perdita and Florizel cast caution to the winds, appearing together at theatres, balls and military reviews with enraptured indiscretion. Mrs. Robinson proudly recalls one incident in which the Prince gave public proof of his amorous favor, as follows:

"On the 4th of June, I went, by his desire, into the Chamberlain's box at the birth-night ball; the distressing observation of the circle was drawn toward that part of the box in which I sat by the marked and injudicious attentions of his Royal Highness. I had not arrived many minutes before I witnessed a singular species of fashionable coquetry. Previous to his Highness's beginning his minuet, I perceived a woman of high rank select from the bouquet which she wore two rosebuds, which she gave to the Prince, as he afterwards informed me, 'emblematical of herself and him.' I observed his Royal Highness immediately beckon to a nobleman, who has since formed a part of his establishment, and, looking most earnestly at me, whisper a few words, at the same time presenting to him his newly acquired trophy. In a few minutes Lord C—— entered the Chamberlain's box, and, giving the rosebuds into my hands, informed me that he was commissioned by the Prince to do so. I placed them in my bosom, and, I confess, felt proud of the power by which I thus publicly mortified an exalted rival."

Perdita was far from being the shy and modest violet that she pretends to have been in her autobiography; evidence more reliable than her own shows that she courted stares and basked in the attentions of the crowd. Notoriety, in fact, was the meat upon which her soul fed. In the piquant volumes of anecdotage left by Miss Lætitia Hawkins, daughter of the literary Sir John who was a friend of Dr. John-

son, particular attention is paid to her amazing repertory of costume, in this vivid paragraph:

"When she was to be seen daily in St. James'
Street and Pall Mall, even in her chariot this varia-
tion was striking. To-day she was a *paysanne,* with
her straw hat tied to the back of her head, looking as
if too new to what she passed to know what she
looked at. Yesterday she, perhaps, had been the
dressed belle of Hyde Park, trimmed, powdered,
patched, painted to the utmost power of rouge and
white lead; to-morrow she would be the cravatted
Amazon of the riding-house; but, be she what she
might, the hats of the fashionable promenaders
swept the ground as she passed."

The Prince of Wales reached his eighteenth birthday August 12, 1780; and on January 1, 1781, he was
established in bachelor apartments of his own. He
was granted this liberty by his father on condition
that he break off with Perdita; he entertained the
suggestion cordially because his fickle heart had
already been caught by another pretty face; and so
Perdita's reign neared its end. About six months
later the blow fell. She had no fair warning; two
days after a rendezvous with the Prince at Kew,
when his love had seemed to her "as boundless as it
was undiminished," she received a note from him
announcing that they "must meet no more."

Poor Perdita's bubble of iridescent fortune burst
so suddenly that she could hardly believe it. "I call
Heaven to witness," she cries, "that I was totally

unconscious why this decision had taken place in his Royal Highness's mind." Her letters asking for an explanation remained unanswered. In despair she decided upon a personal appeal, and so she set out for a journey in her phaëton from London to Windsor, where the Prince was preparing for a ball in honour of his nineteenth birthday. It was a trip not without peril; a highwayman grasped at her ponies' reins on Hounslow Heath, but she drove on recklessly and escaped. When she reached Windsor she asked for an audience with the Prince; but after she had waited for hours she received word through a secretary that he was too busy to be disturbed.

She consulted with Lord Malden, to no avail except to hear him declare the fires that had long smouldered for her in his own bosom; she wrote to the Prince again and again, without reply; and at last she surrendered to the inevitable and bade her romance farewell. She had a brief after-glow of hope when a message came that the Prince would see her in the house of Lord Malden, but it only illuminated Florizel's utter hardness of heart. She says:

"After much hesitation, by the advice of Lord Malden, I consented to meet his Royal Highness. He accosted me with every appearance of tender attachment, declaring that he had never for a moment ceased to love me, but that I had many concealed enemies who were exerting every effort to undermine me. We passed some hours in the most

friendly and delightful conversation; and I began
to flatter myself that all our differences were adjusted. But what words can express my surprise
and chagrin when, on meeting his Royal Highness
the very next day in Hyde Park, he turned his head
to avoid seeing me, and even affected not to know
me! "

In this manner Florizel closed the book of love
with Perdita. The account might have been settled
in a more graceful manner; but the private life of
The First Gentleman of Europe is a long sequence
of such broken vows.

Mrs. Robinson was now in a difficult position.
She had given up her profession and acquired debts
of about 7,000 pounds through faith in the Prince's
constancy. As soon as the news of her dismissal got
abroad, her creditors swooped down upon her with
rapacity. She was advised against returning to the
stage on the theory—utterly mistaken according to
modern examples—that the public would not toler-
ate her after the liaison with the Prince. Florizel's
treasured letters now had negotiable as well as sentimental aspects, and she did not have any scruples
about using them to her advantage. The Prince's
royal papa, always dreading a scandal, promptly
came to time, as this letter of his, written to Lord
North August 28, 1781, bears witness:

"I am sorry to be obliged to open a subject that
has long given me much pain, but I can rather do it
on paper than in conversation; it is a subject of which

I know he is not ignorant. My eldest son got last year into a very improper connection with an actress and woman of indifferent character through the friendly assistance of Ld. Malden; a multitude of letters past [sic], which she has threatened to publish unless he, in short, bought them of her. He had made her very foolish promises [sic], which, undoubtedly, by her conduct to him she entirely cancelled. I have thought it right to authorize the getting them from her, and have employed Lieut.-Col. Hotham, on whose discression [sic] I could depend, to manage this business. He has now brought it to a conclusion, and has her consent to get these letters on her receiving 5,000 pounds, undoubtedly an enormous sum; but I wish to get my son out of this shameful scrape. I desire you will therefore see Lieut.-Col. Hotham and settle this with him. I am happy at being able to say that I never was personally engaged in such a transaction, which perhaps makes me feel this the stronger."

With this price of peace, 5,000 pounds, Mrs. Robinson's creditors were satisfied, but what of current expenses? The Prince's bond for 20,000 pounds still remained; it had not come to maturity, but it was a tangible asset. Close-fisted George III rebelled at paying its face value, and sent a cabinet minister, Charles James Fox, to adjust the demand. The latter undertook the commission with enthusiasm; he languished at the feet of Mrs. Robinson as an admirer for some time; and finally compromised the matter for an annuity of 500 pounds, one-half of which was to descend to her daughter after her death. So it was apparent that Perdita was an excellent business woman, and fared very well from the Prince's shabby treatment of her, in the long run.

The old love being off, she was not slow in finding a new. Before the bond claim had been settled she formed an alliance with Colonel Banastre Tarleton, the cavalry officer who was much cursed by the revolutionists in the southern states of America for his brutal military efficiency. This amour, which went to the length of joint housekeeping, was more permanent than that with Florizel; it lasted for almost sixteen years, during which time Mrs. Robinson devoted herself assiduously and rather successfully to literary endeavour.

Her writings deserve some comment. She has a list of seventeen titles to her credit, including eight collections of poems, a tragedy in verse, a sonnet sequence, a three-decker novel, and four shorter ventures in fiction. She also helped Tarleton with his "History of the Campaigns of 1780 and 1781 in the Southern Provinces of North America." Her autobiography, of course, is now her best-known work. In her life-time her poems were "best sellers" because into their amatory strains the public chose to read frequent allusions to the false Prince.

Mrs. Robinson may be said to have lived three lives—as actress, adventuress and lady of letters, each with a rather passionate completeness. Her career on the stage, though brief, won for her honourable mention in such standard histories as those of Genest and Dr. Doran. In proof of its comprehensive activity, her list of interpretations are worthy of note. From début to retirement they are as follows:

Juliet in Shakespeare's "Romeo and Juliet," "Statira in Nathaniel Lee's "Alexander the Great," Amanda in Sheridan's "A Trip to Scarborough," Fanny Stirling in Colman and Garrick's "A Clandestine Marriage," Ophelia in Shakespeare's "Hamlet," Lady Anne in Shakespeare's "Richard III," The Lady in Milton's "Comus," Emily in Hannah Cowley's "The Runaway," Araminta in Sir John Vanbrugh's "The Confederacy," Octavia in Dryden's "All for Love," Lady Macbeth in Shakespeare's "Macbeth," Palmira in an adaptation of Voltaire's "Mahomet," Miss Richly in Mrs. Sheridan's "The Discovery," Alinda in Robert Jephson's "The Law of Lombardy," Cordelia in Shakespeare's "King Lear," Jacintha in John Hoadly's "The Suspicious Husband," Portia in Shakespeare's "The Merchant of Venice," Fidelia in Wycherley's "The Plain Dealer," Viola in Shakespeare's "Twelfth Night," Perdita in Shakespeare's "A Winter's Tale," Rosalind in Shakespeare's "As You Like It," Oriana in George Farquhar's "The Inconstant," Imogen in Shakespeare's "Cymbeline," Mrs. Brady in Garrick's "The Irish Widow," and Eliza Camply in Lady Craven's "The Miniature Picture."

"Perdita" Robinson and Her Prince

She died December 26, 1800, at the age of forty-two, after a long period of invalidism. Her death-bed request was that "two particular persons" should receive a lock of her hair; they were, presumably, the Prince of Wales and Colonel Tarleton. There is no means of knowing that her last sentimental wish was fulfilled; but if so, one might speculate with some melancholy profit upon the Prince's feelings—provided he had any at all—when he inherited that tress from his one-time Perdita's coiffure, seductive and radiant in the long-ago, now lifeless and ashen-gray.

GREAT LOVE STORIES OF THE
THEATRE

IX

MLLE. GEORGES AND NAPOLEON

IN the prosperous days of the Consulate, when Napoleon took an all-too brief respite from war and led France along the brilliant paths of peace, a girl of tender youth and statuesque beauty made a triumphant début at the Théâtre Français, playing the grand rôles of tragedy. The First Consul, always a connoisseur and a constructive patron of the stage, came, saw and was conquered; the young actress bewitched the Man of Destiny. Thenceforward Mlle. Georges, as this débutante was known, added to her artistic prestige the glamour of historic fame; she will always be remembered as "a favourite of Napoleon."

The relationship between the masterful Corsican and the actress was more than a sordid and venal liaison. Napoleon was notorious for callous amours; there was little romance in his numerous loves; and yet a thread of idyll, of pretty sentiment, altogether strange to his grim character, runs through the story of his dalliance with Mlle. Georges. To him she was "my little Georgina," tenderly petted and caressed while the relationship endured and ever afterward held in affection. For her the association

217

meant reverence, high patriotism, hero-worship; she gave a devoted passion that typified the idolatry of the whole nation. Other women upon whom the Napoleonic fancy settled in a brief caprice—Mme. Branchu, known as "the vestal of the Opera"; Mlles. Duchesnois, Bourgoin and Levard of the Théâtre Français; and various beauties of the court—cried out upon their paramour as a monster and a tyrant after their dismissal; but not so with Mlle. Georges. Between her and the First Consul, afterward Emperor, it was a matter of sentiment, free with her from self-seeking, and with him from brutality.

Ten years after the liaison had been broken off, in the Hundred Days which ended with Waterloo, she sent word to the Emperor that she had certain papers compromising the Duke of Otranto (Fouché). When his emissary returned from the appointment with her, Napoleon asked:

"She didn't tell you that she was in low water, I suppose?"

"No, Sire, she merely spoke of her desire to restore the papers to your Majesty."

"I understand. I also know that she is in difficulties. You will give her 20,000 francs from my purse."

That was at a time when Napoleon needed all the sinews of war at his command, but he was quick to make a tactful sacrifice for the sake of his one-time "little Georgina." And she, after Waterloo, when Napoleon saw nothing but treason and desertion

MLLE. GEORGES

about him, requested the honour of accompanying him into his exile upon the lonely, heat-smitten rock of St. Helena.

In very truth, neither of them had forgotten, though ten tumultuous years of wars and passions had passed since their romantic days. Each was ready to give aid and support in the other's hour of need, for the sake of their sweet memories; and no matter what else may be said of Napoleon's or Mlle. Georges' morals, toward one another they displayed a loyalty worthy of an emperor and a player-queen.

Mlle. Georges was born February 23, 1787, her father being manager and orchestra leader of a nomadic provincial troupe in which her mother played soubrette rôles. Baptismally, the future favourite of Napoleon was Marie-Josephine Weymer, but as her sobriquet of the theatre she chose her father's given name of Georges and by it alone she was known. She went on the stage at the age of five, and displayed such talent as a child that she became the special protégée of Mlle. Raucourt, a veteran of the Théâtre Français, under whose auspices she made her début at that famous playhouse, November 23, 1802, as Clytemnestra in Racine's "Iphigénie en Aulide." She was then only sixteen years old. Within a single season, however, she was transformed from a timid country maiden into a leading tragedienne, courted by princes and toasted for her beauty by all Paris.

Even in her novitiate she was introduced into the

Napoleonic circle. Mlle. Raucourt had the entrée
into consular society, and being an inveterate gadder
whirled her young prodigy about with her to dinners and receptions where the notables congregated.
Although Mlle. Georges did not meet Napoleon
until after her début, she was in touch with his
family as a student. The following passage in her
memoirs curiously foreshadows the romance to
come:

"There were incessant visits; the ministers came,
then all the family of the First Consul—Lucien
[Napoleon's brother], who, like the First Consul,
only loved tragedy; the eminent Mme. Bacchiochi,
a thin and delicate woman who was very much in
the Consul's confidence. We often lunched at her
house with the Consul's mother and Lucien. Then
afterward I had to recite. Lucien used to take part
in the performances, giving me my cues and frequently playing whole scenes by himself."

The débuts of new actresses at the Théâtre Français were great events at the time, because of the
keen interest which Napoleon took in that institution. Mlle. Georges' *première* was stormy; the
crowded house was divided into two camps—one,
the adherents of Mlle. Raucourt and her neophyte,
the other partisans of M. Legouvé, who had coached
a rival, Mlle. Duchesnois. The First Consul was
present with Josephine; here he first saw the beauty
which he afterward wooed and possessed.

Mlle. Georges was supported by the great Talma,

who became her life-long friend. She made a favourable impression in her first scene, but then, feeling the suppressed animosity of her rival's friends and of a clique banded against Talma, stage-fright descended upon her. She struggled along bravely, however, receiving messages from her instructress, who occupied a box, after every scene. Mlle. Raucourt's communications ran in this strain:

"It is going well. Keep firm. There is a cabal. Don't be afraid, but keep on trembling just the same."

In the fourth act she was interrupted with murmurs of disapproval. For a moment the girl lost her head; then she heard Mlle. Raucourt call out, "Begin again, Georgina"; she saw the First Consul join in applause friendly to her; and after two attempts, she carried the speech through above the uproar, during which some of her supporters undertook to punch the heads of the hissing foe. It ended as a success; the First Consul and Josephine sent compliments to Mlle. Raucourt upon her talented pupil.

The début was chronicled by M. Geoffroy, the dramatic critic of the *Journal des Debats,* as follows:

"Preceded upon the stage by an extraordinary reputation for beauty, Mlle. Georges has not appeared beneath her reputation; her face unites to French graces the regularity and nobility of Grecian forms; her figure is that of the sister of Apollo when she advances on the banks of Eurotas, surrounded by her nymphs and raising her head above them. Her whole person is made to be offered as a model to Guérin's chisel. When she caused the first line of her part to be heard, the ear was not as favourable to her as the eyes; the inseparable trouble of such a moment had altered her voice, naturally flexible, wide of compass and sonorous; some defects which could be remarked in the acting and diction must be attributed to the same cause, all of which, however, can be easily corrected. A girl of sixteen who appeared for the first time before such a large and imposing assembly could not have the full use of her faculties; it is sufficient that in the first appearance she showed the happiest disposition and the germ of a great actress. One must wait and not extinguish by carping severity a good talent ready to develop itself. Her very faults have a noble origin; they belong to an impetuosity and an ardour which she does not yet know how to regulate, which precipitate her delivery and movements; for in that beautiful body there is a soul impatient to pour itself out. She is not a statue of Parian marble; she is Pygmalion's Galatea, full of warmth and life, and in some way oppressed by the crowd of new sensations which are rising in her bosom."

Then came new rôles in other tragedies—"Tancrède," "L'Orpheline de la Chine," and "Phèdre" —all of them received with enthusiasm. The girl-tragedienne became the idol of Paris; she was fêted like a princess. Josephine sent her a cloak for the costume in "Phèdre"; Napoleon contributed a purse of 3,000 francs after seeing the performance. But with all this success she kept on living like a simple bourgeois maiden with her parents. Lucien Bonaparte offered her a handsome establishment—under the usual conditions—but she declined.

"What is the good of your house to me without my people?" is the comment made upon Lucien's proposal in her naïve memoirs. "Why, I should die there! I don't want it and refuse it with all my heart."

A Polish nobleman, Prince Sapieha, became interested in her, in a platonic way, and showered gifts upon her, even providing a handsome establishment, with horses and a carriage, for herself and family. According to the etiquette of the day, his tributes were "to the artiste," and they were accepted by Mlle. Georges "as an artiste." The prince seems to have taken a generous paternal interest—and only that—in the girl; and certainly he did much to make her early career comfortable.

She was, of course, besieged by more selfish admirers. One of them announced himself at her dressing room as Mr. Curling Papers, declared himself a hair-dresser, and asked permission to arrange her coiffure. This was granted, in order to get rid of him, and then he was shown the door. But when Mlle. Georges' maid removed the curling papers which the apparent madman had used, she found that they were 500 franc notes—twenty in all. Mr. Curling Papers was some amorous banker incog. But this Zeus of the counting room found Mlle. Georges no easy Danaë responsive to his shower of gold.

All this time Napoleon was much in the girl's mind; he was her chosen hero. She had almost lost her heart to the First Consul from seeing him in his box at her performances. By quoting in her memoirs a conversation between herself and Prince Sapieha, she practically confesses as much:

"Is the First Consul, then, so fond of tragedy?" asked her patron. "He goes nearly every time."

"It is true, but Talma always played with me," she answered, "and the First Consul is very fond of Talma. As for me, I feel more animated when I see him in his box, and he knows it. He must see himself sometimes among those great heroes; I am sure he talks with them. He is so great, too; grandeur suits him so well, and how handsome he is! I should like to see him and speak to him. I am told his voice and speech are very soft. And what a pretty little hand! It is seen to perfection, for he places it in front of his box."

"My dear, you are mad about your First Consul."

"No, I am not mad about him," she protested. "I like and admire him the same as everybody else. You see, when he enters his box, the women rise and applaud him, but still they are not mad about him. It is the enthusiasm of delirium."

Then came the first meeting—at Napoleon's own command. One evening, upon returning home after a performance as Clytemnestra, she found the First Consul's chief valet, Constant, waiting for her with the polite request that she visit his master the next evening at Saint-Cloud, to receive his congratulations. She was sophisticated enough to understand all the possibilities which that message contained, and maiden embarrassment overwhelmed her. She did not know what answer to make, but finally, as she says, "I confess curiosity settled it, or self-love; how do I know?"

She did not have a performance the next evening, but she went to the theatre and waited in a box. At eight o'clock Constant appeared and quietly escorted her into a carriage. Often during the long drive she said to the valet:

"I am dying of fear. You would do well to take me back home and to tell the First Consul that I am indisposed. Do that, and I promise you to come another time."

They reached the palace by a secluded garden approach, and entered through an open French window at which Roustan, Napoleon's Mameluke bodyguard, was waiting. Then Mlle. Georges found herself in a large, brilliantly lighted boudoir. Presently a door opened noiselessly; the First Consul stood before her in the familiar costume—green uniform with red facings, white satin knee-breeches, silk stockings, his hat under his arm.

He took her by the hand graciously, seated her on a sofa, raised her veil and carelessly threw it on the floor, and then began an amiable conversation. Mlle. Georges records his method of breaking the ice and putting her at ease in this fashion:

"How your hand trembles! Are you afraid of me, then? Do I seem terrible to you? I found you exceedingly beautiful yesterday, madame, and I wished to compliment you. I am more amiable and polite than you, as you see."

"How is that, monsieur?"

"I sent you a remittance of three thousand francs after seeing you in 'Émilie,' as a proof of the pleasure you gave me. I hoped you would ask permission to present yourself to thank me. But the beautiful and haughty Émilie did not come."

"I did not dare to take the liberty."

"Oh, a poor excuse! Were you afraid of me?"

"Yes."

"And now?"

"Still more."

He found her timidity amusing, and with pleasant, informal talk tried to assure her that he was no ogre. Then he began to quiz her on all the details of her life, leading up to a demand whence came the expensive gown she was wearing. Without reserve she told him of Prince Sapieha's platonic attentions.

"That is good; you do not lie," he said. "You will come and see me again, and will be very discreet. Promise me."

He made his intentions as a lover manifest, in a
delicate manner, but she, though fascinated in spite
of her modesty, begged for a little indulgence, promising to return the next evening if he wished. He
respected her timidity, and so they talked on, in a
lover-like vein, until five o'clock in the morning,
when she said:

"I should like to go."

"You must be tired, my dear Georgina. Good-
by until to-morrow, then. You will come?"

"Yes, gladly. You are too kind and gracious
for one not to love you, and I love you with all my
heart."

He put on her shawl and veil, and kissed her
good-night on the forehead. Then, like a silly
child, she burst out laughing, with the words:

"You have just kissed Prince Sapieha's veil."

Her tactless remark unleashed the Napoleonic
storm of wrath. He tore the veil into bits; he
trampled the shawl underfoot. A little crystal ring,
inclosing some of Mlle. Raucourt's grey hairs, was
jerked from her finger and crushed by his heel.
After the outbreak the tyrant resumed his aspect of
wooer, saying:

"Dear Georgina, you must not have anything except what comes from me."

He rang for Constant and gave orders. A white
cashmere shawl and lace veil were brought to re-
place the offending gifts of Prince Sapieha, and in
her ears, as recompense for the shattered keep-sake

ring, he placed two superb diamonds. Then he sent her away, after compelling her to repeat her promise for the next day. Upon the homeward drive the sedulous valet fell asleep, snoring terrifically, but the girl was far from slumber. She was facing the crisis of her life and trying to think it out sanely.

"I thought the Consul very charming, but very violent," say her memoirs. "It is to be nothing but an existence of slavery. I am going to give myself without the least hope of liberty, and I am very fond of my independence. Shall I return to-morrow, as I promised him? I am undecided. He pleases me; I find him so kind and gentle with me. But how do I know it is not a caprice? It would be very sad and humiliating to be deserted."

She discussed the problem with Talma during the day. He told her that she was mad to hesitate.

"But he is the First Consul and I am a strolling player," she answered. "He thinks of nothing but glory, and do you believe that glory goes with love? No; I want some one to be in love with me. Should I be happy if I came to love the Consul, to be near him only when he orders, when it pleases him! See, Talma, it is slavery."

"Well, then, get married."

"That's nice advice to give me. I fear slavery, and you wish me to marry!"

So Talma delivered his ultimatum and she accepted it.

"You will go this evening to Saint-Cloud. It is your destiny; follow it. If you do not go, you will do something stupid which will be very serious for you."

Thus, urged by her great colleague, she kept her promise to Napoleon, and when the carriage arrived at the palace she found him waiting for her. To quote again from her memoirs, a document of historical value:

"He loaded me with tenderness, but with such delicacy, with such a restrained ardour, always respecting the modest emotions of a young girl. My heart experienced an unknown feeling; it beat with force. I was attracted in spite of myself. I loved the great man who was surrounding me with such consideration, who was not rough in his desires, who waited the will of a child and bowed to her caprices."

She informed him that in spite of his high station, she did not intend to be a plaything; he answered that she would be his "favourite plaything." And again he yielded to her pleas for postponement. A rendezvous was fixed for the next night, after she had appeared in Corneille's "Cinna," the performance of which he would attend.

When she came upon the stage the First Consul had not arrived. She looked at his empty box, and her heart sank. Feeling herself already abandoned, she began to bungle the rôle in her despair. Finally, however, she heard frantic applause; the people's hero had entered. Then her playing seemed inspired.

Again the carriage drive by night to Saint-Cloud; again the quiet boudoir and the waiting lover. The time for surrender had come, and she yielded to it gladly. When they parted at dawn she said:

"I am afraid of loving you too much. You are not made for me, I know, and I shall suffer. That is written—you will see."

Almost every night Constant called for her with the carriage, and as the liaison progressed she found that her mighty lover's passion increased rather than waned. She was discreet, as Napoleon had warned her; Talma, also an idolator of the Consul, was her only confidant; and yet people began to gossip. Her colleagues at the theatre were envious; acquaintances came to ask her to plead their interests with the ministry. According to the lax moral code of the time, Mlle. Georges was being signally honoured. And as for Napoleon himself, his amours were always discreetly overlooked by his household. The affair with Mlle. Georges, however, succeeded in arousing the jealousy of the complaisant Josephine. In the memoirs of Mme. de Rémusat, a court lady who was intimate with the consular family, this passage occurs:

"Mme. Bonaparte soon learned from the spying of her valets that Mlle. Georges had been, for several evenings, introduced secretly into a small, remote set of apartments in the château. This discovery inspired her with real uneasiness; she told me about it with genuine emotion, and began to shed a great many tears, which seemed to be more abundant than that passing occasion deserved.

"One evening Mme. Bonaparte, more overcome than usual by her jealousy, kept me with her and conversed about her troubles. It was one o'clock in the morning, and we were alone in the salon. The most profound silence reigned. All of a sudden she got up.

" 'I can't stand it any longer,' she exclaimed. 'Mlle. Georges is certainly up there, and I am going to surprise them.' Rather troubled by this sudden resolution, I did my best to deter her from it, but without success. 'Follow me,' she said, 'we will go up together.'

"Then I represented to her that such espionage, being scarcely suitable on her part, would be intolerable on mine. She would listen to nothing, and pressed me so much that in spite of my repugnance I yielded to her will, saying, however, to myself that our expedition would amount to nothing.

"So there we were, both marching silently—Mme. Bonaparte first, very excited, I behind, slowly climbing the carpetless staircase that led to Bonaparte's room. In the middle of our journey a light noise was to be heard. Mme. Bonaparte turned back.

" 'Perhaps it is Roustan,' she said, 'Bonaparte's Mameluke, who is guarding the door. The wretch is capable of throttling both of us.'

"At that word I was seized with a fright which, ridiculous as it doubtless was, prevented me from listening any more; so without thinking that I was leaving Mme. Bonaparte in cruel obscurity, I descended with the candle which I was holding in my hand, and returned as quickly as I could to the salon. She followed a few minutes afterward, astonished at my sudden flight. When she saw my frightened face, she began to laugh, and so did I; but we renounced our undertaking. I left her, saying that the strange fright she had given me had been useful to her, and that I had been very wise to yield to it."

Once in their honeymoon period Napoleon cast his nocturnal caution aside, inviting Mlle. Georges to accompany him on a little outing in the country. Constant called for her at nine o'clock in the morning and drove her to Butard, a hunting place not far from Saint-Cloud. Napoleon arrived shortly afterward, escorted by Caulaincourt, Junot, Bessiéres and Lauriston. After partaking of the usual breakfast coffee in a little pavilion, the Consul and the actress, arm-in-arm, took a simple-hearted lovers' stroll in the woods. She was overwhelmed with the honour, but Napoleon was proud of his young mistress, ordering her to raise her veil as they passed by the four stiffly saluting *aides-de-camp*, each of a general's rank.

He said to her on this occasion:

"At last I see you in daylight; it is not unfavourable to you."

"You are very good to think so," she answered.

"Come, come, no false modesty! Ah, my dear, there are so many women who deceive you by candle-light; and you theatrical people with your rouge are practically masked. But to rise at nine and drive three leagues into the country is an ordeal, and you have sustained it victoriously. You are just as I desired to see you."

They sky-larked like any pair of bourgeois sweethearts during their ramble. It was cold, so he challenged her to a race. The paths were strewn with dead limbs which caught in her skirts, so he kneeled down to clear them away. He was gay; she was happy. That was doubtless the most charming, the most perfect day in their romance.

Mlle. Georges continued to live quietly, in spite of her lofty connection; yet she was often sought out by distinguished men. Talleyrand was friendly with her; visiting potentates, like the Prince of Würtemberg, called upon her behind the scenes and brought her presents. A mysterious Captain Hill of the British army brought her an avowal of passion from the Prince of Wales, promising her a life of luxury if she would leave France. Scorning the marvelous jewels which the soldier offered, on behalf of his high-born master, Mlle. Georges hastened to inform Napoleon of the episode.

"Dear Georgina," he said, "perhaps they wanted to bring to life another Judith."

"You will never be a Holofernes," she declared.

"Reassure yourself; I knew all. You will never see that man again."

When Napoleon changed his residence from Saint-Cloud to the Tuileries, a special suite was arranged for Mlle. Georges above the state apartments, to which, two or three times a week, she was escorted by Constant, through dark passages and up winding stairs. In her company, Napoleon forgot the cares of empire in a kind of boyish merriment.

On a certain evening she came wearing a wreath of white roses. He crowned himself with it—even as he was soon to crown himself Emperor—and exclaimed, as he studied himself in the mirror:

"Ha, Georgina; how pretty I am! I look like a fly in milk."

Another time, when she entered the suite, contrary to expectation, she found it empty. She called out for her lover, but received no answer. Then, at a hint from the valet, she looked under some cushions, to find Napoleon hidden there, laughing like a school-boy.

A pretty lovers' ritual marked the intrigue. They exchanged miniatures, and wore them at their breasts in lockets. She asked for a wisp of his hair, and he submitted to the scissors, protesting merrily. She promised to cut off only four hairs, but when he saw her trophy he exclaimed:

"Oh, the lying little wretch! It is enormous."

After two years of this happy relationship, affairs of state drifted them slowly but inevitably apart. War clouds were lowering on the horizon; England was about to renew the death-grapple with France; Napoleon was marshalling his hosts in camp at Boulogne, preparing for an invasion across the channel; and was also planning for his coronation as Emperor. An evening came when he sent for her to say good-by for a while; he was going to Boulogne to inspect his troops.

"Don't you experience any pain in seeing me go away?" he asked. Then, according to her story:

"He placed his hand on my heart and pretended to tear it out, saying to me in a half-angry, half-tender tone:

" 'There is nothing for me in this heart.'

"Those were his very words. I was on the rack, and would have given everything in the world to cry, but I did not even want to. We were on the carpet near the fire. My eyes were fixed on the fire and the shining andirons, and remained fixed there like a mummy's. Whether it was the glow of the fire, of the irons, or of my feelings, two great, enormous tears fell on my breast, and the Consul, with a tenderness I am unable to express, kissed them. I was so touched to the heart with this proof of love that I began to sob with real tears."

Before Napoleon left her that evening, he stuffed her lap full of bank-notes, saying, "I don't want my

Georgina to be without money in my absence."
When she counted them she found that he had given
her 40,000 francs.

She was lonely during his absence; the Thèâtre
Français appeared empty to her when the First Consul was not in his box; the doom of her first love
seemed to be ringing in her ears. To Talma she
made the threat that if Napoleon did not receive her
upon his return, she would leave Paris.

She kept her word, but not immediately. She
saw him again, and often, but with arrangements
for the coronation on his mind, he was not as atten-
tive and devoted as before. Little lovers' disagree-
ments arose; once a fortnight passed without his
sending for her, and so when Constant appeared
with the usual message, she declined. The next
day she attended a performance at the Théâtre Français, sitting in a box opposite Napoleon's. Presently Murat, the gallant cavalry officer, joined her.

"Cast your eye on the Consul's box," said Murat.
"He looks at you often, pretending to listen to 'Les
Femmes Savantes.' "

"Ah, I am very flattered, I assure you," she answered flippantly, "but as a matter of fact it doesn't
interest me at all."

"Has there been a quarrel, then?"

"One has not the right to quarrel with the Consul, but one has the right to remain one's own self.
That is what I am doing."

"Come, wrong-headed one," he advised, "you re-

236

fused yesterday, did you not? You will consent to-morrow."

Then he suggested a drive in the Bois, and she accepted, taking a jealous pride in leaving the theatre under the very eyes of Napoleon with one of his generals. He sent for her the next day, and she obeyed, but with no joy in her heart. She was cold and serious, though he was as gay as usual. A few days later he asked her to come again. This time he had a paternal, and not a lover's manner. He said:

"My dear Georgina, I have to tell you something which will grieve you. I shall not be able to see you for some time to come. Well, have you nothing to say?"

"No, I was expecting it," she replied. "I should have been mad to believe that I could have occupied a place, I do not say in your heart, but in your thoughts. I have been a simple distraction; that is all."

"It is charming of you to say that; you prove your attachment, and I love to know you love me. But I will see you again, I promise you."

"I shall not profit by your kindness. I shall go away."

"You will not make that mistake. You would lose your future."

"My future! I have none. It matters very little to me; I shall go away."

She took her troubles to Talma, and received his

kindly comfort. A month later Napoleon crowned himself Emperor. She rented some windows which afforded a view of the procession, saw her imperial lover drive past in his gilded carriage with Josephine by his side, and then went home saying to herself: "It is all over."

Her love burned out into ashes then; she realized that the end had come, and undertook to cure her heart-break with work and distractions. Five weeks later the Emperor sent for her, and she found him apparently unchanged; but these visits, unsought by her, became less and less frequent. Finally, when a lady of Josephine's retinue—the same Mme. de Rémusat whose memoirs were quoted above—was named by gossips as Mlle. Georges' successor, they ceased altogether.

In May, 1808, Mlle. Georges carried out her threat of deserting Paris. Attracted by offers of engagements and imperial favour in St. Petersburg —these glittering inducements were held out by Count Tolstoy, the Russian ambassador—she set out for that northern capital. Napoleon ordered her arrest, but she crossed the frontier before his command could be carried out.

Her artistic success in St. Petersburg was as great as it had been in Paris, and, having put her affection for Napoleon out of her heart, her amorous conquests were also extensive. Her patriotic worship remained loyal, however, and in 1812, when St. Petersburg celebrated the withdrawal of the invading French from Moscow, she refused to illuminate her windows, according to the general order of the Czar, who remarked: "She is behaving like a good Frenchwoman."

While the Grand Army was on its terrible retreat she left St. Petersburg for Sweden. After a brief stay in Stockholm, she journeyed to Dresden, then in possession of the French, and there, as friends, she and Napoleon met again. He sent for the company of the Théâtre Français and ordered a repertory of his favourite tragedies, with Mlle. Georges in her greatest rôles. After the performances he would talk with his one-time sweetheart and with Talma, the admired tragedian, of Corneille and Racine, and the brilliant days at the Théâtre Français under the Consulate. Such was his diversion upon the very eve of the battle of Leipsic.

Napoleon ordered Mlle. Georges' restoration to all her rights in the Comédie, which she had forfeited by her desertion to Russia, with full salary for her years of absence. After her offer to share his exile had not been accepted by the British authorities she resumed her career in Paris, though she was dismissed from the Comédie for five years, soon after the new royalist régime came into power, because she appeared with a bouquet of violets— which were under the ban as a Bonapartist flower. When pardoned she appeared again at the Français and its companion theatre, the Odéon. Her middle career was identified with the heyday of the romantic drama; and her mature beauty was thus celebrated by Théophile Gautier:

"The arc of her eyebrows, traced with incomparable purity and fineness, stretches over two black eyes full of fire and tragic brilliance; the nose is narrow and straight, cut with oblique nostrils passionately dilated, and joins the forehead with a line of magnificent simplicity. The mouth is powerful, bent at the corners, and superbly disdainful, like that of an avenging Nemesis waiting the hour to unchain her lion with the brazen talons. This mouth, however, has charming smiles, expanding with quite imperial grace, and one would not remark, when she wishes to express tender passions, that she had just launched an ancient imprecation or a modern anathema. . . .

"Mlle. Georges seems to belong to a prodigious and vanished race. She astonishes you as much as she charms you. One would call her a wife of Titan, a Cybele, a mother of gods and men, with her crown of embattled towers. Her construction has something Cyclopean and Pelasgian. One feels on seeing her that she remains like a column of granite to bear witness to an annihilated generation, and that she is the last representative of the epic type. She is an admirable statue to place upon the tomb of tragedy, buried forever."

She gave a farewell performance May 27, 1849, appearing as Clytemnestra, the occasion being marked by an artistic clash with the rising Rachel, who was also on the bill. On December 17, 1857, she had a genuine farewell, playing Cleopatra in "Rodogune." She died January 11, 1867, at the age of eighty, her last years having been spent in poverty. Emperor Napoleon III assumed the expenses of her burial in the cemetery of Père-Lachaise, as a sentimental heritage from his greater namesake.

Throughout her long life the glamour of Napoleon's love for the stately young girl she had been clung to her. She spoke of him often, and always with reverence.

"But it was not the lover she evoked," wrote Frederic Masson, "it was the Emperor. She no longer saw the man he had been for her, but the man he had been for France, like those nymphs who, honoured for an instant by the caresses of a god, never regarded his visage, dazzled as they were by the blinding light of his glory."

GREAT LOVE STORIES OF THE THEATRE

X

THE FOLLIES OF "BECKY" WELLS.

THE loves of famous actresses run a wide gamut of themes—from the sentimental to the tragic, from the ecstatic to the pathetic. In the life-stories of these dear, dead women there is only one phase of broad human appeal lacking, that of humour, which is naturally alien to the grand passion. But in the escapades of "Becky" Wells, a bizarre, moon-struck comedienne of the late Georgian period, that element is to be found. Its mirth is a little grotesque, perhaps, its laughter strained and high-pitched, close to the tears of hysteria; but humour it remains. For Becky was the merriest, maddest eccentric that ever walked the borderland between cleverness and insanity.

She was a very popular player in London at the close of the eighteenth century. Her success was intermittent, but her undoubted talent might have won enduring and respectful regard if her own unbalanced exploits had not muddled her career into a tragi-comedy. As it is, her memory is chiefly preserved by her own amazing memoirs, as well as in the autobiographical accounts of James Bernard, a minor actor, and Frederick Reynolds, a minor playwright of her times; and that less as an actress than as a crack-brained elf whose adventures were almost too absurd to be true.

Professionally, she was an expert in rôles of the ingénue and comic simpleton type. Her greatest characters were Becky Chadwallader in Samuel Foote's "Author," produced in 1780, and Cowslip in O'Keefe's "Agreeable Surprise," staged in 1781. So completely were these parts identified with her that the sobriquets of "Becky" and "Cowslip" followed her through life. She also appeared in such forgotten plays as Ticknell's "The Camp," Colman's "The Jealous Wife," David Garrick's "The Irish Widow," and Hoadly's "The Suspicious Husband." The loftier realms of the drama she invaded as Imogen in Shakespeare's "Cymbeline," Lady Randolph in John Home's "Douglas," and the name-part of Rowe's "Jane Shore," with excellent effect. Incidentally, she was the original Cecilia Loftus, for her "imitations" were a staple attraction of the British stage as long as she flourished before the footlights. That record will summarise her histrionic career; now for her escapades.

Becky was born in 1759, her maiden and ungarnished name being Mary Davies. Her mother went on the stage to find a means of livelihood for their family, after the head of the house had made a sudden transition from humble toil to raving lunacy; and she followed the maternal example when very young. The girl played Juliet in the provinces when she was eighteen, and promptly married her Romeo, a fledgling actor named Wells. The bestowal of his name was almost the only husbandly duty which he fulfilled toward her, for soon after the wedding, according to her memoirs, he sent her back to her mother with this note:

"Madam: As your daughter is too young and childish, I beg you will for the present take her again under your protection; and be assured I shall return to her soon, as I am now going on a short journey, and remain, yours, etc."

Becky does not seem to have missed him in the slightest degree; he never returned to her, for he had eloped with one of her bridesmaids; she went on her own way in single blessedness, and prospered accordingly. Portraits of her at that period show an engaging sprite of faëry beauty, blonde, laughing, roguish-eyed, half simple and half shrewd of expression. James Bernard, who cast her for Becky Chadwallader in "Author" merely because she was girlish and pretty, says that he dispelled her doubts concerning her ability to play the rôle by advising her to put her thumb in her mouth and look like her usual self. By this method, he assured her, she would completely realize the playwright's ideal. She obeyed and scored a hit which soon took her out of the provinces and into London.

Becky's amours began with Edward Topham, an officer in the Life Guards who had a happy knack of dashing off epilogues and prologues, and also an established reputation for eccentricity. His clothes were always at the opposite extreme from the reigning fashion; his poses were notorious at all the clubs. Topham permitted his playwright friend, Frederick Reynolds, to clap him, a character ready made, into farce after farce; and he seemed to enjoy this advertisement of his foibles.

After he and Becky began to keep house, without any pretense at the proprieties, Topham founded a daily newspaper called *The World*. His editorial policy was revolutionary; he was the first of the yellow journalists. He revelled in scandals and impertinent gossip, served up in the elegancies of his graceful style; he published a serial comic story which increased the circulation by 1,000 copies a day, which was flamboyant prosperity for a primitive Georgian paper; and he followed it with a prolonged correspondence upon fistic affairs between the gladiators, Humphreys and Mendoza. Obviously, he was born too soon, this fellow Topham.

Becky was his associate editor; she not only wrote for *The World* but also attended to its literary and business direction when he went into the country to recreate his overtaxed brain, as he frequently did. From his rural retreat he would write to her such notes as these:

"I hear with great pleasure that the numbers of *The World* printed on Friday were 2,600. There's credit for you, you old Pud."—"Take care of yourself, and when you have been quiet some time, take

care of *The World."* — "Simon can be of use, I
see, and seems to have a knack of writing fashionable
fiddle-faddle; in regard to which you may promise
him, if he does well, he shall have the special privilege of mentioning himself."

At the trial of Warren Hastings, before the House
of Lords, Becky sat in the press gallery every day
busily taking notes; and before she went to the theatre in the evening she dictated a full report of the
speeches and proceedings to clerks in *The World* of-
fice. That was no small "assignment," and journalists of to-day, if they had access to the musty old files
of *The World,* would congratulate Becky's shade
upon her skill in "covering" it. Another manifestation of her literary talent was collaboration with
Topham upon a farce called "The Fool," the best
parts of which, he acknowledged like a gentleman,
were of her invention. Meanwhile her popularity
with theatre-goers waxed mightily, in proof of which
one Anthony Pasquin, a versifier of the period, may
be quoted. He paid tribute to her in his "Children
of Thespis," as follows:

"Come hither, ye sculptors, and catch every grace
  That Fate interwove in a heaven-formed face;
  For 'tis Wells, the resistless, that bursts on the sight,
  To wed infant rapture and strengthen delight.
  When she smiles, Youth and Valour their trophies resign;
  When she laughs she enslaves—for that laugh is divine."

But with her success, Becky's eccentricities began

to develop amain, possibly accelerated by her association with Topham. For instance, she suffered from a delusion that every man she met, or saw at a distance, fell in love with her out of hand. More than that, she was for having Topham challenge them all, and fight with them by the half-dozens, for daring to look upon her with eyes of languishing adoration. George III was among her imaginary victims, and when that addle-pated monarch took a sea-voyage along the English coast, at medical advice, she pursued him loyally in a hired yacht. The king was pleased at first by this evidence of devotion; he would hang over the bulwark watching Becky's sail by the hour, nodding his paretic head solemnly and exclaiming: "Mrs. Wells—Wells—Wells! Good Cowslip—fond of the water, eh?" Finally, however, he became bored and then alarmed, for Becky's yacht hovered near his with such nagging persistence that he had doubts as to whether it were a delusion or reality. According to James Bernard:

"Whenever his Majesty cast his eye over the blue element, there was the bark of Becky, careering in pursuit of him; the infatuated woman reposing on the deck in all the languor and sumptuousness of Cleopatra. The royal attendants now began to suspect her motives, and the sovereign became so annoyed at his eternal attendant that whenever he espied a sail he eagerly enquired: 'It's not Wells, is it?' or on perceiving the dreaded boat: 'Charlotte, Charlotte, here's Wells again!' "

In 1790 Becky was arrested for debt. She is careful to explain in her memoirs that this pecuniary difficulty resulted from her generosity in lending an undesirable brother-in-law money enough to educate him as a surgeon and send him to India; but whatever the cause she was in almost constant fear of the bailiffs through the rest of her life. Topham was not in London when she was apprehended, so she sent for his companion, Frederick Reynolds. That gentleman fulfilled his obligation of friendship toward Topham first by securing her release from prison and then by eloping with her. To escape her other creditors they went into hiding in remote farm-houses, and then, tiring of seclusion, they voyaged to France. Topham seems to have counted himself well rid of Becky, whose vagaries were becoming too expensive, and to have held Reynolds, as his rescuer, in higher esteem than ever. He made an arrangement with her creditors, however, which permitted her return to London, and politely notified Reynolds that he might bring his prize home. Having found France, then in the throes of revolution, no paradise, they did not delay in terminating their romantic exile. Becky went back to the stage immediately; but, as Reynolds deposes:

"Within a few months of our arrival in London, the wild and eccentric character of my fair fellow-traveller, which had lately been subdued by her pecuniary distresses, again broke forth with additional violence. In a romantic spot in Sussex she formed a hermitage, and like Charles the Fifth or Madame de la Vallière, she determined, in the full blaze of her power and beauty, to lead a life of seclusion."

Her brief experiment as an anchorite was chiefly remarkable for a *fête champêtre,* which she gave to satisfy the curiosity of the country-side before going into complete retirement. The "quality" of the county was invited to attend, in masquerade costumes, and Becky entertained them with a *tour de force* of her theatrical talents, singing, dancing, acting, and imitating. She became the toast of all the neighbourhood squires; never was there a livelier or more popular hermit. Then she went back to the glitter of the London stage, and for a while she fluttered gayly on the crest of her fame. Suddenly, however, she startled Reynolds with the announcement that she had discovered she was mad, and made him accompany her to the sanitarium of Dr. Willis, in Lincolnshire. This was the physician who had treated George III's tottering reason with some success, and who, though regarded as a quack by his colleagues, seems to have had excellent modern methods for handling neuropathic and psychiatric cases.

Becky lived in one of the farm-houses of Dr. Willis's estate as a patient for several months, visited occasionally by Reynolds; and then, at her insistence, he took her for another journey into the wilds. They went to a desolate district on the coast of Norfolk, populated by smugglers. The inhabitants were in some doubt as to the character of these well-dressed strangers, and it was believed that they were either government spies or refugees from France. Becky decided to satisfy their curiosity in full measure; she announced that she was Queen Marie Antoinette and that her companion was the Dauphin. The peasantry believed her devoutly; Reynolds writes:

"I was much astonished to see the farmer, his wife, and all his dependents, and many of the neighbouring peasantry, advance toward me, bowing and curtseying with the most profound respect. Becky accompanied this grotesque and outlandish group; and to the increase of my amazement began with much seriousness and theatrical gesture to address them in broken English. The surrounding confusion was such that I could catch nothing except the frequently repeated words, 'Dauphin' and 'Jacobin.' But not a syllable she uttered seemed to be lost upon her awe-struck auditors, who continued to approach towards me with ever lower and more awkward obeisances; when the farmer, advancing before the others, motioned them to keep back, and then falling on his knees, he hastened to disburthen his brain by exclaiming in a voice of thunder: 'Dang the Jacobites! Long live the Dolphin!'"

They held royal court for an evening, with hand-kissings and genuflections; but when the manager of a small theatre ten miles distant dashed up to implore a "royal command" for a performance, they decided that the jest was becoming too notorious. That night Marie Antoinette and the Dauphin secretly abdicated and fled.

How Becky separated from Reynolds is unknown; perhaps she was arrested for debt too often to suit his fancy; but at any rate, the affair died a natural death. One night, for old time's sake, she went to see a performance of his play, "How to Get Rich," and as she arose to leave, after the final curtain, a man who had been sitting in the adjoining box courteously remarked that he had refrained from interfering with her pleasure, but that he must now do his duty and escort her to the Fleet prison. In that grotesque institution, whose humours and hideousness are perpetuated in the pages of Charles Dickens, she met her second matrimonial fate.

Shortly after she had been placed in pawn there, Joseph Sumbel was added to its assemblage of characters. He was a young Oriental Jew whose father had been prime minister to the Sultan of Morocco. He was rich, and his sojourn in the Fleet was not brought about by debt but by a contempt of court, in stubbornly refusing to settle with his brother over a disputed inheritance. Sumbel entered the Fleet like an eastern prince, attended by a gorgeous retinue of Moorish servants; and Becky, looking on from the gallery, was much impressed by the sight. Sumbel's eye must have caught hers, as she stared in admiration, for within a few days she received an invitation to dine with him, suitably chaperoned, in his quarters. It was not long before he had proposed marriage and had been accepted, provisionally; Becky informed him that since she did not know whether her husband were living or dead, there might be some barrier to their union. They consulted lawyers who were unable to find any trace of the missing Mr. Wells, and who advised that the only way in which to make the wedding legal was for Becky to espouse the religious faith of her betrothed. This she did, and so the two strange beings were married in the Fleet. Becky says that four rooms were illuminated for the occasion, that the ceremonies lasted for a week, and that the net cost of the nuptials was 500 pounds. The *Morning Post* of October 16, 1797, chronicled the event, in part, as follows:

"On Thursday evening last the marriage ceremony in the Jewish style was performed at the Fleet, uniting Mrs. Wells, late of Covent Garden theatre, to Mr. Sumbel, a Moorish Jew, detained for debt in that prison. The bridegroom was richly dressed in white satin and a splendid turban with a white feather; the bride, who is now converted to a Jewess, was also attired in white satin, and her head dressed in an elegant style, with a large plume of white feathers. Mr. Sumbel's brother assisted at the ceremony, dressed in pink satin and a rich turban and feather. The apartments were brilliantly illuminated with variegated lamps, according to the customs of the Jews. The rest of the company who attended were Jews, in their common habiliments —as old-clothesmen. But with the exception of the guests, everything had the appearance of eastern grandeur."

That account must have been substantially accurate, even though it has a flavor of the Arabian Nights, for Mr. Sumbel saw fit, in a letter to the editor, to correct only the statement that he was imprisoned for debt instead of contempt of court. But Becky was aggrieved by a suggestion in the article, omitted in the quotation, to the effect that her conversion was more a matter of notoriety-seeking than of conviction; she wrote to the *Morning Post* in this vein:

"Sir:—In your paper of Thursday last it was said —'Mrs. Wells was always an odd genius, and her becoming a Jewess greatly gratifies her passion for eccentricity.' In answer to this, I beg the favour to insist in your paper that it is not any passion for eccentricity that has induced me to embrace the Israelitish religion—it is studying and examining, with great care and attention, the Old Testament, that has influenced my conduct. Excuse me for giving you the trouble, but I beg you will insert the following passage from that book:

" 'Thus saith the Lord of Hosts: In those days it shall come to pass that ten men shall take hold of all the languages of the nations, even shall take hold of the skirt of a Jew, saying, we will go with you, for we have heard that God is with you.'—Zechariah, ch. viii, verse 23.

"By giving the above a place you will much oblige,
"Your humble servant,
"LEAH SUMBEL (late Mary Wells)."

A few days after the wedding they were freed, for Becky persuaded her new husband to bend his stubborn neck and purge himself of his contempt by settling with his brother, to the tune of 20,000 pounds, and to pay her own debts in addition. Then they took a house in Pall Mall and established themselves in almost regal state. She soon discovered, however, that being the wife of an Oriental plutocrat was no bed of roses. He displayed a furious jealousy, possibly with some cause, for Becky could never make her eyes behave. If she dared to look across the footlights into the audience at the theatre, he would knock her down as soon as they returned home. If a servant or tradesman even so much as touched her hand, he was promptly crushed to earth. He gave her costly jewels, but—

"Though the diamonds I wore, of immense value, were allowed me on state days and bonfire nights, on my return home they were taken from me (not in the most delicate manner) and committed to the care of the iron chest. I was, on no pretense whatever, allowed to see them except in his presence; and as to money, I was never suffered to receive even a shilling in my pocket, for fear I should run away."

Sumbel, in short, was madder than Becky; the man was really a raging lunatic, but being a little cracked herself, she did not notice it at first. His violence was not limited to her, and presently, fearing prosecution for an assault, he went into hiding in an obscure cottage. When this life became monotonous, she persuaded him to make a journey into Yorkshire; but travelling incognito, without his Moorish entourage and in English dress, irritated him extremely; and his only consolation, she declares, was to don his eastern attire after they had found shelter for the night in some wayside tavern, and to sit cross-legged on the floor, while the landlord and servants stood at gaze, awe-stricken and speechless.

They managed to get along together for a while, however; and there was even an interval of perfect domestic peace when nothing happened to perturb Becky except the flooring of a servant or two, now and then. But finally Sumbel tired of London and decided to return to Morocco. He spent 20,000 pounds, Becky declares, in brass cannon as a gift to the Sultan; bought expensive presents for other notables among the Moors; and rehearsed her carefully in the various exotic ceremonies which she would have to go through with on her arrival at Mogadore.

Then, after all preparations had been made, she rebelled against expatriation. He tricked her into coming aboard the vessel which he had chartered, and would have sailed away with her, willy-nilly, if she had not discovered his plot at the nick of time and gone ashore in a tender. He abandoned the voyage, but occupied himself with threatening to kill her and then commit suicide. Once he fired a pistol at her as she lay in bed, upon which she had him bound over to keep the peace and then deserted him. Pleas for forgiveness, protestations of affection, and attempts to have her incarcerated in a madhouse all failed him, so he gave up in disgust and divorced her. His method of securing a legal separation was peculiar; all that he did was to hand her a slip of paper upon which was written the first verse of the twenty-fourth chapter of Deuteronomy:

"When a man hath taken a wife and married her, and it comes to pass that she hath no favour in his eyes because he hath found some uncleanness in her, then let him write her a bill of divorcement and give it in her hand, and send her out of his house."

The London newspapers commented upon this domestic disaster as follows:

"Mr. Sumbel, the Moorish Jew who about a year ago married Mrs. Wells, has lately stated in a public advertisement that Mrs. Wells is not his wife, and that he will not pay any debts she may contract. The grounds he gives are, first, that the ceremony was not a legal Jewish marriage; secondly, that Mrs. Wells was not capable of becoming a Jewess, without which no marriage could take place; and thirdly,

259

that she has broken the Sabbath and the Holy Feast, by running away from Mr. Sumbel in a post-chaise and eating forbidden fruit—namely, pork griskin and rabbits."

Becky promptly wrote to the editors, defending herself against the more serious charges, declaring that she herself would bring suit for divorce and maintenance because of Sumbel's wicked and inhuman treatment of her; and concluding: "Mr. Sumbel himself eats pork, and even rabbits, which shocked Mrs. Sumbel much."

Then he refused to pay the rent on their house, declaring that she was responsible for its lease. He was sued by the landlord; his counsel argued in his defense that he was not a Jew but a Mohammedan, but failed to cloud the issue; and a verdict was rendered against him. But rather than settle the bill, he quickly drew all his money out of the London banks, secured a passport, and took ship to Denmark. Thus Sumbel passed out of Becky's life; she disposes of him in this whimsical paragraph:

"I have since learned from a gentleman that he went to Altona in Denmark, where he built a large street at his own expense; and that for the last years of his life his sole amusement was fishing; but the place where he enjoyed that amusement was rather singular. He had a very long room built for the purpose, in which was a large reservoir of water that contained fish of various descriptions; and he would sit whole days angling in it. If the fish did not bite quick enough to suit his Moorish temper, the water was let off, and they were beaten to death with a large stick."

Becky began to go down hill after Sumbel's disappearance, although her memoirs indicate that she endured the vicissitudes of her stormy destiny cheerfully enough. Hers was a buoyant spirit, and the only deep grief of her life was over her separation from her three daughters, who were carefully raised by their illustrious father, Mr. Topham. She was devoted to these girls, who had all of their mother's beauty and charm, whenever she remembered about them. Upon getting rid of Sumbel she made a trip into the country to see them, but Topham, with all the virtue of the reformed rake, ordered her away. She roamed about the roads near their house in hope of catching a glimpse of them until she had worn out her last pair of shoes, when she gave up in despair and returned to London.

Arrests for debt now became more frequent, and engagements fewer. Her memoirs, written with the collaboration of some hack, were published by subscription in 1811, but she had spent the proceeds before the edition came from the press. She had to appeal to the Theatrical Fund for relief, which was freely granted. Then poor Becky dropped out of sight and London knew her no more as a public character.

Ten years later James Bernard, returning from a long sojourn in America, met her near Westminster

Bridge, London. He describes that strange encounter as follows:

"Though old and faded, she was still buoyant and loquacious. A young, rough-looking male companion was with her, whom she instantly quitted to welcome me home. After about five minutes' conversation on past and present times, I begged not to keep her from her friend any longer. 'Friend!' she replied, putting a construction on the word which I by no means intended. 'He's no friend! He's my husband!' It was now my turn to stare; and I inquired whether he was in the profession. She took him by the hand, and dancing up to me through the stream of coal-heavers, porters and men of business that were passing, sang with great good-humour:

" 'And haven't you heard of the jolly young waterman,
   That at Westminster bridge used to ply?' "

That glimpse of Becky, cheerful in adversity, is the last trace of her which posterity can find. Five years afterward she was reported as dead. Doubtless she passed into the presence of the Great Prompter, after pitifully bungling the farce of life, in some sailors' lodging house, with a song on her lips.

GREAT LOVE STORIES OF THE
THEATRE

XI

DORA JORDAN AND THE DUKE OF CLARENCE

"HAD he left me to starve, I never would have uttered a word to his disadvantage."

Of such tenderness was the fidelity of Dora Jordan, even in the anguished hour of her dismissal by the paramour with whom she had lived in conjugal, if not marital, happiness, for twenty years. He was the Duke of Clarence, afterward William IV; she was a comedienne; but in that poignant crisis the player is revealed as far more noble than the man of royal blood. Of all actresses whose names are associated in illicit union with the titled great Mrs. Jordan is, in fact, the most worthy of respect. To her honours as an artist, there may be added, in no less degree, that homage due a lofty spirit of devoted womanhood and maternal sacrifice.

She sat at this Duke's table as the matron of his house with such dignity that prudes and princes alike accepted her as wife rather than mistress. She bore him ten children, and was to them all that the name of mother could mean. She supported the establishment when his own income was insufficient. For their common needs and for the generous endowment of their brood, she slaved at her profession long after she had wearied of the player's fame. When she was bluntly told to go, she made no outcry, published no letters, wrote no memoirs; but withdrew in quiet grief, giving her betrayer complete absolution. A few years later she died, a wretched recluse, almost in want, the rich earnings of a prosperous career drained away by her beloved, devouring children.

Dora Jordan is not to be considered, however, merely as a pathetic instance of royal ingratitude; apart from that chapter of her life, she was one of the greatest and most successful actresses of the English stage. For three decades her name was magic by which the managers could conjure up crowded houses at will; and in competition with the dominating Mrs. Siddons she held her ground in the public favour with ease. To the tragic muse of "the incomparable" she triumphantly opposed the comic; and if her more famous rival was the Melpomene of the time, she was just as genuinely the Thalia—a sobriquet, indeed, by which she was widely known.

Curiously enough, in spite of her brilliant public and romantic private life she has been neglected by latter-day annalists, where actresses of less talent and achievement have found biographers by the score. That very neglect, however, makes her all the more grateful as a theme.

Before her story is taken up in detail, she may be

introduced as an artist, in the estimate of Charles Lamb, who wrote of her in his essay, "On Some of the Old Actors":

"Those who have only seen Mrs. Jordan within the last ten or fifteen years can have no adequate idea of her performances of such parts as Ophelia, Helena in 'All's Well that Ends Well,' and Viola. Her voice had latterly acquired a coarseness, which suited well enough with her Nells and Hoydens, but in those days it sank, with her steady, melting eye, into the heart. Her joyous parts—in which her memory now chiefly lives—in her youth were outdone by her plaintive ones. There is no giving an account how she delivered the disguised story of her love for Orsino. It was no set speech that she had foreseen, so as to weave it into a harmonious period, line necessarily following line, to make up the music—yet I have heard it so spoken, or rather read, not without its grace and beauty—but, when she had declared her sister's history to be a 'blank,' and that she 'never told her love,' there was a pause, as if the story had ended—and then the image of the 'worm in the bud' came up as a new suggestion— and the heightened image of 'Patience' still followed after that, as by some growing (and not mechanical) process, thought springing up after thought, I would almost say, as they were watered by her tears. . . . She used no rhetoric in her passion; or it was Nature's own rhetoric, most legitimate then, when it seemed altogether without rule or law."

Mrs. Jordan, like Peg Woffington and a long line of London's favourite comediennes, was born in Ireland. She inherited the theatrical temperament from her mother, and in her sixteenth year (1777) she made her début in Dublin, playing Phœbe in "As You Like It." There, at the outset of her career, professional success was joined with personal misfortune. The manager of the Dublin theatre, one Richard Daly, was an unmitigated scoundrel who practised upon the innocent girl a system of seduction in which, through long experience, he was an adept. By frequent advances of salary he involved her in debt, and then threatened her with prison until she succumbed. By this vile means he held her in serfdom for several years, but at last, in 1782, with her mother, brother and sister, who were dependent upon her, she fled like a criminal to England, in order to place herself beyond his clutches.

Tate Wilkinson, of the discursive "Wandering Patentee," was her salvation. She and her people were almost destitute when application for an engagement was made to him at Leeds; he recognized the mother as having played Desdemona to his Othello in Dublin twenty-four years before, and was charitably disposed. Did she play tragedy, comedy, or opera? he asked. "All," she replied mildly, with no pretense to special merit for such versatility. Tate gasped politely, hemmed and hawed, thought it over, and then demanded an example of her quality—a few lines from any rôle she might choose. She begged to be spared an immediate trial, because of her fatigue and nervousness, but the tactful Tate, apparently acceding, ordered a bottle of wine, began to gossip about old days in Dublin, and soon, under the influence of his geniality, she was reciting Calista, in Rowe's "The Fair Penitent," across the table. Then the manager's doubts vanished; it was arranged forthwith that she should have an engagement at fifteen shillings a week, and should make her first appearance a few days later as Calista. She stipulated, or her mother did for her, that after the tragedy had ended she should sing the ballad of "The Greenwood Laddie," and although Tate had observed no symptoms of comic facility in his "discovery," he consented, with some reluctance, to this peculiar arrangement. When the day of test came, he was pleasantly surprised, as he admits in "The Wandering Patentee":

"I was not only charmed, but the public also—and still more at what I feared would spoil the whole, the absurdity of Calista, after her death, jumping forth and singing a ballad; but on she came, in a frock and a little mob cap, and sang the song with such effect that I was fascinated—for managers do not always meet with jewels, but when they do, and think the sale will turn out for their own advantage, you cannot conceive, reader, how it makes their eyes sparkle."

For the next three years she was a popular lead-

ing woman at Leeds and the other provincial theatres on the York circuit, in which Wilkinson had an
interest. She received her *nom de théâtre* of Dora
Jordan, as well as her introduction to English audiences, from that manager, according to tradition.
Her true name was Dorothy Bland, and she had
been accustomed to play either as Miss Francis or
Miss Phillips, cognomens taken in recognition of
her mother's side of the house. Fear of giving offense to her relatives—remittances and legacies
from whom were hoped for but never received—
caused a decision to revise her nomenclature.
Dorothy was naturally contracted to Dora, and Wilkinson, more by accident than design, did the rest.
He is quoted by an associate as telling how he happened to officiate at the mummer's baptismal font,
in this fashion:

"Why, I said, my dear, you have crossed the
water, so I'll call you Jordan; and, by the memory
of Sam! if she didn't take my joke in earnest and
call herself Jordan ever since."

The persuasion of "Gentleman" Smith, from
Drury Lane, who was gratifying his sporting tastes
by a visit to the races at York, turned Mrs. Jordan's
ambition toward the London stage. In the autumn
of 1785 she secured a modest engagement at Drury
Lane to play "second parts" to Mrs. Siddons in
tragedy, on a salary of four pounds a week. Hardly
more than a month had passed when, through her
appearance as Peggy in "The Country Girl"

(adapted by Garrick from Wycherley's "The Country Wife"), she established herself as an independent favourite. One of the newspaper reviewers took this measure of her endowments:

"She is universally allowed to possess a figure, small perhaps, but neat and elegant, as was remarkably conspicuous when she was dressed as a boy in the third act. Her face, if not beautiful, is said by some to be pretty, and by some pleasing, intelligent, or impressive. Her voice, if not peculiarly sweet, is not harsh; if not strong, is clear, and equal to the extent of the theatre. She has much archness, and gave every point of the dialogue with the best comic effect. She is a perfect mistress of the *jeu de théâtre,* and improved to the uttermost all the ludicrous situations with which 'The Country Girl' abounds. From such premises there is and can be but one conclusion, that she is a most valuable acquisition to the public stock of innocent entertainment."

James Boaden, the only satisfactory chronicler of her life, speaks of her, "when she burst upon the metropolis," in this manner:

"Perhaps no actress ever excited so much laughter. The low comedian has a hundred resorts by which risibility may be produced. In addition to a ludicrous cast of features, he may resort, if he chooses, to the buffoonery of the fair; he may dress himself ridiculously; he may border even upon indecency in his action, and be at least a general hint of *double entendre,* to those whose minds are equally impure.

But the actress has nothing beyond the mere words she utters, but what is drawn from her own hilarity, and the expression of features, which never submit to exaggeration. She cannot pass by the claims of her sex, and self-love will preserve her from any willing diminution of her personal beauty. How exactly had this child of nature calculated her efficacy, that no intention on her part was ever missed, and, from first to last, the audience responded uniformly to an astonishment of delight. In the third act they more clearly saw what gave the elasticity to her step. She is made to assume the male attire; and the great painter of the age [Sir Joshua Reynolds] pronounced her figure the neatest and most perfect in symmetry that he had ever seen."

Then for twenty-four busy years she enjoyed uninterrupted popularity. Although her special talent was for comedy, particularly in romping, hoydenish and "breeches-rôles," she ran through almost the entire repertory of the British stage, playing the ephemeræ of the day, the comic masterpieces, and the standard tragedies. Her "takings" were enormous for the time; her second season alone brought 5,000 pounds into the coffers of Drury Lane. She was admired by the *cognoscenti* as well as by the mob. Macready said:

"With a spirit of fun that would have outlaughed Puck himself, there was a discrimination, an identity with her character, an artistic arrangement of the scene, that made all seem spontaneous and accidental, though elaborated with the greatest care."

Leigh Hunt wrote this critical appreciation of her contagious laughter:

"Her laughter is the happiest and most natural on the stage; if she is to laugh in the middle of a speech, it does not separate itself so abruptly from her words as with most of our performers. . . . Her laughter intermingles itself with her words as fresh ideas afford her fresh merriment; she does not so much indulge as she seems unable to help it; it increases, it lessens, with her fancy; and when you expect it no longer, according to the usual habits of the stage, it sparkles forth at little intervals as recollection revives it, like flame from half-smothered embers. This is the laughter of the feelings; and it is this predominance of heart in all she says and does that renders her the most delightful actress in the Donna Violante of 'The Wonder,' the Clara of 'Matrimony,' and in twenty other characters."

In 1787 Mrs. Jordan formed an alliance, so steadfast for a time that it was regarded as a marriage, with Richard Ford, a hybrid barrister-actor. Three years later the Duke of Clarence, just returned from that service in the navy which afterward gave him the appellation of "The Sailor King," fell in love with her and began to woo in a downright nautical fashion. His offers were flattering, and Mrs. Jordan, feeling insecure in the unkept promises of Ford, who had proved to be a worthless parasite on her bounty, gave them careful consideration. She afforded the latter an opportunity to merit her continued matronly devotion by marrying her, accord-

273

ing to his professed intention; but he, with a hint of venal purpose, chose rather to cater to the ducal interest by waiving his pledge. Boaden explains his heroine's action in this change of protectors, as follows:

"Mr. Ford was elevated by some persons into an injured and deserted man; they neither knew him, nor his privity to the advances made by the noble suitor. They had never seen him at the wing of the theatre, and thrown their eyes, as he must have done, to the private boxes. Mrs. Jordan was not a woman to hoodwink herself in any of her actions—she knew the sanctions of law and religion as well as anybody —this implies that she did not view them with indifference. And had Mr. Ford, as she proposed to him, taken that one step farther, which the Duke could not take, the treaty with the latter would have ended at the moment."

In 1790 Mrs. Jordan became the morganatic Duchess of Clarence, and for two decades the connection was so domestic and so permanent that all England regarded it with toleration. The couple seemed more truly husband and wife than thousands of others whose union was of Book and ring, as well as "in the sight of Heaven."

The Duke was then rated as of small political importance, for not until the death of the Duke of York, in 1827, did he become the heir presumptive. With his two older brothers between him and the crown, he was thought to be out of the running; he had to content himself with the trivial function of Ranger of Bushey Park, not far from London; and —what was more embarrassing—with an unprincely income. At Bushey, therefore, Mrs. Jordan took up residence with him, enjoying country life between theatrical engagements and rearing lusty children, in whom he took as keen a family interest as she. Her other offspring—she had borne one daughter to the evil Daly and three to the caitiff Ford—were with her, accepted by the Duke without a trace of step-fatherly grudge. There was room for all, including the ten young ducal scions who blessed the liaison, in capacious Bushey House. That mansion was indeed a happy home, with "olive-branches" enough to found a village.

Contemporary gossip had it that the Duke allowed Mrs. Jordan 1,000 pounds a year; but whatever the sum, she spent all, and as much again of her own earnings, for the maintenance of the establishment and the support of her children. Old George III is said to have advised his son in the matter of finances:

"Hey! hey! What's this? What's this? You keep an actress—keep an actress, they say."

"Yes, sir."

"Ah, well, well! how much do you give her, eh?"

"A thousand a year, sir."

"A thousand! A thousand! Too much, too much! Five hundred quite enough, quite enough."

Then, according to this probably apocryphal anecdote, the Duke wrote to Mrs. Jordan suggesting such a reduction of her income. All the satisfaction he received from her in regard to the proposed economy was a strip torn from the bottom of a play-bill, carrying the motto: "No money returned after the rising of the curtain." That ribaldry, however, does not sound at all like Dora Jordan.

The Duke certainly drew freely upon his mistress's personal funds, though for domestic, not wastrel, purposes. Journalistic paragraphers boldly satirised his dependence upon her salary. In 1791 one of the newspapers printed this item:

"The connection between *Little Pickle* and her new FRIEND has been paragraphed in every public shape, and unless something extraordinary should ever occur, may now be dropped. We have only to add that, as *Banker to her Highness,* he actually received her *week's salary* from the *Treasurer* on Saturday last!!!"

In that incident a rhymster masquerading as "Pindar Junr," found inspiration for a pungent epigram:

"ON A CERTAIN PERSON'S RECEIVING A THEATRICAL
SALARY"

"As Jordan's high and mighty squire
    Her play-house profits deigns to skim,
Some folks audaciously enquire
    If *he* keeps *her,* or *she* keeps *him!*"

Mrs. Jordan came to consider her work in the theatre merely as a means of securing domestic ease for herself and family, although it is of record that as soon as she set foot on the stage, all of the spirit and enthusiasm of youth returned to her, and she acted as if inspired. In letters to friends she would speak of her tours as "prosperous cruises"; and in 1809 she wrote to Boaden:

"I am quite tired of the profession. I have lost those great encitements, variety and emulation. . . . Without these it is mere money-making drudgery. . . . From the first starting in life, at the early age of fourteen, I have always had a large family to support. My mother was a duty. But on brothers and sisters I have lavished more money than can be supposed, and more, I am sorry to say, than I can well justify to those who have a stronger and prior claim on my exertions."

The Duke did all in his power to make a fair return for her affection and her toil. He read dramas which were submitted to her in manuscript; he played the devoted husband admirably; he insisted that his friends should receive her on equal terms with himself. Visitors to Bushey were numerous, and they all came away declaring that they had seen the finest family in England. In this letter of the Duke, answering an inquiry regarding Mrs. Jordan's health, there is the manner of honest conjugality:

"The papers have on this occasion told the truth,

for she was last week for some hours in danger; but now, thank God, she is much better, and I hope in a fair way of perfect recovery. It is my present intention to set out on the 23rd inst. for the seaside, in order that Mrs. Jordan may bathe for six weeks. As the place we mean to go to is no great distance from the Isle of Wight, and if you have nothing better to do, I shall be very happy to see you there, and Mrs. Jordan has likewise desired me to say as much."

When entertainments were given at Bushey, Mrs. Jordan rose to the occasion as if born the great lady. If the duke could be the true yeoman husband, she was equally the Duchess in the presence of society. Take, for example, this excerpt from a newspaper account of the celebration in honour of the Duke's forty-first birthday, which names her as surrounded by the Hanoverian court:

"At seven o'clock the second bell announced the dinner, when the Prince of Wales took Mrs. Jordan by the hand, led her into the dining-room, and seated her at the top of the table. The Prince took his seat at her right hand, and the Duke of York at her left, the Duke of Cambridge sat next to the Prince, the Duke of Kent next to the Duke of York, and the Lord Chancellor next to his Royal Highness. The Duke of Clarence sat at the foot of the table. . . . The Duke's numerous family were introduced, and admired by the Prince, the royal Dukes, and the whole company; an infant in arms, with a most beautiful white head of hair, was brought into the dining-room by the nursery maid."

Among her stage associates Mrs. Jordan, who was singularly free from the player's characteristic vanity, deported herself with earnest simplicity, as if she had no associations with the great world. Occasional sarcastic comment upon her royal connection was, of course, inevitable, no matter how uninvited. Once, when she displayed some dissatisfaction at rehearsals, the manager remarked:

"Why you are quite grand, madam—quite the Duchess to-day."

"Very likely," she answered, "for you are not the first person to-day who has condescended to honour me sarcastically with the title."

That very morning, in fact, she had discharged an Irish maid for impertinence, and had been berated violently. Biddy had banged one of the shilling-pieces of her wages down upon a table and had screamed:

"Arrah, now, honey! With this thirteener won't I sit in the gallery!—and won't your Royal Grace give me a curtsey!—and won't I give your Royal Highness a howl, and a hiss into the bargain!"

Another choice anecdote of Mrs. Jordan tells how she brought an austere revivalist into a mood of indulgence for her anathematised profession. He had seen her giving alms in the streets of Chester to a poor widow, and stepped up to her, offering his hand, with the words:

"Lady, pardon the freedom of a stranger, but would to God the world were all like thee."

She drew back mischievously, and declared:

"No, I won't shake hands with you."

"Why?"

"Because you are a Methodist preacher, and when you know who I am, you'll send me to the devil!"

The minister protested his complete sympathy with her and her deeds of charity, but she answered:

"Well, well, you are a good old soul, I dare say; but I don't like fanatics, and you'll not like me when you know who I am."

"I hope I shall."

"Well, then, I'll tell you. I am a player, and you must have heard of me. My name is Mrs. Jordan."

He was staggered by the announcement, but with a sad clerical smile he still held out his hand, saying:

"The Lord bless thee, whoever thou art. His goodness is unlimited. He has bestowed on thee a large portion of His spirit. And as to thy calling, if thy soul upbraid thee not, the Lord forbid that I should."

He then gave her his arm and escorted her to her lodgings. In parting he shook hands with her again, and added:

"Fare thee well, sister. I know not what the principles of thy calling may be; thou art the first I ever conversed with. But if their benevolent practises equal thine, I hope and trust, at the Great Day, the

Almighty will say to each—Thy sins are forgiven thee."

In 1809 it was reported that Mrs. Jordan and the Duke of Clarence had separated after a quarrel. She serenely denied the rumour, and wrote to a friend in this strain:

"With regard to the report of my quarrel with the Duke, every day of our past and present lives must give the lie to it. He is an example for half the husbands and fathers in the world; the best of masters, and the most firm and generous of friends. I will, in a day or two, avail myself of your kind offers to contradict these odious and truly wicked reports."

Two years afterward, however, out of a clear sky, the fate of all princely paramours crashed down upon her, and the home of so many affectionate ties crumbled like a house of sand. She was playing at Cheltenham when a letter came from the Duke, asking her to meet him at Maidenhead—to exchange ultimate farewells. After receiving this death-sentence to her happiness, she passed from one fainting fit into another, but she would not cancel the night's performance, which was to be the last of the engagement, and bravely rallied her strength to go through with it.

The piece was "The Devil to Pay" (ominous title), a scampering farce in which she played Nell, a character with which her comic genius had long been identified. She kept up the pretense of gaiety until a scene in which Nell, accidentally intoxicated, breaks out into a gale of riotous laughter. Here poor "Thalia's" mirth failed her; when she attempted to laugh, she began to sob bitterly, and was unable to control her grief. Only the resourcefulness of Jobson, the actor who was playing opposite her, saved the scene; he deftly altered his lines to meet the situation, remarking:

"Why, Nell, the conjuror has not only made thee drunk; he has made thee *crying* drunk."

As soon as the curtain fell, Mrs. Jordan hurried to her coach, without stopping to change her stage costume, and went to keep her last appointment with the Duke. What words were spoken, what tears were shed, at that forlorn interview are unknown; at any rate, it was, definitely and finally, the end.

The Duke's sudden abandonment of Mrs. Jordan has never been satisfactorily explained; his most unctuous biographers either get up a weak case for him, or gloss over the incident altogether. His desire to make a wealthy marriage, in order to strengthen his social and political position, is believed to have been the cause of her dismissal; for he is known to have canvassed the field of eligible English heiresses, about that time, not halting at commoners if the dowry seemed promising, and to have proposed to a few of them in vain before he married Adelaide of Saxe-Meiningen in 1818. Mrs. Jordan's letters to Boaden illuminate chiefly the emotional side of the episode; they show her heart as pure gold. These confidences, written immediately after the parting, deserve extended quotation; they present a stricken woman, heroically trying to defend a still-beloved traitor:

"My mind is beginning to feel somewhat reconciled to the shock and surprise it has lately received; for could you or the world believe that we never had, for twenty years, the semblance of a quarrel! But this is so well known in our domestic circle, that the astonishment is the greater! Money, money, my good friend, or the want of it, has, I am convinced, made him, at this moment, the most wretched of men; but having done wrong, he does not like to retract. But with all his excellent qualities, his domestic virtues, his love for his lovely children, what must he not at this moment suffer!

"All his letters are full of the most unqualified praise of my conduct; and it is the most heartfelt blessing to know that, to the best of my power, I have endeavoured to deserve it. I have received the greatest kindness and attention from the Regent, and every branch of the Royal Family, who, in the most unreserved terms, deplore this melancholy business. The whole correspondence is before the Regent, and I am proud to add that my past and present conduct has secured me a friend who declares he will never forsake me. 'My forbearance,' he says, 'is beyond what he could have imagined!' But what will not a woman do who is firmly and sincerely attached? Had he left me to starve, I never would

283

have uttered a word to his disadvantage. . . .
And now, my dear friend, do not hear the Duke of
Clarence unfairly abused. He has done wrong, and
he is suffering for it. But as far as he has left it in
his own power, he is doing everything kind and
noble, even to the distressing himself."

.   .   .   .

"I fear I must have appeared unmindful of your
many kindnesses, in having been such a length of
time without writing to you; but really, till very
lately, my spirits have been so depressed, that I am
sure you will understand my feelings when I say, it
cost me more pain to write to those interested about
me than to a common acquaintance; but the constant
kindness and attention I meet with from the Duke,
in every respect but personal interviews (and which
depends as much on my feelings as his), has in great
measure restored me to my former health and spirits.
Among many noble traits of goodness, he has lately
added one more, that of exonerating me from my
promise of not returning to my profession. This he
has done, under the idea of its benefiting my health,
and adding to my pleasures and comforts."

.   .   .   .

"I lose not a moment in letting you know that the
Duke of Clarence has concluded and settled on me
and my children the most liberal and generous provision; and I trust everything will sink into obliv-
ion."

Whatever that "liberal and generous provision"

was, Mrs. Jordan remained on the stage. Her vast flock of children—five lordling sons of expensive education, and nine daughters in need of marriage portions—demanded unflagging industry of her. For the next four years (1811-1815) she kept on in the harness of her art. Other things arose to harass her; two of her most cherished sons, who had served with distinction in the Peninsular campaign, were court-martialed for insubordination and sent out to India; while the dissolute husband of her eldest daughter, born of her Irish misfortunes—a Mr. Alsop—drained her income and involved her in financial entanglements. In the autumn of 1815 she retired from the stage and went to France; and in July, 1816, she died at Saint-Cloud, aged fifty-four. Toward the end she seemed to be in need of funds, and her total estate was valued at less than 300 pounds.

When the news of her death, in apparent poverty, became public, a hue-and-cry of criticism was raised against the Duke of Clarence, and the subsequent scandal went on for about twenty years, bringing him to the throne as William IV (1830) in no favourable light. He was defended against the charge of ingratitude, of course; his own private secretary, an official of the mint, undertook to prove to the nation that his settlement upon Mrs. Jordan and her children was 2,300 pounds per annum, and that it would have been 4,400 pounds if she had not continued on the stage; also, that she had signed in blank, for a member of her family (presumably Alsop), certain notes which had been treacherously filled out for huge sums, the payment of which had exhausted her resources. Another pleader for the crown declared that Mrs. Jordan merely "took a whim to affect poverty."

These financial aspects of the lamentable affair would become tiresome if the conflicting documentary evidence, pro and con, were to be recited at length; and William IV, moreover, is too dead a king to waste time over, either in exoneration or condemnation. Mrs. Jordan's lack of ready funds, in her last, sad days, doubtless was due largely to her generous sense of duty toward her children, who were too numerous for even a royal treasury to support in the sumptuous manner to which they were born.

The brood of Bushey Park, named Fitzclarence, may be given biographical record as follows: George Augustus Frederick Fitzclarence, created Earl of Munster in 1831; Henry Fitzclarence, captain in the British army, died in India, in 1817; Lord Frederick Fitzclarence, Lieutenant-General, and Colonel of Thirty-sixth Regiment of Foot; Lord Adolphus Fitzclarence, Commander of the Royal Yacht; Lord Augustus Fitzclarence, Rector of Mapledurham and Chaplain to the King; Lady Sophia Fitzclarence, married Lord De L'Isle and Dudley in 1825; Lady Mary Fitzclarence, married General Fox in 1824; Lady Elizabeth Fitzclarence, married the Earl of Errol in 1824; Lady Augusta Fitzclarence, married (first) Hon. J. K. Erskine in 1827; and (second) Lord John Frederick Gordon in 1836; and Lady Amelia Fitzclarence, married Viscount Falkland in 1830.

The four daughters by Mrs. Jordan's earlier liaisons naturally led more obscure lives. She provided each, however, with a marriage portion of 10,000 pounds, and one of them achieved the distinction of mating with a general. The Fitzclarences preyed upon their royal father—though they found his cupboard bare enough—after their mother's death; but the eldest son, honoured above the others by being made an earl, found life not to his liking and committed suicide. The rest received handsome annuities from Queen Victoria when she came to the throne in 1837. This payment of their father's domestic debt and peace-offering to the shade of their ill-treated mother was much applauded by the nation.

There is an element of the uncanny in Mrs. Jordan's end; her death itself is clouded by mystery. Her only companion in France was the former governess of her children. This woman wrote to one of the daughters, Lucy, announcing Mrs. Jordan's death; three days afterward another letter was received from her, stating that Mrs. Jordan was still alive, earlier advices to the contrary notwithstanding, but that she was critically ill; then came a third, repeating the bulletin of death. General Hawker, the daughter's husband, started for France at once, arriving at Saint-Cloud several days after the burial. So far as identification was concerned, the ex-governess was the only person who could testify at first hand; and her own letters argue that she was not particularly reliable.

So it was not strange that rumours should spread, denying her death. Many people even declared that they had seen her in London; and for a time Mrs. Jordan was, like Oscar Wilde only a few years ago, celebrated as a *revenant,* legally dead and yet walking the earth in the very flesh. All this might be dismissed as old wives' tales if matter-of-fact James Boaden, her friend for eighteen years and her loyal biographer, did not corroborate them with his personal testimony. He, too, saw Mrs. Jordan after her death and interment at Saint-Cloud. He says:

"Indeed, about the period in question there was a notion that, so far from her being dead, Mrs. Jordan had been met by various persons in London, and I myself was very strongly impressed with a notion that I had seen her. The dear lady was not an every-day sort of woman. Not that there were not persons who resembled her; for some such I knew who had more than a slight resemblance in features, and who, to enhance their own attractions, copied her smile, and a peculiar action of the mouth, which was full of effect, and pointed an ironical sentence. But there is a physiognomy so minute,

288

if we will observe, as to decide the almost indifferent actions of the human character. She was near-sighted, and wore a glass attached to a gold chain about her neck; her manner of using this to assist her sight was extraordinarily peculiar. I was taking a very usual walk before dinner, and I stopped at a bookseller's window on the left side of Piccadilly, to look at an embellishment to some new publication that struck my eye. On a sudden, a lady stood by my side, who had stopped with a similar impulse; to my conviction it was Mrs. Jordan. As she did not speak, but dropped a long white veil immediately over her face, I concluded that she did not wish to be recognised, and therefore, however I should have wished an explanation of what so surprised me, I yielded to her pleasure upon the occasion, grounded, I had no doubt, upon sufficient reasons.

"When I returned to my own house, at dinner time, I mentioned the circumstance at table, and the way in which it struck me is still remembered in the family. I used, on the occasion, the strong language of Macbeth, 'If I stand here, I saw her.' It was but very recently I heard, for the first time, that one of her daughters, Mrs. Alsop, had to her entire conviction, met her mother in the Strand, after the report of her death; that the reality, or the fancy, threw her into fits at the time; and that to her death she believed she had not been deceived. With her, indeed, it was deemed a vision, a spectral appearance at noon-day, which I need not say was not my impression in the *rencontre* with myself."

What might have been disclosed if Mr. Boaden had not been too polite to speak to the apparition? The incident with its flavor of Poe, sends one's imagination groping in the dark for an answer.

Mrs. Jordan's influence, like her physical form, seemed to live after her; she was not soon forgotten, either in London or at her old home of Bushey. Ten years after her death, Charles Mathews, the elder, called upon the Duke, who was then married, to receive felicitations upon his performance of the day before. He was ushered into the room where the ducal couple had breakfasted, and his attention was immediately fastened upon a life-sized portrait conspicuously placed over the chimney-piece. It was a speaking likeness of Dora Jordan.

The Duke had kept her—in counterfeit—by his hearth-stone, even though a German Princess had filled her place! The actor stared impolitely, but no offense was taken. His host expressed a hope that no one else in the world had so good a portrait of Mrs. Jordan, and then, after a pause, he said with deep feeling:

"She was one of the best of women, Mr. Mathews."

So the spirit of the woman who had been banished was still strong at Bushey House, after all.

GREAT LOVE STORIES OF THE THEATRE

XII

MARIE DORVAL AND ALFRED DE VIGNY

ALFRED DE VIGNY was a poet born to the wreath of bays. Handsome, aristocratic, reserved, sensitive and spiritual, he may be called the Milton of French literature. His was a rich and splendid imagination which dwelt in serene heights above the sordid world.

Marie Dorval was an actress born in a troupe of roving players. A fascinating, impulsive, undisciplined personality, with a great gift for violent emotional acting, she became a tragedy queen, a Mrs. Siddons, of the Parisian stage. She was, for a time, a rival in the Comédie-Française of Mlles. Mars and Georges, whose fame, however, has been more enduring than hers. Like them, she was a woman of notorious love affairs.

The destinies of these two, the austere poet and the ardent actress, crossed, and there ensued a romance, a "grand passion," which makes one of the most absorbing stories to be found in theatrical memoirs. It is exotic and bizarre; it begins in idyll and ends in tragedy; it contains contradictions of temperament which a novelist of psychological bent

293

might seize upon as material for a master-work of analysis in the human heart.

Vigny achieved youthful fame, with a poem called "Éloa," which tells of a sentimental angel who became fascinated by the sins and agonies of Satan. Curiosity causes her to visit him; compassion turns into love; and though recognising his malignant nature, she surrenders to his seductions. Clasped in the arms of the outcast archangel, the fair, frail Éloa sinks downward toward Hell, while the faithful seraphim look on in tears.

That work of his imagination Vigny, through his liaison with Marie Dorval, was destined to live out in personal experience, with the rôles reversed; he himself was his own angelic Éloa, and the actress the destructive spirit. For a time theirs was an inspiring and stimulating love; Vigny's most brilliant and productive years were those spent with Mme. Dorval; but it ended with a brutal shock of disillusion and a long aftermath of disgust. The poet's dream was shattered beyond repair, and wounded to the soul, he withdrew into a retirement that endured until his death twenty-eight years afterward. The world heard little from him after his break with Mme. Dorval; his career was interrupted; and only posthumous publication of his poems renewed his fame. Then, in a magnificent work called "La Colère de Samson," he seemed to be hurling from the grave a last, bitter cry of contempt at the woman who had betrayed his devotion.

MADAME DORVAL

Marie Dorval and Alfred de Vigny

Vigny sprang from a family of the *petit noblesse* which had survived the French Revolution. In 1814, when but seventeen years old, he entered the army. Boyish portraits of him in the scarlet and gold of a King's Musketeer reveal a gracious, winsome character—a debonair soldier with the gentle heart of a poet. He remained in the service until his thirtieth year, when he resigned his commission as captain to devote himself entirely to the literary career in which, between campaigns, he had already made notable progress. Two years afterward, he encountered the fateful Dorval.

Of this actress's early history, it may be said that she passed directly from the cradle to the stage; that at the age of twelve she was married to a man old enough to be her grandfather, who disappears from her memoirs at an early date; that after much provincial experience she hazarded a début in Paris, when twenty years old (1818), in "Pamela"; and that she rapidly rose to a commanding position on the French stage. The impression which she made upon Jules Janin, the leading critic of the time, at the occasion of her first decided success—in "Thirty Years, or A Gambler's Life"—may be recorded. He wrote:

"The budding Mme. Dorval had a personality to justify the strongest sympathies. She was frail, imploring, timid; she wept amazingly, with desolation, with agonies, with an overwhelming delirium."

In a flagrant melodrama called "The Incendiary,"

295

Dorval touched the spark to Vigny's heart. Her rôle was that of a devout girl, the tool of a plotting prelate, who burns down a factory owned by an enemy of the church, believing that her crime will find merit in heaven. The climax came in a scene where the girl, under arrest, comprehends the enormity of her offense, and confesses to a village *curé*.

"Crouched down upon her knees like a repentant Magdalene," says a chronicler of the period, "Dorval stared at the *curé* with great, dim eyes; she wept; she mourned like a frenzied woman suddenly smitten with conscience; and through the twelve minutes of the scene, the audience was breathless with emotion. It was a triumph of hallucination and mysticism upon the stage."

Himself a mystic, Vigny became enraptured with Dorval, as she appeared in this drama, and attended the performance night after night. It seems that he had already made her acquaintance; the previous season, upon seeing her at the *première* of Casimir Delavigne's "Marino Faliero," May 30, 1829, he had demanded an introduction, and had announced himself an admirer of her art. At this time Vigny was making Shakespeare known to the French stage by poetic translations, and even before the production of "The Incendiary," he had presented Dorval with a copy of his version of "Othello"—in which Mlle. Mars was playing Desdemona—dedicated to her in sonorous verses.

When his infatuation began, through the agency of

that play of ominous title, Vigny had been married for several years to a hypochondriacal English-
woman—Lydia Bunbury—for whom he always
showed the most chivalrous regard, but whom he
did not love. A worshipper of all things English,
he had carried his philanglican tendencies to the
absurdity of this conventional, mismated union, in
which there was no ardour on either side.

Dorval herself had been a wife, a mother, and a
free adventurer in the realms of love. Though a
little younger than Vigny, she was infinitely more
sophisticated. He was a cold, chaste dreamer,
as naïve as a child; she was a woman of vast experience, practised in the amorous arts of which he was
a fastidious novice. She was all emotion; he all
imagination. Yet the adoration which he offered
lifted her for a time to his own spiritual level. As
one of Vigny's biographers puts it:

"When at the age of thirty-two she saw kneeling
at her feet this gentleman of ancient lineage, his
charming face framed in his blonde and curly hair
and delicately lighted up by the tender azure of his
eyes, she experienced a sentiment she had never felt
before. It seemed to her as if a cup of cool well-
water had been lifted to her burning lips."

And so, for several years they remained like a betrothed couple, in a pure, sentimental relationship
—a poet and his muse, a nun and Sir Galahad.
The wits of Paris sneered or smiled, but the lovers
heeded not. Through the feverish whirl of theat-

rical life they drifted along like a pair of angelic creatures in one of Vigny's own poems.

Temperamentally, they were as dissimilar as could be imagined. Dorval was animated, expansive, frank, unrestrained. Vigny was cold, self-contained, irreproachable of manners, impeccable of habit. Sainte-Beuve declared that "he lived in a perpetual, seraphic trance." This friendship, therefore, was like linking Carmen to a puritan.

Intellectually and emotionally, however, they were akin; or at least, they had points of contact which explain this platonic beginning. Both of them had a strain of religious mysticism in their natures; both had the same artistic predilections; for Vigny's poetry was all in the key of grief, pity and tenderness, while she excelled upon the stage in the depiction of those very emotions. Like the Breton race from which she came, Dorval was superstitious. Vigny, on his part, had a kind of blind, superstitious faith in destiny. His youth had been nurtured on the Scriptures, and she always turned in her hours of trouble to the Psalms or the Imitation of Christ.

Yet there was also this vital difference between them: her emotions tended toward immediate expression in action, and his toward repression in dreams. She was an actress with the moral malaria of Paris in her blood; he was a poet of the ideal. These anomalies are to be taken into account in explaining the catastrophe of their romance.

Marie Dorval and Alfred de Vigny

Vigny's courting was typical of the man, and it piqued Dorval's interest keenly, for she was accustomed to being pursued by rough hunters of women. His attentions were delicate; his discretion was scrupulous. There were, at first, no protestations of love or friendship; no bouquets at the theatre; no sentimental excursions; no compromising rendezvous. After their separation, Dorval once said: "He never once asked me out to dinner." His gifts were those of critical praise in the reviews; his confidences concerned his art and her own. In the *Révue des Deux Mondes,* 1831, he wrote of her:

"Mme. Dorval has the secret of the most poignant tears, the most penetrating emotions, in tragedy; and she has just proved that the easy tone and finished style of comedy are also familiar to her. She seems like an actress from Covent Garden or Drury Lane, with all the profound reveries and feeling of Mistress Siddons; and now she has added to this tragic gift (the greatest in the theatre) another of subtle observation of manners. Hers is a well-rounded talent, of which the future is indeed vast."

Dorval maintained an establishment in Paris where she reared her three children with fond maternal care, and there Vigny came to see her, by appointment, or when he was certain to find her alone. The talk of their *tête-à-têtes* ran to literary and theatrical topics, though personal confidences doubtless played a part in this platonic wooing. From Vigny there came no hint of passion, no suggestion of a relationship other than the intellectual.

The actress was captivated by this respectful homage; after her experiences with the rapacious males of her circle, adoration as a muse came to her as a fresh and precious tribute. She was flattered; she felt a secret pride in being treated like a duchess, in being addressed as "my angel" by a rapt-eyed poet. With this delightful comradeship she experienced, for a time, a return to the long-lost purity of maidenhood.

Alexandre Dumas, the elder, had been one of Dorval's light-o'-loves before Vigny came upon the scene, and when she followed the poet into the realms of the ideal, the old musketeer of the pen still besieged her with advances. There is on record a letter from Dorval to Dumas, written two years after her friendship with Vigny began, which proves her temporary regeneration.

"You may depart without seeing me," she said, "and I will accept your adieux; or you may come to visit me, and I will receive you as a friend, ill from a disease which though painful is not of long duration. I promise to see you upon your return, if you will promise, on your part, to love me only as M. de Vigny loves me."

Under the influence of Dorval, Vigny became a dramatist. He had already made a début upon the Parisian stage, before he fell in love with her, by his translations of Shakespeare's "The Merchant of Venice," "Romeo and Juliet" and "Othello," yet these were tributes from a poet to his master rather than indications of a definite bent toward the theatre. Naturally, however, his interest in the actress led him to undertake vehicles for her use, and so he ventured out of the peaceful realms of poetry into the battlefields of the drama.

With her in mind for the heroine, he wrote, first of all, a melodrama in prose called "La Maréchale d'Ancre." It was a poison-and-dagger story of the seventeenth century, reeking with the plots and counterplots of Concini and Borgia. He was unable to place her in the leading rôle, however, and when the piece was finally produced several years afterward, at the Odéon, the second endowed theatre of Paris, Mlle. Georges, her rival, was the central figure. Vigny was greatly chagrined by the intrigues which defeated his purpose; how he made amends to her the following letter tells:

"I am sending you two copies of 'La Maréchale d'Ancre,' madame. It is a poor corpse which might have revived under your interpretation, but that happy event was not in the cards. I will come to dine with you to-night, according to your gracious invitation, and am, Your thousand-times devoted
"DE VIGNY."

Thus Vigny's first play for Dorval was ill-starred, from his lover's point of view. Before he wrote another, their platonic dalliance had become a fierce liaison of passion. His dream had been for a bond of the spirit, not of the flesh—but one does not play with fire and remain unscorched, particularly when the flame is a woman of Dorval's temperament. She finally wearied of intellectual love, and began to fret against the platonic ideal. Her impulsive emotions at last refused to be content with elusive sentimentalities.

Shortly after the "Maréchale d'Ancre" episode, Dorval is known to have exclaimed to some of her companions of the theatre, in a fit of petulance: "Would that M. de Vigny were human!"

That was the beginning of the end. Her rule as muse was nearly over, and her reign as mistress was about to begin—at her own prompting. The only wonder of it all is that the event was postponed so long. One night when she was nervously overwrought—according to the anecdote of a player of the period who knew her well—she looked Vigny full in the eyes, and asked with provoking mockery:

"When will the parents of Monsieur the Count come to ask my hand in marriage?"

She did not have to repeat the cynicism a second time. Vigny folded his wings and came down to earth at once.

They went into a honeymoon which continued for months, a trance of amorous delights, tempered and refined by the mysticism in which both were adepts. Mme. de Vigny—the perpetually ill and complaining Lydia Bunbury—knew of her husband's in-

trigue and condoned it; Mme. Dorval was responsible to no one for her liberties with the moral code;
and so the liaison flourished openly. Paris exclaimed "At last!" and made epigrams about the
virtue of poets.

By that time—the year was 1833—Dorval had
lost her youthful charm; she was no longer beautiful; but she had a personal fascination which tran-
scended physical perfections. In Vigny's journal,
published after his death, there is a description
of her which reveals the depths of his infatuation.
He makes it impersonal, but Dorval is written in
every line:

"An inspired actress is charming to watch at her
toilet before going upon the scene. She talks of
everything under the sun with ravishing exaggeration; she loses her head over trifles; cries, laughs,
groans, smiles, becomes angry, caresses—all in a
single minute. She says she is sick, suffering, well,
weak, strong, gay, melancholy—and she is nothing
of the kind. She is impatient as a blooded race-
horse at the barrier; she shows off her paces; looks
in the mirror, puts on her rouge, removes it again.
She tests and heightens her expression; she tests her
voice by speaking loud; she tests her soul by passing
through all the sentiments; she intoxicates herself
with the art of the scene in advance."

During his first raptures, Vigny wrote for Dorval
a one-act comedy sketch called "Quitte pour
'la Peur," which she played at a benefit in her own

behalf, May 30, 1833. After this trifle, which was successful, his stimulated genius busied itself with a greater work, which was rapidly completed and which marks his high-tide as a dramatist. This was the tragedy of "Chatterton," written at fever-heat in seventeen days. Into the mournful story of the English boy-poet, Vigny put all of his high faith in the poetic mission, but into the rôle of Kitty Bell, the young woman who befriends Chatterton in his garret, he put Dorval, as he saw her with love-dimmed eyes. His own stage directions describe the rôle, which became Dorval's greatest achievement, as follows:

"Kitty Bell, a young woman, gracious and elegant by nature more than by education; reserved, religious, timid of manner, trembling before her husband, unreserved only in her maternal love. Her pity for Chatterton is growing into love; she feels it and struggles against it; the constraint which she imposes upon herself becomes more and more severe. Everything must indicate, as soon as she steps upon the stage, that an unexpected shock, a sudden terror, might cause her instant death."

Baffled in his intention to see Dorval in "La Maréchale d'Ancre," Vigny, now the masterful lover where before he had only been the reserved admirer, took a firm stand in the case of "Chatterton." His influence had just secured for his mistress an engagement with the Comédie-Française, and he declared that no one in the company, not even the great Mars or Georges, was capable of playing Kitty Bell—no one but his beloved Dorval. Pressure was brought to bear upon him, but he refused to change his decision, insisting upon his author's privilege to select the leading player according to his own wishes. The intrigue which followed ran up to the throne of Louis Philippe himself, but without any effect upon the consecrated lover.

Dorval, though a favourite with the public for years, through her engagements at the Porte St. Martin, had not yet been granted the intimacy, the confidence, and the admiration of her colleagues in the "house of Molière." To them she was still an interloper; and Mlle. Mars, seeing in her a growing rival, never lost an opportunity of defeating this upstart of the boulevards. Mars, moreover, had power in high places. So when it was announced that the author of "Chatterton," from which much was expected, had gone over the heads of Mars and Georges, and selected Dorval as the creator of the rôle of Kitty Bell, the director and the trustees of the national theatre set up a great cry of scandal. Then Vigny delivered this ultimatum:

"Whether it be scandalous or not, such is my will, and I intend that it shall be carried out. Otherwise, my piece will go to join Mme. Dorval at the Théâtre Porte St. Martin."

Several days afterward, the minister of the Beaux-Arts department, under whose jurisdiction the

Comédie-Française fell, met Vigny in the foyer of the Opera, and began diplomatic negotiations:

"It seems, Monsieur the Count, that you are on the eve of a great success. I congratulate you upon the happy event, and also upon having Mlle. Mars as your principal interpreter."

"Will your excellency permit me to say," remarked Vigny haughtily, "that he has been misinformed? It is not Mlle. Mars but Mme. Dorval who will create the rôle of Kitty Bell, and I can assure you that she will be magnificent."

"Mlle. Mars, however, has certain rights, and royal interest," protested the minister.

"Perhaps Mme. Dorval may not have won them yet, but they will be hers the day after, I swear to you."

Then Louis Philippe, strongly prejudiced in favour of Mlle. Mars, took a hand in the affair. Vigny was invited to a ball at the Tuileries, and between two dances, the bourgeois King condescended upon him in this subtle manner:

"Permit me, M. de Vigny, to present my felicitations upon the success which is in store for you, and also for your happy choice of Mlle. Mars as interpreter. She is an admirable actress, and we will go, the Queen and I, to applaud her in this new creation."

But the poet failed to truckle to royalty.

"If Your Majesty will deign to pardon me," Vigny answered, "it is not to Mlle. Mars that I have confided the rôle of Kitty Bell. I have thought it necessary to pass her by in favour of Mme. Dorval, a great actress herself and one who possesses precisely the grace, the poetry and the passion with which I have endowed my heroine."

Then with cutting *hauteur,* Louis Philippe replied:

"I hope that your determination may prove profitable to you—but I fear that it will not be very acceptable in the theatre."

Upon that score the King was a true prophet. All the people in the cast of "Chatterton" were conspiring against Dorval, and they did not hesitate to show their discontent to the author at rehearsals. Dorval and Vigny had to endure many an affront or *double entendre* in order to make headway with the work. One day the players found installed upon the stage the traditional spiral staircase down which Kitty Bell fell to her death. A cry of derision went up.

"What is that machine for?" they exclaimed.

"That machine," Dorval answered good-naturedly, "is the staircase down which I must tumble *(dégringoler)* in order to die at the bottom. It is a beautiful scene; you will see."

The company exchanged winks, and went out singing:

"*Tra la la la, elle dégringole, comme à la Porte St. Martin.*"

Thus did the dwellers in the "house of Molière"

hoot at scenic realism as worthy only of the lurid melodramas produced at the Porte St. Martin, whence Dorval had come.

The players rehearsed with their usual zeal, though their frigid attitude toward the author and the interpreter of Kitty Bell was maintained. *"Dé-gringoler"* became a catch-word of derision with them, and they waited impatiently to see Dorval perform the acrobatic feat of tumbling down a spiral stairway, as the climax of a tragic scene.

"Will you *dégringolez* this morning, madame?" M. Joanny, who was cast for the rôle of the Quaker husband, John Bell, would ask with sarcasm.

"No, monsieur, not to-day."

"Good; we will have patience."

The day for the dress rehearsal came, and still Dorval had not performed the *dégringolade.*

"Do you *dégringolez* to-day?" inquired the ironic Joanny.

"I'll try."

"Very well, madame."

But when the cue came, Dorval quietly picked up her skirts and tripped down the stairs in regulation manner. She seated herself upon the last step, smiled at Joanny, and said:

"This is the spot where I die."

"But, madame," he objected, "I want to see your *dégringolade* in order to determine my own attitude of horror."

"Bah! To look on while some one dies is not

such an unusual or difficult thing. Everyone knows how, my dear fellow, and after having listened to me, with all your talent in your own rôle, you will not be embarrassed by seeing me die. In short, monsieur, if you must know, I intend to keep secret until the first performance the movement of this scene upon which we—the author and I—are counting. It must be an effect of complete surprise."

Dorval and Vigny attained their end. The surprise was sudden and overwhelming.

When "Chatterton" had its *première,* in June, 1834, *Tout-Paris* was present. Political passions, literary jealousies and amorous intrigues rubbed elbows in the foyers and whispered in the loges. The King himself, with all his court, was in the audience.

The play was successful from the opening scene, though it ventured farther into the field of pure thought and submerged feeling than that audience, accustomed to the gross melodrama of the romantic school, had ever gone before. Written in the simplest prose, it was steeped with the mystical passion, subtle, silent, never expressed, between Chatterton and Kitty Bell. As the Quakeress, Dorval was admirable; she completely realised the words of Kitty Bell's husband: "The peace that reigns about you has been as dangerous to the spirit of this dreamer as sleep would be beneath the white tuberose."

But while the applause grew, there was with it a

feeling of restraint; the mysterious dénouement, known only to the actress and her lover, was anxiously awaited. At last the episode came when Kitty Bell, feeling a premonition of tragedy, rushes feverishly up the spiral stair to throw open the door of Chatterton's room. As she saw the poet's lifeless body, Dorval recoiled in horror, with a piercing scream; then, half-swooning, she tottered backward against the balustrade, and fell, or rather glided, down the steep, winding flight, like a wounded dove, reaching the bottom in her death-agony.

The audience, recovering from the supreme thrill of that tragic moment, burst into a wild tempest of applause for Dorval. As the conquering actress advanced to the footlights, hand in hand with the children in the play, to receive the homage, a bouquet of flowers, thrown from the royal box, fell at her feet. Even Louis Philippe, the prejudiced monarch, had succumbed to her genius.

And when Dorval went toward her dressing room after the curtain had fallen, glowing with the triumph of the evening, she encountered Joanny, who had played the Quaker husband with great authority, waiting to greet her.

"I have come to ask your pardon, madame," he said. "You were sublime to-night, and I shall never forget the expressive spectacle which you have just given us."

The impulsive Dorval embraced her reformed enemy affectionately, crying:

"My dear, clever colleague, you are as great in heart as in talent!"

With which she gave him the flowers that had fallen from the royal box.

The next morning the dramatic critics raved about "Chatterton" and Dorval. As is often the case in Parisian journalism, Vigny reviewed his own play for one of the newspapers; and here was his rhapsody upon his mistress:

"She constantly recalls the maternal virgins of Raphael. Without effort she takes poses like them; like them, also, she carries, holds or puts down her children, who never seem to be separated from their gracious mother, offering to artists' eyes groups worthy of their study, which appear unstudied. Her voice is tender unto sorrow and despair; her soft and melancholy words are those of forlorn pity; her gestures those of ministering devotion; her glances never stop asking heaven for mercy in misfortune; her hands are always ready to clasp themselves in prayer. One feels that the impulses of her heart, restrained by duty, will be mortal as soon as love and terror have conquered her reserve. Nothing could be more innocent and naïve than her ruses and coquetries to persuade the Quaker to talk of Chatterton. She is gentle and modest up to the surprising outburst of energy, of tragic grandeur, of unexpected inspiration, when fright, at the climax, brings out all her loving woman's heart. She is poetic in every detail of this rôle, which she caresses fondly. In fine, she proves herself the most accomplished talent of which the Théâtre-Français can boast."

Thus were the names of Dorval and Vigny united before the public gaze with the brilliant ritual of a great dramatic triumph. With "Chatterton" their love rose to its zenith—and shortly thereafter fell to its ruin.

It would seem as if Dorval's passion for Vigny should have been strengthened by their artistic union upon the boards. She owed her strongest rôle to him; and more than that, to his influence, and his fidelity in the face of intrigue, she owed an established position, on equal terms with Mars and Georges, in the Théâtre-Français.

But at the very time when she should have been most loyal, she turned traitor, through one of the curious contradictions of character not uncommon among women of her type. While still loving Vigny, she deceived him. He discovered her treason, in December, 1835, renounced her absolutely, and hid his heart-break in a grim, stern retirement, whence he never emerged.

The facts in the case are more or less obscure. The gossips of that time held that Dorval had yielded to the importunities of Alexandre Dumas. Jules Sandeau, a man of letters who had been the *bel ami* of George Sand, and from whom that writer had taken part of her pen name, has also been mentioned in connection with the incident. There is better ground, however, for believing that in a moment of abandon, while on a provincial tour, Dorval began a fugitive affair with a handsome young actor, M. Gustave, afterwards called M. Melingue, whom she discovered at Rouen and helped to a career on the Parisian stage. No matter who the man was or what his station, the one definite, vital fact in this sordid aspect of the romance is that Dorval recklessly inflicted upon her poet-lover a wound that never healed and that he never forgave.

For some months before the rupture, it had been common scandal that Dorval was resuming her old wanton habits, and Vigny was sneered at as a deceived lover, until he swept the actress out of his life. There is extant, in the hands of a Parisian collector of autographs, a brief series of letters which discloses the awakening of his jealousy, the first pangs of his agony. They even hint at condonation, on his part, of one or two offenses before his pride mastered his love and caused him to leave her forever. A few quotations from these documents will throw a little light upon this poet's tragedy:

"Upon returning from your home, at one o'clock —I have come back a thousand times more heartbroken than in all these past days. How you wound, how you torture me, my beautiful angel! My poor, dear sweetheart, how you are humiliating me! You think that you will have Louise [a maid or companion] write to me occasionally while you are on tour? If you wish to kill me with chagrin,

that is the right way. No, no, no! I must have
your own handwriting, the trace of your own arm
upon the paper, every day—every day of my life.
. . . Ah! what cruelty to accuse me of not having
been of enough service to you in the theatre! You
know my life—could I have done more? You are
going to see presently, if you will give me confidence
in yourself, what I shall do for you. . . . I beg
of you, my beautiful Marie, instead of frightening
and threatening me as you did to-night, to reassure
me of the future, so that I may be able to think and
write for you."

He kept his promise; he wrote "Chatterton" for
her; he secured for her an engagement with the
Comédie-Française so that she might be free of provincial tours. But still she failed him.

The morning after that piteous letter had been
written, he awoke to send another:

"I was overpowered with fatigue last night, and
slept heavily. I was astonished to awake and find
my pillow, my cheeks, my eyes, wet with tears. I
had dreamed some horrible thing that made me
weep. You made me unhappy last night, my beautiful angel; it is indeed yourself who should not be
jealous. I love you greatly, and with a continual
apprehension."

Later, while she was still on tour, he wrote:

"The other day, when I went to see Volnys at the
Théâtre-Français, I felt a veritable fright at being
there without seeing you, and I was obliged to de-

sert my loge. I shall go no more to the Français. What were you doing that night? Who knows if you were not in flirtatious conversation with some new lover? Take care! I will know it. Take care!"

Such letters as these mark the suffering of Vigny before he turned in rebellion and threw off the yoke. In one place he asks pathetically: "Do you still remember the color of my eyes?"—that being the first thing, according to amorous lore, which lovers forget.

But after his emancipation, when in his bitter retirement he blasted Dorval's memory with the majestic "Colère de Samson," what a contrast! He sang, in the stately rhymes of the classic French alexandrine, here given in English blank verse:

> A strife eternal rages in this world,
> In every place upon which God looks down,
> Between the wiles of Woman and the heart of Man;
> For she's a thing impure in flesh and soul
> That preys upon Man's need for gentle love.
>
> .   .   .   .
>
> Thrice she has sold the secrets of my life,
> And thrice has wept for me deceitful tears,
> Which could not hide the rage within her eyes,
> Shamed as she was still more than deep-amazed
> To find herself discovered yet forgiven.*

---

* Une lutte éternelle en tout temps, en tout lieu,
Se livre sur la terre, en présence de Dieu.

Vigny refused Dorval the satisfaction of knowing that he remembered her, even in this fashion, and held the poem for publication after his death (1863). On her part she soon repented of her infidelity, and when she found that the poet was lost to her forever, she was inconsolable—for a time. George Sand, in "The Story of My Life," tells of Dorval's hysteria, of her black disgust with life, of her threats to abandon the stage. This mood finally passed, however, and she went on in the old reckless way.

But she could never forget Alfred de Vigny, and on her death-bed (1849) she committed to her daughter's care a package of his love-letters, which she had kept for fifteen years, with a solemn injunction that they should never be published. And the man who would have been with her at the end, if she had appreciated his devotion in the proper manner, did not even emerge from the seclusion of his retirement to attend her funeral.

It was indeed a tangled, sorry web of life and love that this actress and this poet wove together.

> Entre la bonté d'Homme et la ruse de Femme,
> Car la femme est un être impur de corps et d'âme.
>
> .   .   .   .   .
>
> Trois fois elle a vendu mes secrets et ma vie,
> Et trois fois a versé des pleurs fallacieux
> Qui n'ont pu me cacher la rage de ses yeux,
> Honteuse qu'elle était plus encore qu'étonnée
> De se voir decouverte ensemble et pardonnée.

INDEX

INDEX

A

Index

Boileau, 36, 40, 41, 43, 44, 45, 49.
Bonaparte, Josephine. See Josephine.
Bonaparte, Lucien, 220, 223.
Bonaparte, Napoleon. See Napoleon.
Boswell, James, 150.
Bouillon, Duchesse de, 46, 47, 130, 131, 132.
Bouret, Abbé, 131, 132, 133.
Bourgogne, Hôtel de, 31, 32, 35, 43, 46, 47.
Bourgoin, Mlle., 218.
Boyer, Abbé, 31.
Bracegirdle, Anne, 81, 85-107.
Branchu, Mme., 218.
Brereton, William, 196.
Brie, Mlle. de, 47.
Buckhurst, Charles, Lord, 10, 11, 12, 14, 66.
Buckingham, Duke of, 2, 66.
Bunbury, Lydia (Comtesse de Vigny), 297, 302.
Burford, Earl of, 20.
Burke, Miss Billie, 8.
Burlington, Lord, 86, 87.
Burnet, Bishop, 25, 60, 61.

C

Calista in Rowe's "Fair Penitent," 269.
"Camp," Ticknell's, 246.
"Captivity," Mary Robinson's, 195.
Carwell, Mrs. See Querouaille, Louise de.
Castlemaine, Countess of, 2, 7, 12, 13, 18. 19, 22.
"Catiline," Ben Jonson's, 9.
Catherine of Braganza, Queen, 13.
Caulaincourt, General, 232.
Champmeslé, Marie de, 29-51, 56.
Champmeslé, Sieur de, 30, 36.
Chantilly, Mlle. See Favart, Justine.
Chapelle, Claude Emmanuel Luillier, called, 37.
Charles I, 44.
Charles II, 1-26, 55, 56, 57, 58, 60, 64, 79.
Charles V, Emperor, 252.
Charlotte, Queen, 199.
Châtelet, Mme. du, 182.
Chatterton, Thomas, 79.
"Chatterton," Vigny's, 304, 305, 307, 309, 311, 314.
"Chercheuse d'Esprit," Charles Favart's, 164.

Chevillet. See Champmeslé, Sieur de.
Chevreuse, Duchesse de, 174.
"Children of Thespis," Anthony Pasquin's, 249.
Churchill, Sarah, 106.
Cibber, Colley, 25, 58, 87, 91, 93.
Cibber, Susannah, 192.
"Cinna," Corneille's, 229.
Clairon, Mlle., 120.
"Clandestine Marriage," by Colman and Garrick, 212.
Clarence, Duke of (afterward William IV), 265-290.
Clavel, 114, 115, 116, 117, 137.
Cleopatra in Corneille's "Rodogune," 241.
Clermont-Tonnerre, Comte de, 39, 40, 48.
Cleveland, Duchess of. See Castlemaine, Countess of.
Cleveland, Duke of, 19.
Clive, Kitty, 152, 153.
Clytemnestra, in Racine's "Iphigénie," 219.
"Colère de Samson," Vigny's, 294, 315.
Collier, Jeremy, 94.
Colman, George, 246.
Comédie-Française, 30, 47, 114, 119, 135, 136, 166, 178, 239, 293, 304, 306, 314.
Comédie-Italienne, 166, 178, 180.
"Comical Revenge," Etherege's, 65.
"Comparison between the Two Stages," Charles Gildon's, 102.
"Comus," Milton's, 212.
"Confederacy," Vanbrugh's, 212.
Congreve, William, 65, 85-107.
Constant, valet of Napoleon, 225, 227, 230, 232, 234, 236.
"Constant Couple," Farquhar's, 143, 144.
Consulate, the, 217.
Conti, Prince de, 185.
Cordelia in Shakespeare's "King Lear," 192, 196, 212.
Corneille, Pierre, 29, 33, 43, 44, 46, 68, 114, 119, 239.
"Country Wife," William Wycherley's, 271.
"Country Wife," Wycherley's, 271.
Covent Garden, 299.
Cowley, Hannah, 212.
Cowslip in O'Keefe's "Agreeable Surprise," 246.

Index

Index

Index

Index

Index

Index

327

www.ingramcontent.com/pod-product-compliance
Lightning Source LLC
Chambersburg PA
CBHW022149010726
47493CB00002B/407